what I didn't say

what I didn't say

Keary Taylor

First Paperback Edition: May 2012

The characters and events portrayed in this book are fictitious. Any
similarity to real persons, living or dead, is coincidental and not intended
by the author.

Taylor, Keary, 1987 –
What I Didn't Say : a novel / by Keary Taylor. – 1st ed.

Summary: When high school senior, Jake Hayes, loses his ability to
speak, he'll learn to deal with being mute and find a way to tell Samantha
Shay that he's loved her for forever, even if he can't talk anymore.

ISBN 978-1475156454

Printed in the United States of America

For Justin

Orcas Island

Airport

Eastsound (Town)

West Beach

Moran State
Park

Golf Course

Lake

Rosario

Doe Bay

Deer Harbor

Olga

Ferry Landing

10 months 'til the Air Force

3 weeks since school started

There were three things that I knew for sure about Orcas Island:

One: The people here were generally weird. Half its residents were your run-of-the-mill hippies. The other half was a mix of extreme liberals, hermits, and multi-millionaires. Then there was a dash of us "normal" people.

Two: I came from the biggest family on the island. Seven kids made our family stand out and everyone on the island knew who the Hayes' were.

Three: I knew everyone here just a little too well.

As I walked through the halls of Orcas High School, I could tell you the name of every single face that passed by. I could tell you that Christie Rose had lost her first tooth biting into a spoonful of macaroni and cheese in first grade. I could tell you that Henry Asher had peed his pants the first day of kindergarten. I knew that Miss Pence who taught ancient world history attended hippy dance parties regularly in the buff. I'd rather not say how I knew that one. And then Principal Hill was a die-hard Star War's fan and had half a garage full of action figures, posters, costumes, and way too real looking light sabers.

On an island this size, with its whopping 5,000 residents, there are no secrets.

"Hayes!" my best friend since the first day of kindergarten, Carter Hill, called from behind me. A second later his hand slapped down on my shoulder. "Your family doing the team dinner tonight?"

"My mom's been cooking nonstop since last night," I said as I stopped in front of my locker and yanked it open. "You know how she gets about these things."

"Hey, I'm not complaining. Your mom's the only one who actually makes enough food. I'm not full until I feel like I'm going to hurl," Carter laughed as he dug into his locker, which had been next to mine since freshmen year.

"Just try to make it to the back yard this time, okay?" I sighed. The carpet had smelled off for weeks after last year's team dinner.

"We talking about Carter's epic dinner hurl?" Rain Jones asked, opening his locker that was just a few down from ours as the warning bell sounded.

"Unfortunately," I said as I pulled out my AP history book and stuffed it into my frayed backpack. I should have let Mom get me a new one at the beginning of the year when she offered.

"We eating in the backyard again?" Rain asked, unabashedly staring at my sixteen-year-old sister Jordan as she walked by.

"Dude," I said, shaking my head at Rain. "Don't do that in front of me. It's gross."

"What?" he said, still staring after her. "She's hot."

"Seriously, just stop," I said as I closed my locker and headed toward class. Rain whistled after Jordan, in an attempt to draw a punch out of me. He wasn't going to get the satisfaction.

The AP history class wasn't exactly full. With only thirty-seven students in the senior class, a good handful of those on the verge of already dropping out, even though we were only three weeks into the school year, and another good handful full-time potheads, that didn't leave many qualified to enroll in any AP classes. All five of them that our tiny school offered.

"Hey, Sam," I tried to keep my voice cool as I slid into my desk.

"Hey, Jake," she smiled as she glanced over at me just briefly.

"You coming to the game tomorrow night?" I wiped my palms against my shorts. Why was I sweating so bad?

"Depends on how much homework Mr. Hill gives us today," she rolled her eyes.

It was a well-known fact that Samantha had the heaviest school load out of all the students in the high school. She was enrolled in every single AP class, except for European History, which she had aced last year, and if I remembered correctly, she also had several independent study classes. She was on track to be the valedictorian.

"It's homecoming. Would be a shame to miss it."

Samantha gave me a little smile before her eyes darted back to her book. Her mind was already elsewhere.

I tried to turn my attention to Principal Hill's lesson on some war, or maybe it was about US economics? All I could think about was the way Samantha shifted in her

3

chair, how her dark auburn hair fanned across her shoulder, the way she held her face in her hand.

Someday I'll tell her, I thought.

I still couldn't figure what that final week of school last year had been about. Samantha had been almost... flirtatious? My eyes would meet hers unexpectedly; she'd stand just a little too close at times. She even invited me to go to a movie with her and her friends, which I had quite unfortunately had to bail out of last minute due to family drama. Thanks Jenny...

But this school year? Nothing. It was like Sam was no more than an acquaintance. She was all school work and no wandering eyes.

"Earth to Jake Hayes," a voice from the front of the room called.

My eyes snapped up to Principal Hill's face, where he stared at me expectantly. "Care to tune in for a while?" he asked, one of his dark eyebrows arched.

"Sorry, Principal Hill," I said, opening my book and trying to look busy with a notebook and pen. The class chuckled. I felt my face flush as I glanced over at Samantha. She had a tiny smile on her lips, but she kept her eyes glued to the pages of her book.

Day dreaming about Samantha Shay was about as good as day dreaming about catching the eye of a Victoria Secret model or maybe the Princess of some far away land. It wasn't that I was too ugly to stand next to Sam. *No one* caught Sam Shay's eye, at least not anymore.

Everyone knew the only thing Sam could see was school work and the finish line that was graduation. It was bizarre. A girl as pretty as Sam didn't usually equal such enormously big brains and educational commitment.

She was smarter than all of us. And it only made me want her more.

I tried to stand as straight as I could as I walked through the doors of Orcas High School for the first time as a real student. I had yet to really hit a growth spurt. I didn't want to be confused for an eighth grader.

My older sister, Jenny had shuffled off to her friends the second we stepped out of the car, leaving me on my own.

I'd never admit I was beyond freaked out about my first day of being a freshman.

I gave a little sigh of relief when I saw Rain walking toward the front doors. I jogged to catch up with him, slapping him on the shoulder with my palm. We shared one of those looks, like we were both scared out of our minds, but were pretending to be cool.

We stepped through the doors we would walk through a million times over the next four years. I half tripped over myself when I saw a girl with dark auburn hair that hung down to her waist talking with Principal Hill.

She had the most amazing end of summer tan and she sported super pink lip gloss.

"I told you, I've already finished Algebra two at my old school in Portland," she said. She sounded like she was trying to keep her voice even.

"Who's that?" I asked Rain as we walked across the commons.

"Never seen her before," Rain answered. "Dude, there's a little drool, there." I suddenly felt Rain's finger on my chin. I slapped his hand away without even looking away from the girl.

"I'll talk to the Pre-Calculus teacher, but for now, you're going to have to go into the Algebra two class. Here," Principal Hill's eyes suddenly flashed to my face, making me jump. "Jake!"

Rain and I stopped and walked back toward Principal Hill and the girl.

"Jake, this is Samantha Shay, she and her mother just moved here. Would you mind showing her to her first period class?"

Samantha's eyes met mine. Even though I could tell she was frustrated, she gave a warm smile. Her entire face lit up.

"Yeah, I'd be happy to," I responded. Had I not been so totally engrossed with the girl in front me, I might have noticed Rain making small gagging sounds.

Samantha looked back at Principal Hill. She was trying hard not to roll her eyes at him. "Guess I'm set. Thanks for all your help." She then met my eyes again, that smile spreading on her face once more.

"You guys better get moving," Principal Hill said as the warning bell sounded.

Just because I was a freshman didn't mean that I didn't know my way around the high school. With how involved John and Jenny were, I'd been in the school more times than I could count.

"Thanks for showing me around," Samantha said as we started up the stairs to the second floor. Rain had already made some excuse and went off to do something with his empty locker. "I still can't get over how weird this school is. It's so tiny."

"Yeah," I said, hoping I could think straight enough for the new girl to not think I was an idiot. "It's pretty small. You came from a bigger school?"

"Yeah," she said with a laugh. I couldn't help but smile when she did. "The high school I would have gone into down in Portland was a 5A school."

"Wow," I said, chuckling as we turned down the hall. "I can't even imagine going to a school that big."

"You grew up here?" she asked as we stopped in front of a random door. She dug her class schedule out of her bag and handed it to me.

"Yeah," I said as I looked it over. She had English first period, just down at the end of the hall. We started towards it.

"So, are you like, super smart, or something?" I asked, handing her schedule back to her. Most of her classes were ones only juniors took.

She shrugged, her face turning slightly red. "Maybe I'm just weird, but I like school."

"Not weird," I said as we stopped in front of her classroom. "Someday we'll all be working for people like you."

She laughed and I mentally patted myself on the back.

"Well, thanks for showing me to my class, Jake..." she trailed off.

"Hayes," I filled in. It was weird having someone on the island not know who I was. "Jake Hayes."

"Nice to meet you, Jake Hayes," she said, her smile blinding me.

"You too, Samantha Shay," I said, stuffing my sweaty hands in my pockets.

"Sam," she said, placing her hand on the door knob.

"See you later, Sam." I smiled as I walked away.

Sam may have just stolen my fourteen-year-old heart.

24 hours 'til the Homecoming game
10 months 'til Air Force

The Hayes house wasn't exactly tiny. When one has seven kids, each with a personality just a little too big for their own good, one had to have a lot of bedrooms and space. But with the entire OHS football team and a good handful of other parents in the house, the walls were in danger of being knocked out and the roof collapsing on us all as we weaved in and out of each other.

I sometimes wished my parents would send the younger kids to friends' houses or something when we had these dinners. I could be grateful that at least John and Jenny were away at college. That was two less bodies. But that still left us with Jordan, sixteen; Jamie, thirteen; James, ten; and Joshua, seven. But my siblings were almost a part of the team. They didn't seem to care if their ages were in the should-not-be-cool-cause-you're-like-this-big range, and most of the team was pretty cool with them.

"Jake!" Mom yelled from the kitchen. Her light-brown, curly hair was sticking in every direction, giving her a crazed but warm look. "Take this to the table."

"This" translated to a huge bowl that contained a salad, a scalding hot dish that contained something I didn't even recognize, and another huge bowl full of rice. It was pure luck that I made it to the table without dumping something hot on someone's head. Dad then instructed me to herd the thirteen chickens we owned back into the coop. I seriously hoped none of them had laid any eggs in the yard. There was nothing like ruining a team dinner by stepping on some hidden rotten egg in the yard.

Sadly that had happened before. The same night Carter had barfed in the living room.

"Excuse me, Blake Shaw?" I heard Mom scold from inside. "You know better than to use language like that. I don't care if you're a teenager and a football player. You will not talk like that in my house."

"Sorry, Mrs. Hayes," I heard Blake apologize. "It won't happen again."

"It better not, or I'll wash your mouth out with soap, and don't think I won't."

I chuckled as I closed the door to the chicken coop. Mom had no tolerance for foul language, something she engrained so well in her children I had literally never let a swear word slip passed my lips, ever, even when I was just with my friends. She'd instilled the same values in half the kids on this island, since half of them had spent a good amount of their summer in our house or backyard.

Finally it was time to sit down and eat. Not only had Mom cooked enough to feed the army that was the football team, she could have fed a whole other army. Everyone spoke too loud as we reached around each other for food, endless taunts and pep talks rose up about the game the next day.

The people on the island may have been weird, but they were generally good people. You didn't find people like that in other parts of the country. You wouldn't find someone who would ask if your pet alpaca was feeling better after a bout of suspected chicken pox. You wouldn't find people who would unexpectedly bring over dinner or show up to clean your house just cause your mom wasn't feeling too great. When you needed help, you'd get all your friends out, as well as a dozen strangers, sometimes whether you wanted them or not. The people on the island took care of one another.

As I looked around at them all, I felt just a little twinge of self-doubt in my decision to leave the island so soon after graduation. I'd always been so excited to leave this tiny island and its tiny and weird people.

Until that night, with my departure looming so close, I didn't think I'd miss any of them except Samantha.

5 months ago

2 months 'til the end of junior year

Every time I finished a solo flight it felt like I was on some kind of drugs. I always wondered if that was what feeling high was like.

I couldn't stop smiling as I walked from the Bronco to the front door. I didn't even notice how our huge, eleven passenger van was missing, Mom and the younger kids out somewhere for the night. I closed the door behind me and peeled my jacket off.

"That you, Jake?" Dad called from the back door leading out from the kitchen into the backyard. I could smell something floating through the house. Steak? Dad didn't grill steak often. With so many mouths to feed, steak got a little expensive.

"Yeah," I said, following my nose. "Just finished flight number seven." I found Dad closing the door to the backyard behind him, carrying a plate with two monstrous sized steaks. "One of those for me?" I asked hopefully. My stomach instantly started growling.

"Yep," Dad said, setting the plate on the counter. "Your mom is out with a few friends, and your siblings are off playing with the other island hooligans."

"Just the two of us tonight?" I didn't hide my surprise. I couldn't remember the last time it had just been me and Dad in the house. Dad just nodded.

We didn't say a whole lot as we piled food onto our plates that was sure to clog our internal workings. When they were fully loaded, we headed to the loft and Dad turned on a basketball game.

Half way through dinner, and just after the second half started, Dad nudged something on the coffee table with his toe. "This came in the mail for you today."

I glanced to the table, and suddenly froze, the fork halfway to my mouth. It said *Air Force* on it in big, bold letters.

"You want to talk about that?" Dad asked, breaking his eyes away from the game to look at me.

Letting out a big sigh, I set my fork down on my plate.

"You thinking of joining the Air Force?" Dad asked when I took too long to answer.

"Yeah," I responded, my eyes not quite meeting his.

"How soon you think you'd join?"

"I was thinking pretty soon after graduation," I said, not sure if I should be nervous about this conversation or not. I'd only decided for sure that I was going to join a few days ago. I'd requested the information from the Air Force's website long before then. "Like, September?"

Dad's eyes glanced back to the game when the commercial ended. "You sure about it?"

I swallowed hard, meeting Dad's eyes again. "Yeah, I'm sure. I'm ready to see more of the world. I'm not afraid. And I love flying more than almost anything else."

Dad just nodded. A smile slowly started growing on his face. "Okay. I'm proud of you Jake. That's an honorable thing to do."

14

I couldn't help but smile, my entire body finally relaxing.

"But you might want to talk to your mother about it sooner than later. It might take her a while to warm up to the idea."

I stuffed more steak into my mouth. "Thanks, Dad."

Out of the thirty-seven seniors at Orcas High School, every single one of them had been at the homecoming football game. It was a Friday night, the sky was cloudy, threatening to rain, a picturesque September day on Orcas Island.

The Vikings had crushed Tree Hill Baptist High, thirty-two to eighteen. I had scored four of those touchdowns. And I celebrated with twenty-four of my senior classmen.

"Jake!" Carter shouted from across the bonfire. "Catch!"

I barely got my hands up to block the Budweiser can from hitting me square in the face.

"And that's how we won the game today!" Carter cheered, the rest of the crowd cheering and shouting with him. I shook my head and laughed as I watched Carter grab another beer from the cooler at his feet and chuck it at Rain.

The entire football team was at the party and if we got caught we were screwed for the rest of the season. I could think of nothing worse than having the cops roll up. We were on track to win districts this year. I had told Rain and Carter they were stupid for throwing this party, and yet there I was, drinking with the rest of them.

Ignoring my mother's voice in the back of my head, the one that was always there whenever I was doing something I knew I shouldn't, I popped the top of the can. Carter joined at my side and slapping his hand on my shoulder said, "Race you to the bottom?"

"Chug," Rain started chanting. "Chug! Chug!"

"It's on," I taunted. Not hesitating, my lips met the lip of the can and tipped it back.

The alcohol burned my throat as it went down, and everything in me wanted to cough it back up. But I'd never admit this was only the third beer I'd ever had in my life. The one I'd finished not three minutes ago was my second.

Crushing the can in my fist as the last drop slid down my throat, I threw it at the ground and raised my arms in triumph. Carter coughed as he choked on his, laughing.

"That's how we do it, Hayes!" Rain egged on, beating on my back. "Maybe you aren't as innocent as we all believed you to be."

"Shut up, man," I shoved Rain, laughing with the rest of the crowd.

We'd all flocked to Rain's house out in Deer Harbor, nearly at the end of the world on Orcas Island. The Jones' had owned the twenty acres of ocean front property since the early nineteen hundreds, which was lucky. Rain's hippy parents would never have been able to afford a place like this on their own.

And lucky for the student body of the high school, they were down in Portland for some sort of hippy convention about saving salmon, or ferns, or the cross-eyed, two toed crane, or something granola like that.

None of us would ever admit it, but parties like this happened all the time on the island. There was nothing to do on an island so tiny, so parties with red plastic cups and glimmering glass pipes were the frequent solution.

"I seriously can't believe you guys invited all of these people," River said as she stopped at Rain's side, giving him the look of death. It was hard to believe they were twins, with River's nearly black long hair, and Rain's nearly white-blond hair. They couldn't have looked less alike.

"And yet I see you have a red plastic cup in your hand," Rain taunted her. "Quit being a kill joy."

"Whatever," she said with a very dramatic roll of her eyes. "Jake, don't get so drunk you can't make it to the dance tomorrow. I spent way too much on my dress for you to get too wasted to not wake up tomorrow. I won't be stood up."

"Yes ma'am," I saluted her. She winked at me once and walked back toward their borderline historic house.

"It is a little weird that *she* asked *him* to the dance, right?" Carter asked, unabashedly staring after River. Carter tended to get a little depressed when he smoked weed.

"Dude, when are you finally going to grow a pair and just ask her out?" Rain asked, his voice exasperated. I just shook my head, everything starting to feel a little fuzzy. I'd heard this argument more times than I wanted to count.

"River would never go out with me," Carter said in a nearly wistful voice. "She doesn't go out with anyone."

I wondered if I was the only one who knew *why* she didn't go out with anyone. River would never admit she batted for the other team. I only found out when I happened to see her holding hands with another girl when I was off-island once. I'd been weirded out for weeks. Eventually

18

River figured out I knew. After a very awkward conversation, I agreed to keep her secret, and the two of us went back to being friends as usual.

And I had agreed to take her to the dance when River blackmailed me with Samantha. She knew I'd never have the balls to ask Sam, so I either take River, or she spilled the beans about how I really felt about Sam.

Girls fought so dirty.

The first drops started to fall from the sky, the clouds above us thick and heavy. It would have been pitch black outside had it not been for the raging bonfire. You didn't get to experience that kind of darkness unless you lived in a remote place like Orcas.

"We all know it isn't hard to beat Hill in a drinking match," Blake Shaw said as he lumbered over to us. He was easily the most built kid in the school, dark as night, and probably six foot five. "You ready to take on the Shaw?"

"*The* Shaw, huh?" I challenged my teammate. "Bring it."

I took the can Blake offered and popped the top. Rain counted us down.

I hadn't stood a chance.

"And *that's* how the Shaw does it!" Blake bellowed, hurling his empty can into the fire, raising his arms into the air and turning in a circle. The girls all cheered for him. Blake struck a pose, flexed his biceps and kissed each of them.

"Who wants a piece of the Shaw?" he called, nodding and winking at them.

"Wow," Carter shook his head. "Is he for real?"

We all laughed, each grabbing another beer from the cooler. I watched as Norah Hamilton, the only girl with enough money to supply the booze, eyed me from across the bonfire, and slowly made her way toward us.

"Watch out Jakey-boy," Rain teased. "The tigress is on the prowl again."

"Shut up," I hissed. I felt my stomach clench, and I was pretty sure it wasn't from the alcohol.

"Hi, Jake," Norah practically purred as she swished her dark brown hair off of her shoulder. Her French manicured fingernails wrapped tightly around her plastic cup. "So when are you going to take me flying in that lawyer boss's plane?" She bit her bottom lip in a way that made my hindered brain ache, and not in a good way.

"Brent's pretty strict about who I'm allowed to take up in his plane with me," I half lied. Once the liability release was signed, Mr. Carol let me take whoever I wanted up.

"Come on," she said, reaching out for the front of my jacket. "You've got to be the youngest pilot ever. You need to take me up before you leave for the Air Force."

"Uh," I struggled to make my brain form an answer. I really hoped the alcohol wouldn't make me say something I regretted. I probably should have listened to Mom's voice in the back of my head. "Maybe. We'll see."

"You really shouldn't run off to the Air Force," Norah said as she stepped a little closer, her nose only inches away from mine. "You know a lot of people die in the services, don't you? It would be a shame if that pretty face didn't live past its nineteenth birthday."

"Uh, yeah," I said, trying to disentangle myself from Norah. My speech was starting to sound just a little slurred. "I'll keep that in mind."

"Be careful up in those skies," she practically whispered next to my ear. She pressed her perfectly glossed lips to my cheek just for a moment, her hand dropping to my belt.

"Uh! Okay, got it!" I shouted as I jumped away from her. She simply winked and walked back to her pack of friends.

I felt a shiver run through me that I didn't like.

"Oh, Norah the Whora has her sights on Jakey-boy!" Rain said just a little too loudly, high-fiving Carter.

"Could you guys just shut up?" My words were slurring a little more.

"Chill out, Hayes," Carter said, clasping me on the shoulder. "We all know you're saving yourself for Samantha."

I got quiet at the mention of Samantha's name, a hard knot tying itself around my chest. Samantha was one of the few students who weren't at the party. She was probably at home studying.

"No defense," Carter said, squeezing my shoulder again. "It must be true love."

"Shut up," I said again, letting myself sink to the ground. It felt a bit like I was standing on a dock down at the marina instead of solid ground.

"Just say it, my friend," Rain said, sitting on the ground next to me, another can between his hands. "You'll feel better if you get it out."

My drunken brain didn't even register or care that he was still mocking me. "I've been trying to drop the hints since the beginning of last year, but does she respond? No!" I said just a little louder than I should have.

"Oh Samantha!" Rain sang out in a terrible mock country voice. Carter slipped his phone out of his pocket and pointed it in our direction. I didn't even care that he was recording this.

"Oh Samantha," Rain continued. "Why isn't Jakey-boy good enough? With those beautiful green eyes and hair like sweeping... chocolate?" he held the note out long and dramatic.

"Oh Samantha," I joined Rain, singing in harmony. "I've been watchin' you fo so long," I sang. "Waitin' for you to come around. Cause don't you know Samantha, that I love you?" I hadn't even realized that I'd fallen onto my back until I was looking up at Carter and his recording cell phone. "I love you Samantha," I said with a lazy smile, straight into the phone.

"And sent," Carter said, sliding it back into his pocket. I felt my phone vibrate in my pocket as I received the video Carter had just recorded.

"Okay, lover boy," Rain said, pulling me back to my feet. "It's time to go tell her. This is just sad."

"Tell her?" I said as Rain pulled my arm around his shoulder to keep me on my feet. "Tell who what?"

"Tell Samantha just how much you love her," Carter said as he put his arm around me from the other side.

I hesitated, my foggy brain processing their words. It sounded like a pretty good idea. "Okay!" I declared, standing up a little straighter. "Okay! I'm gonna' tell her! Tonight! Right now!"

"Yeah!" Rain and Carter both cheered. Carter reached into his pocket for his keys. "I'll drive!"

"Aren't you drunk too?" I tried to be reasonable in an unreasonable state. "And high?'

"Not nearly as drunk as you," Carter laughed. "And I'm not *that* high."

The three of us called good-bye to the party and made our way to Carter's rust-bucket of a truck. The doors squealed painfully as they were forced open. Carter slid into the driver's seat, Rain scooted into the middle, and I followed him in and slammed the door shut. Reaching into his pocket, Carter pulled his cell phone out and set it on the dash.

The engine just squealed when Carter tried to start it up.

"Come on, you piece of crap!" Carter yelled uselessly at it as he slammed his fist on the dash. His phone jumped violently. "We're on an important mission!"

A moment later it turned over.

"Where does she even live anyway?" Carter asked as he worked his way back to the road. "I've never been to Samantha's house."

"Me neither," I said, leaning my forehead against the cool glass. It felt good. "Some place at the end of Enchanted Forest Road."

And so the three of us set out, driving down the winding road. Carter turned up the radio. I squeezed my eyes closed. Everything sounded too loud.

Behind my eyes I could picture Samantha, her dark hair, her warm brown eyes, her tiny nose, and perfectly smooth skin. I had loved her since I saw her the first day of our freshmen year. I'd developed crushes on other girls, sure, over the last three years. But it always came back to Samantha Shay. Always.

I'd just never had the guts to tell her.

Samantha was intimidating. She was smart, by far the smartest girl in our school. She was confident. She was an athlete, at least until this year, when her school schedule became too crazy to try and balance sports and classes.

And during an English class last year, she and Mr. Morrison got into a debate. We'd been reading some book that I no longer remembered, and one of the issues was about love. Samantha's argument was that she didn't believe in love.

No one in the class doubted she really didn't believe in love after she finished her argument.

Thus I had never told her.

But that was going to change tonight. As Rain had put it, I was finally going to grow a pair.

Just as we went around a sharp bend in the road, Carter's phone started blaring some rap song. At the exact same time, it slid off the dash and onto the floor.

"Got it," Carter and Rain said at the same time, both reaching toward the floor.

"Hey," I muttered as I squinted out the front window. "Watch out for that deer."

"What?" Carter mumbled, briefly glancing at the windshield before turning his eyes back to the floor of the truck.

"Watch out for that deer!" I yelled. I saw its eyes grow wide and white as we barreled towards it. Reaching over for the steering wheel, I jerked it to the right, narrowly missing the animal.

Carter slammed on the breaks just after I jerked the steering wheel. The back end of the truck skidded, turning us in a half circle. The truck swerved wildly and there was a loud pop as the front passenger tire burst. For one second the truck was airborne. There was the sickening sound of metal crunching and the next second it felt as if my head had been ripped off.

Blackness crept in on the edges of my vision as a shaky hand rose to the source of the pain. Glass was embedded into my arms and face, but that wasn't what really hurt. My fingers met cold steel. I traced my fingers up the metal.

And then my fingers met my own bloody flesh, just a few inches under my chin. The steel and my skin were connected.

I passed out.

Even though I couldn't see her, I could smell her. Not the girl I really wanted to see, but my sister Jordan. I always told her she wore too much perfume. It wasn't that it smelled bad, she just wore too much.

My eyes struggled to open, my entire body sure Jordan was going to jump on me, or dump a glass of ice cold water over my head to wake me up. She was evil like that sometimes. But for some reason my eyes didn't want to open. In fact, my entire body seemed pretty unwilling to do anything.

"Hey, Mom," I heard Jordan say. "I think he's starting to wake up."

I heard the sound of shuffling feet, accompanied by beeping and a bunch of other sounds I didn't recognize. A sliver of light appeared as my eyelids struggled to open.

It felt weird when I breathed.

"Jake," I heard the familiar sound of my mom's voice. "Jake, are you awake?"

I tried to tell her that I was, but it felt like my throat was swollen to the point of almost being sealed shut.

"Mom," I heard my other younger sister, Jamie, hiss. "He can't now, remember?"

My eyes slid open just a little more, seeing my mom's face blanch. She was sitting on the side of whatever surface I laid on and it took me a moment to realize that I wasn't lying on my own bed. The lights above me were all wrong.

I finally registered the other faces in the room, all eight of them. My big, crazy family. Three brothers and three sisters, and both parents.

A stream of tears rolled down Mom's face as she looked at me, my eyes now fully open.

I would have panicked at that sight. Mom didn't cry. But then I realized where I was.

I was in a hospital.

A hospital room that was decorated with seashells and cartoony sea creatures.

A small whimper escaped Mom's throat and she reached for Dad's hand. Johnson Hayes, father to all seven of the children in the room, just stared at me in a maddening way.

I opened my mouth to ask *"what's going on?"* when searing pain ripped through my throat. My hands shot to it, but my entire body screamed.

"Don't move, Jake," Jordan cried, her hands flashing to pull my hands away. My fingers brushed what felt like gauze at my throat before she pulled my hands back. "Don't."

On instinct, I went to ask *"what happened?"* when the pain ripped through me again. My eyes turned frantically to my family.

Something had happened to me. The last thing I remembered was my stupid drinking haze, and something about a deer.

Having everyone stare at me, not saying a word was going to drive me insane. I felt panic eating at me, a kind of terror I had never felt before. And it hurt too much to ask what had happened.

So I simply pointed at my oldest brother, the oldest child in our family, John. Giving me a meaningful look, John cleared his throat.

"You were in a car accident, Jake," John said with a husky voice. "Do you remember that?"

I tried to make my frantic thoughts focus for a second, to think back to the last thing I remembered. I was sure it was the deer. And then I remembered the sound of the tire popping. And the feeling of steel too close to my skin.

I nodded.

"Carter was trying to find his phone or something, he said you jerked the wheel so he wouldn't hit a deer. Apparently he was drunk, guess you all were," John's voice hardened a little in anger. I felt my heartbeat quicken.

"John," Mom managed to get out. "Are you sure we shouldn't wait until the doctor gets back to tell him?"

I shook my head, just a little. More pain ripped through me. But I didn't care. I had to know what had happened. Now.

John nodded his head, understanding. "You guys swerved off the side of the road. There was a pretty big ledge where the truck went off. The truck slammed to the ground and rolled onto its side. You all rolled..." his voice cut off for a second. John placed a fist over his mouth and tried to clear his throat. A single tear slipped down his cheek. "You all rolled... You rolled onto the side of the truck. Right onto a t-post. It broke right through the passenger window. It..." John didn't seem able to talk anymore.

"The t-post skewered you, right through the neck," my older sister Jenny said. Jenny had never been afraid of anything, not even to deliver the earth-shattering news. "It might have been okay, but with the truck tipped, Carter and Rain piled on top of you, and it made it worse."

My head was spinning. I felt sick. I was pretty sure I was going to throw up but tried with everything in me not to. Just trying to talk was torture. I couldn't imagine what having the contents of my stomach come up would do to me.

"That's enough, you guys," Johnson said, speaking for the first time. "No more until Dr. Calvin gets here."

I wanted to protest, to demand that they tell me every little horrifying detail, now. But I knew something was so beyond wrong, so wrong that I couldn't form even a single word.

"It's going to be okay, Jake," seven-year-old Joshua said, climbing onto my bed and laying his head on my chest. Despite the pain in my arms, I placed my hand on Josh's back and rubbed small circles into it.

My arms hurt from all the cuts and stitches. I then remembered the window had shattered on the passenger side. The side I'd been sitting on.

A nurse opened the door to the room, asking if we needed some help.

"Could you call Dr. Calvin?" Johnson asked her quietly. "Jake's awake."

"He'll be right down," she answered, giving me a sad glance.

I tried to block it all out as we waited, all the beeping, the weird smell, the hard bed. The downfallen expressions every single one of my family members wore. I imagined I was back at the football game, catching that interception and making a break for the goal line. And I imagined Samantha, exactly where she had been in the stands, cheering the Vikings on.

I imagined her screaming my name as I made a touchdown.

"Jake?" a voice called, tearing me from my daydream back into reality. My eyes lifted to a man with the shiniest shaved head I'd ever seen. Grey eyes looked back at me from behind silver wire rimmed glasses. "I'm Dr. Calvin. I've been taking care of you for the last four days."

Four days?

I'd lost *four days*?

"I assume your family explained what happened?" Dr. Calvin asked as he pulled up a rolling stool. The room was starting to feel very crowded with ten people in it.

"Just the accident," Mom spoke up. Her voice still sounded rough. Josh hopped off the bed and crawled up into Jenny's lap.

"Okay," Dr. Calvin said, digging through a manila folder. He pulled out a few pieces of paper and handed them to me. I took the pages but didn't look at them. I simply waited to hear the news that could be nothing but crushing.

"First off, I have to say that you're very lucky to be alive."

I closed my eyes for a moment. It's still really bad when a doctor says that.

"The post that crashed through the window in your friend's truck lodged into your neck. It came in through

30

here," Dr. Calvin lightly touched his fingers to the side of my neck. "And came out here," he touched another place on my neck, not quite center on the front of my neck. "When your friends crashed down on you, it shifted the post and it embedded itself right in your vocal chords. It also did significant damage to your wind pipe."

I gave a hard, painful swallow. The fire that ripped through me would never be as painful as the words I knew the doctor was going to say next.

"Your vocal chords were essentially ripped out," the doctor said simply, his face all too serious. I wasn't sure if I appreciated his direct approach or not. "You were in surgery for five hours, we tried the best we could to repair the damage. We managed to repair your esophagus, got you breathing on your own again. But..."

The room started spinning around me, my head feeling like it might float away from the rest of my body.

"I'm afraid we weren't able to save your vocal chords."

Small black spots swam on the edges of my vision.

"Jake," the doctor half sighed. "With how extensive the damage was, and with how the pole hit your neck, we had to remove the vocal chords completely, what little there was left to remove. You're..." he trailed off. I wondered how many times a day he had to deliver life destroying news. "You're not going to be able to talk again."

I let out a long breath when Dr. Calvin finally said it. The words I knew were going to be said as soon as I had tried to speak.

Dr. Calvin started talking about treatment plans, my recovery over the next few days, options about my future, how I was lucky I hadn't been paralyzed, but I didn't hear any of it, not really. Everything dropped away, and the world fell very quiet and still.

One by one, I saw the things I loved dropping away.

The Air Force.

Football.

Oddly enough, school.

But mostly, Samantha.

I'd never gotten to tell her.

"Here," a voice said, pulling me back into the room again. Jordan pushed a spiral notebook and a pen across the bedside table to me. "You can write down anything you have to say."

I looked up at my sister, so close in age to myself, only eleven months apart, and tried to manage a small smile. I looked around the room to see everyone looking at me expectantly. I realized Dr. Calvin had left.

"Are you okay, Jake?" ten year-old James asked. I just stared at him blankly.

"Hush, James," Mom hissed. She wiped at her eyes with a tissue. I wished she would stop crying. I could count on one hand the number of times I had seen my mom cry and they had all been when someone had died.

I wasn't dead.

Trying to turn the attention away from me, I reached for the notebook and opened the cover. The pages stared up at me, too white and too crisp. It felt wrong, that those perfect pages would have to do my imperfect talking.

Carter and Rain? I wrote in sloppy handwriting. My entire arm ached when I used it.

"They're both okay," Mom answered, finally seeming to pull herself together. "Carter's left arm is broken, Rain got a good handful of stitches. But they're both okay."

"You got the worst of it, since the truck landed on your side," Jenny said.

I nodded my head, trying to act like I didn't care about that last part.

We in trouble for the drinking?

"You better believe you're in trouble," Mom shot, back to her normal self. "What were you doing at a party like that Jacob Hayes?"

A smile nearly cracked on my lips as I just gave a shrug. All the siblings laughed.

"I can't believe you all went and did a stupid thing like that. I'll let your teammates tell you all the drama there tomorrow," Mom shook her head.

?

"Everyone wants to see you," Jordan answered. "A lot of people are coming down on a bus tomorrow after lunch. They're catching the one o'clock ferry."

How many coming?

"Probably half the school," she answered, reading my scribbled handwriting. "My cell phone hasn't stopped ringing the last four days. I'm up to over a thousand texts, all asking about you."

I took another painful swallow. I didn't want the entire school seeing me like this. But I couldn't say that, and it felt too incriminating to write it down.

"Don't worry about that right now," Mom said as she sat on the side of my bed again, taking my cut up hand in hers.

33

"You should probably get some rest. Why don't you all go get some dinner and let Jake get some sleep?" she said to the rest of the family. "I'll stay with him."

I'm okay, Mom, I wrote. You don't have to stay.

"No sweetie," she said. "You're not okay. And I'm not going anywhere."

I simply gave her a small half-smile and let my eyes start to slide closed as my family shuffled out the door.

4 1/2 days since the accident
10 months 'til Air Force?

I woke up with my hands wrapped around my neck, drenched in sweat, and trying to scream my lungs out. I couldn't remember what I'd just been dreaming about, but Sam's face lingered in front of me like vapor steam from the shower.

I looked around, trying to orient myself. Muted light started peaking around the curtains, hinting at grey skies that never fully left Washington State it felt like.

In all the chaos that had been the previous day, I hadn't thought to ask where or what hospital I was at. We didn't have a hospital on Orcas so I had to be somewhere off-island. Searching the room, my eyes sweeping past my mother's sleeping form on a couch, I looked for any indicator.

There was a mug sitting near the hand washing sink that read *Seattle Children's Hospital*.

Great. I was just months from being a legal adult and I was in a children's hospital.

Feeling the call of nature, I cautiously slid my legs over the side of the bed. Everything in my body screamed against me not to move. As I looked at my legs, poking out from underneath a baby blue hospital gown, I saw they were covered in mushroom clouds of green and yellow.

Taking a deep breath, and grabbing the IV tower that was attached to me with clear, snaking tubes, I pushed myself to my feet. My muscles felt weak and a bit like rubber. It was embarrassing what a few days in bed had done to me.

The lights in the bathroom blinded me for a second as I flipped them on. The cleanness of the space was almost startling at first. When you share a bathroom with four siblings, you didn't get the luxury of a clean one too often.

As I sighed in relief, I wondered how I'd managed this the last four days. That was something I didn't want to dwell on too long.

"Jake?" Mom groggily said. "Jake?" this time her voice sounded a little more panicked.

I was about to call *"just taking a leak in here"* when the reality of everything hit me again. I flushed the toilet. Nothing like having a toilet speak for you.

Mom dashed into the bathroom, her eyes wild, just like her hair.

"I didn't expect you to get up by yourself," she said, her expression calming. She leaned in the doorway and crossed her arms over her chest. "You feel okay?"

I took a breath to speak, but then just nodded my head in response. I stepped around her, back into the room. I was already feeling tired just taking the few steps to the bathroom.

"Dr. Calvin said you'd be feeling weak for a while, since you haven't had any solid food for a few days. He said you might be able to eat sometime next week."

Great. As if everything else weren't going to be bad enough, I couldn't eat now either.

I shuffled over to a chair that sat pushed into the corner of the room and gently lowered myself into it.

Mom handed me the notebook and pen, an expression of sadness and almost anger mixed on her face. I took it from her, attempting to manage a half-smile. I didn't think it worked though.

I flipped the notebook open to a blank page. *Where is everyone else?*

"They've been spending nights in a hotel a few miles away," Mom answered, sinking into the hospital bed. "Your siblings are going back to the island tonight. They've missed a bunch of school. They'll be heading back on the bus with the rest of your classmates. Shelly's going to stay with them tonight."

Shelly Smith was our next door neighbor and all five of her kids were long gone and raised. She'd been a surrogate grandmother to me and my siblings whenever she was needed.

"A bunch of your friends called last night, after you fell asleep," Mom said. The way she said it, the way her eyes didn't quite meet mine was awkward. "They wanted to see how you were doing."

I nodded. I suddenly felt awkward too.

Life had changed. Had it changed me? What else was about to change in the future?

You look like you could use a shower, I wrote, half in an attempt to relieve the tenseness, half because she really did look like she could use one.

"Thanks, you little brat," Mom laughed, glaring at me. I chuckled, but no sound came out.

That had been the weirdest part about everything so far.

"But you're right," she said as she sniffed at her arm. "I do kind of smell." She stood and kissed the top of my head. "There are family showers on one of the upper floors. I'll be back soon, okay?"

I nodded again and watched as she grabbed some of her stuff and walked out the door.

Things felt too quiet as soon as the door slid shut. It felt like the silence was pushing in on my eardrums. I looked around for the remote to the TV. My eyes froze on the bedside table, on a few of the papers Dr. Calvin had given me the day before.

Being Mute, the title read.

The word seemed to echo in my head, over and over.

Mute

    Mute

      Mute

I had never thought about that word much before. There were just certain words that you know, but you never really think about, never really consider what they mean.

"Mute" was one of those words.

And suddenly I felt like that word had been slashed into the skin across my neck with a blade.

Or maybe written in permanent, black marker across my forehead:

Hi, I'm Jake Hayes, and I'm MUTE.

I searched for the remote with more aggressive intent, determined to block my own thoughts out. I finally found it dangling from a power cord on the side of the bed and started flipping through channels with furious fingers.

The rest of the family got back to the hospital just after nine. It was easy to tell no one had been sleeping well, and everyone was just a little irritable. But they came prepared to entertain me. Jordan had bought a few card games, Joshua made up his own kind of Pictionary game, Dad brought a few action movies.

I wondered how much being in the hospital was costing the family. We had insurance, but the ferry was two hours from the hospital and then it was another hour on the ferry, and then a twenty minute drive to our house once you got on the island. They weren't driving back and forth to get all these things. Everything they were bringing for me was brand new. And housing seven people in a hotel couldn't be cheap.

My dad being an electrician didn't make us super rich. We weren't poor exactly, but we were careful with our money.

How much work had Dad had to miss because of me?

The day rolled by slowly, it was nothing but torture to watch each of them eat their lunches, even if it was crappy hospital cafeteria food. My stomach growled. The liquid pumping into my system didn't exactly make me feel full.

And I watched as the hands on the clock kept ticking steadily forward, the school bus arrival time of three o'clock creeping steadily nearer.

When Jordan arrived that morning she brought along my cell phone, which had been recovered from the accident. The screen was badly cracked where it had been smashed in my back pocket, but it did still work.

It wouldn't stop vibrating on the bedside table. It seemed like every ten seconds it flashed that I had a new text message from someone. I ignored them all.

I had just gotten out of the bathroom, the entire family gone, when there was a knock on the door. I just managed to sink into a chair, grateful for the sweats and tee-shirt Mom had gotten for me, when the door opened and in popped Rain and Carter.

"You still alive in here?" Rain tried to joke, his voice not quite pulling it off. I just tried to give a smile and nodded them in. They were followed by about a fourth of the student body of Orcas High School.

My breathing picked up a bit as I watched faces file in. There were so many people crowding into the room that I couldn't even see the people toward the back. My heart started hammering.

Rain, Carter, River, and Blake all sat on the bed, in the closest proximity of me. And every one of them stared right at the bandages on my neck.

It was a long awkward moment.

Finally, I pulled the notebook into my lap and clicked the pen open.

Hey everyone, I wrote. I held it up for them to see.

"Hey, Jake," they all murmured, forced looking smiles spreading on their faces. They all seemed to realize that they were supposed to be saying or doing something cause suddenly a bunch of them were asking how I was, saying how glad they were that I was okay, how sorry they were that this happened.

I'm okay, I guess, I wrote. Sore.

They all nodded, sadness filling each of their faces. It was irritatingly quiet again for a long moment.

Was it always going to be like this? With everyone, from now on?

"Dude, I'm really sorry," Carter finally spoke up, his eyes tortured. He cradled his casted arm with his hand. "If I hadn't been so drunk I would have just left my phone on the floor, instead of throwing us off a cliff."

I squeezed my eyes closed, shaking my head just slightly. I didn't want their apologies. I was pretty wasted too, I wrote. Technically I was the one who threw us off the cliff.

"I shouldn't have thrown that party in the first place," Rain said in a hoarse voice. He had a row of stitches above his left eyebrow, a few more on his chin. "It was a totally stupid thing to do."

I shook my head again. How screwed are we?

"The whole football team got suspended," Carter answered, his voice rough. "The rest of our games got canceled this year, with no team left to play. Dad was beyond pissed."

Carter had probably gotten the worst of the wrath, being the principal's son, and the quarterback of the football team.

"Everyone's excited for you to come back to school though, Jake," River chimed in. It was nice to see her face wasn't as downfallen as everyone else's. She was trying harder than everyone else. "There's a special assembly planned for you and everything."

Great... I wrote.

That made everyone laugh. Or at least fake a laugh.

It was nice to see them look a little more normal.

But they all kept staring at my throat.

It's going to be a pretty impressive scar, right?

"That's not funny, man," Rain said, shaking his head at me.

I'd be laughing, I wrote in shaking, almost angry letters.

"Jake, stop," River said, looking at me with hard eyes.

And then the crowd that occupied the room shifted, and through the bodies, I saw her, standing back near the door. Samantha.

My stomach knotted and I felt nauseous. My throat tightened and I suddenly felt like I couldn't breathe.

I didn't care that most everyone in my school was seeing me like this. Most of them didn't matter, and I didn't care what they thought about me.

But I didn't want Samantha Shay seeing me like this.

Something started beeping on the monitor attached to my IV tower and a nurse suddenly pushed her way through the crowd.

"Your pulse is getting a bit higher than we'd like it," she said as she checked the machine, pressing her fingers to my wrist. That was just making things all the more humiliating. I wanted nothing more than to curl up in that chair and disappear. "You should get some rest. All of you should probably say your good-bye's."

I finally met their eyes, seeing the fear and uncertainty in each of their faces. They were looking at me like I might explode or die right then and there. Again, I felt like the word MUTE was carved into my throat, blood and gore dripping from the letters.

"Hang in there, man," Rain said as he stood. He gave me an awkward hug, as did Carter, his cast feeling heavy and hard on my back. River's hug at least felt real. I wanted to die as countless other's either waved good-bye or gave an awkward embrace. But with each one I pulled more and more away. I didn't even return the hugs after River's. I started to glaze them all out.

"Bye, Jake," a sweet voice said as bodies filed out the door. My eyes rose to meet Samantha's. She looked at me sadly, but for once, it felt like she was really seeing me.

Something in me hardened.

It had taken nearly getting decapitated for Sam to finally really notice me.

I didn't even say, or rather write or wave good-bye as she gave me one more sad look and left, closing the door behind her.

Screw them all.

Especially Samantha.

"Would you take our picture?" Carter asked, his voice hopeful, as he shoved the camera at an unsuspecting tourist.

"Sure," the man said, clearly a bit annoyed but trying to force a smile. He accepted the camera.

Carter draped an arm around Rain and pointed out to Indian Island with the other. He gave me the look of death, like "just go along with it". I tried really hard not to roll my eyes. "Going along with it," I pointed out toward the water and plastered a big, fake smile on my face.

"One… two… three."

"Thank you," Carter said in a very feminine voice that made Rain scoot away from him as fast as he could.

The guy just raised his eyebrows at the three of us and continued toward town.

Carter immediately busted up laughing and the three of us kept walking down the narrow sidewalk.

"This is lame," I said, shaking my head and pushing my sunglasses up.

"Let's be German next," Carter said. "I come from far country, you show me good American time, yeah?"

"Seriously, you're not going to find any tourist girls to hook up with," Rain said, stuffing his hands in the pockets of his shorts. "It's all old, rich ladies in the summer."

"No, it's not!" Carter protested as he scrolled through the pictures on his camera. "There was Gloria from Maine last year!"

"There is no Gloria!" Rain and I both said at the same time.

"She's not real," Rain said, shaking his head and laughing. "You totally made her up."

"Where's the proof?" I said, my eyes scanning the crowded streets and sidewalk. It was amazing how many people flocked to our tiny island in the summer.

"Gloria was real," Carter said, his jaw tightening, just as it always did whenever "Gloria" was brought up. "And that night was magical."

"Magical is right," Rain said as we crossed the street. "As in not real."

"Oh, oh! Twelve o'clock!" Carter said, nodding his head at an older couple coming down the sidewalk straight for us.

"Come on, man," I moaned. "This is mean."

"No, it's entertaining," Carter said, getting his camera ready. "Excuse me!" It was too late. Carter was a German traveler from a faraway land. "You take our picture?"

"Ah," the man said, his face lighting up. "Welcher Teil von Deutschland sind sie?"

Carter's face blanched, obviously panicking. "Uh, never mind."

He took off running down the sidewalk.

The couple watched as he ran off, then glanced back at me and Rain with confused expressions.

"Excuse our friend," I said with a sigh.

"He was in a car accident recently," Rain said, his voice totally serious. "He's been a bit… off, ever since."

Without waiting for them to question us further, me and Rain took off after Carter, the both of us trying to hold our laughter back.

"Ah, crap," Rain said as he checked the time on his phone. "We're supposed to pick River up from Diana's house in like two minutes. Where's Carter?"

By now we'd reached the park in the middle of town. Considering it was Saturday, that meant it was filled with booths and tents for the farmer's market. Hippy gardeners, potter's, jewelry makers, glass-blowers, and other entrepreneurs spread themselves out across the expanse of grass. And the entire place was flooded with tourists.

Rain and I started wandering the aisles, poking around for Carter.

"You two look like you're looking for someone," a familiar voice said through the crowd.

I looked up to see Samantha, a basket over one arm, holding a big floppy straw hat down on her head with the other. She wore a breezy, white summer-dress and bright pink flip flops.

She looked amazing.

"You seen Carter?" Rain asked, speaking when I seemed to lose my ability to do so.

"Yeah," she said, a brilliant smile flashing on her face. "I saw him near the food tents, talking to some girl."

Rain and I exchanged a look.

"Take us there?" I said, feeling like I might pass out from how nervous I felt asking such a simple question. I was turning into a freaking joke around Sam.

"Sure," she smiled again. "Come on."

Sure enough, we found Carter, talking to some skanky looking girl who had to be at least twenty. I had to give him credit, he had her laughing, even if she was way too old for him.

"Come on," Rain said, dragging Carter away. "River's waiting for us, and you do not want to enrage my Amazon-warrior sister."

"Seriously?" Carter protested as Rain pulled on the back of his shirt. "I told you I'd find a tourist to hook up with!"

"I don't think you'll be hooking up with her," Sam said as she glanced back toward the girl. We all looked back at her to see a very muscled guy wrapping his arms around the girl. The guy's eyes met Carter's and his jaw flexed and his nostrils flared.

"Run," Rain said. Without another word, he and Carter took off in the direction of Carter's truck. I just shook my head as I watched them go.

"Isn't that your ride running for his life?" Sam asked as she stopped at one of the produce tents.

"I met them at Teazers," I said, picking up one of the apples Sam was studying. Pulling out my wallet, I paid for two of them. I handed one to Sam and bit into mine.

"Thanks," she said, flashing another warm smile that made my knees want to give out. "Have you tried the horchata from the Mexican food stand?"

I shook my head as I swallowed the bite of apple.

"It's divine," she said, and we headed back in that direction. "It's going to ruin you though. All other horchata is going to taste disgusting after you try this."

I chuckled as I followed her. "Ruin me."

12 days since the accident
No more Air Force...

Things got quieter over the next week. John and Jenny went back to college, from Jordan on down they went back to the island. Even Dad had to get back to work. It was just me and Mom. And a million nurses, a million physical therapists, and one psychologist.

Mom had tried staying with me that first therapy session. She said she wanted to help me learn how to cope with my new "lifestyle." I liked the psychologist a little more when she wouldn't let Mom into her office.

But it was all the same crap that I had expected to hear when I learned I was going to be visiting her. Life was going to be hard, but I still had a lot to live for. I shouldn't give up and I shouldn't give up on my dreams, but maybe adjust them.

Blah, blah, blah.

All I heard was pity and a lot of rehearsed lines.

I was told I would be released by Saturday, a full twelve days after the accident. Then on Thursday I started burning up with a fever of 104, and they decided to hold me prisoner for a few days longer.

Despite being in a children's hospital, I almost didn't mind. The world inside the walls of the hospital were a bit like an alternate reality. Almost like I was only unable to speak within those walls. As soon as I stepped outside of them, reality was going to finally sink in, that this was real, and my voice wasn't going to come back.

I didn't mind holding reality off.

Because not being able to talk for the rest of forever felt like an unbearable amount of time. I couldn't even comprehend it.

Even though I was in the hospital, and even though I had just had a life-changing event happen, Mom didn't let me completely pretend I didn't have to do school work anymore. She'd called each of my teachers, had Dad bring down all my school work and books, and every afternoon after the vampires were done with me, she drilled and hounded me until my homework was done.

There'd been a note from Principal Hill that we'd talk when I was ready to go back to school about adjusting my schedule.

Great. Special treatment. Just great.

It didn't take long to fill that first notebook, the one Jordan had given me. My messy handwriting stained the pages, big and blocky so everyone could read it easily. Several pages were ready to fall out, after being flipped to so often. Pages that said things like "thank you", "I'm tired", and "where's the remote?"

Mom dared to leave my side for about an hour one day and came back with a stack of fifteen notebooks, a rainbow of colored covers.

I just shook my head when she set them down.

My paper voice.

It both seemed that Monday came all too fast, and couldn't get there soon enough. But at ten in the morning, Dr. Calvin came in and told us I was going home that afternoon.

My bandages were also ready to be removed.

I sat on the bed with my hands pressed firmly between my legs so no one would see them shaking as Dr. Calvin sat on a stool in front of me with latex gloves on his hands. I couldn't look at his face as he started to remove the bandages. I just stared at the ceiling tiles, determined I was going to find at least one cobweb.

"Now, Jake," Dr. Calvin said. Something tugged just slightly on my neck. Tape, hopefully. My stomach churned. "You're still going to be really tender for a few weeks. You're going to have to take it easy. Your doctor on the island will remove these stitches at the end of the week, but again, be careful. No scarves or turtlenecks, or anything that will stay in contact with your neck for an extended period of time. You want to make sure you keep out any chances of infection."

Dr. Calvin wadded up a bunch of bandaging and threw it into the trash, followed by his gloves.

Everything was finally off.

Dr. Calvin looked toward the end of the bed, at the mirror that hung on the wall. So did Mom.

I knew they were waiting for me to look at it.

I closed my eyes for a moment, feeling my heart pound in my chest. My skin prickled as I broke out into a sweat.

Seeing the evidence of the t-post's implantation in my throat was just one more way of making this whole nightmare real.

Don't be a pussy, I thought to myself. *Just look at it.*

Holding my breath for a second to calm down, I nodded my head just once. I pushed myself to my feet and walked over to the mirror.

My eyes couldn't help but immediately jump to my throat. Or what was left of it.

The skin there was a mess. A big line of stitches ran from the right side of my neck, zig-zaging up, trailing to the left. There was a large hole on the right side of my neck. The side where the post had entered.

I tentatively reached a hand up, lightly touching my fingers to the hole.

The skin that covered it looked weird. Like it wasn't really my skin.

"That's the skin graft," Dr. Calvin explained, coming to stand by me. "You'll find things feel a little different. That's because the vocal chords are gone. It's going to take some getting used to."

I continued staring at myself and nodded absentmindedly.

I had been right when I joked with my friends earlier. It was going to be an impressive scar.

"You okay, Jake?" Mom asked.

I blinked suddenly, realizing I hadn't done so since I first looked in the mirror. I nodded, my throat feeling tender.

Dr. Calvin nodded as well, watching my face, like he was expecting me to freak out at any moment.

I kind of wanted to freak out. But my body felt sort of weird. Almost like I was on some kind of drug that didn't let me fully feel pain.

"Okay, then," Dr. Calvin finally said, turning back to Mom. "If you'll just sign these papers you'll be good to go. Jake's medication is in that bag there and the rest of it will be delivered to your house in a few days."

"Thank you for everything, Dr. Calvin," Mom said.

I just kept looking in the mirror as Dr. Calvin left and Mom set to gathering up our stuff.

They were *gone.* The pieces of me that made my voice work were *gone.*

What did they do with body parts after they'd been removed from the body?

"Jake," Mom said from the door. I finally looked over at her, seeing her with her arms loaded with our bags. "You ready?"

I looked back at myself just once more.

It was time to get back to reality.

I nodded and walked over to her, grabbing my backpack from her hand and slinging it over my shoulder. She gave me a long look, studying my face and eyes. She offered a small smile and placed a hand on my cheek.

"Let's go home," she said quietly, rising up on the balls of her feet to press a quick kiss to my forehead.

We stepped out the door and let it slide quietly closed behind us.

It seemed weird that I had changed so much the last two weeks but the world hadn't. Seattle still looked the same as we made our way to the freeway, so did Everett and Mount Vernon. Mom ran into the grocery store in Anacortes before we got to the ferry to grab a few things. I stayed in the car.

You still coming home today? Rain texted.

Yeah, I replied. *We're catching the three ferry.*

Hope the boats aren't too crazy so you can get on.

Dr. gave us a med pass, we'll get on, I answered. *Stupid tourists.*

Seriously. Can't wait to see you man. Carter says hi.

Tell him hi. See you soon.

Truth was, I didn't really want to see anyone any time soon.

Just one more way to make this all real.

Glancing up, I saw Mom pushing a shopping cart out of the store. Pushing my nerves back, I slid the phone back into my pocket, and got out to help her put the groceries in the back of the car.

The ferry wasn't as bad as it had been a few weeks ago. Now that it was mid-October, most of the summer tourists were headed back to work or school, but there were still the real old-timers who liked this time of year when the weather was still fairly warm but it wasn't quite so insane. Not that it mattered, we got on the ferry just fine with Dr. Calvin's medical priority load pass.

Mom and I didn't talk much as we slowly loaded onto the massive ferry. Before that day we would have gone up onto the passenger deck as soon as we parked, but that day we both just hunkered down and pretended to be asleep as the ferry cut through the waters of the Pacific Ocean.

Normally I hated the three o'clock ferry because it stopped at both Lopez and Shaw Island before going to Orcas, so it took forever to get home, but that day there weren't enough islands to stop at before the ferry pulled into the dock.

The ferry workers lowered the ramp and secured the boat with bored and well-practiced movements. And then car engines roared to life, a trail of red taillights flashing on in a row.

And finally we were waved forward and the tires met the narrow roads of Orcas Island.

Home.

But everything about home was going to be different from then on.

We didn't get a mile away from the ferry landing when a gigantic sign on the side of the road came into view.

Welcome Home Jake! it read. There were large hearts painted on the white paper, handprints, and signatures from what looked like half the island.

A small little smile threatened to break on my lips. I noticed that Mom had a tiny smile on her face as we drove passed it.

The narrow road slowly wound through the trees and fields. Driving on the island was a little different than it was driving on the mainland. When the fastest road was only forty, no one was ever in a huge hurry. We were back on island time.

We pulled into the driveway, finding another gigantic paper sign taped to our garage door. This one read *We Love And Miss You, Jake!*

A small smile did finally crack on my face when I found Samantha's name written on it, in big orange letters.

I helped Mom carry the bags in, stepping through the front door.

About a million balloons were hugging the ceiling in the living room. A thousand cards lay on the coffee table, a handful of stuffed animals were lined up in the window seat.

"Well look at that," Mom marveled as she stepped in behind me. She actually laughed. "I think your school missed you."

I just nodded, taking it all in. This hadn't just been my high school. This had been the whole island.

"Wow," Mom called from the kitchen. "Look at that stack of dishes." She laughed.

I walked into the kitchen with the groceries to see what she was talking about. There was a stack of casserole dishes, mixing bowls, and Tupperware with names I recognized written on them. It looked like our family had been well-fed while Mom was with me.

"Jake?" I heard a voice from upstairs. A second later it sounded like a heard of buffalo were pounding down the stairs. I was suddenly attacked in a dog-pile of a hug that sent all of us to the ground.

"Hey! Hey!" Mom yelled, pulling Joshua and James off of me. "The stitches, the stitches!"

"Sorry, Jake," they both said in unison, pulling me to my feet. I just tried to laugh, and punched both of them in the arm.

"I'm so glad you're home," Jamie said, coming at me a little more gracefully. She pulled me into a hug. I felt pathetic that it still hurt just a little whenever someone touched me.

"Ugh," Joshua said, eying my throat. "That's so gross!"

"Josh!" Mom gasped, wrapping a hand over his mouth. "You can't say stuff like that to him."

"It is pretty disgusting," James said, eyeing it up close.

"James!" Jamie shrieked, slapping at his arm.

I pulled out the small notebook I now always carried in my pocket. *He's right,* I wrote. *It is pretty nasty.*

Jamie just sighed and rolled her eyes as she walked out of the kitchen. "Boys," she said as she disappeared back up the stairs.

I was glad to see that not everything had completely changed. Jamie still acted like a thirteen year-old girl. The boys were still honest, gross boys.

"Does it hurt?" Joshua asked, released from Mom's grasp.

Not too bad, I wrote. It felt weird trying to communicate like this. Like the whole conversation was in slow motion. It felt like I couldn't quite write fast enough.

"Cool," Joshua replied lazily, wandering into the living room to watch TV.

"Homework, young man," Mom yelled, neck-deep in the fridge. The whole family swore she really did have eyes in

57

the back of her head. Joshua just sighed and turned to go up the stairs to his bedroom.

And just like that, the whole family seemed to go back to normal. I stood there in the kitchen for just a moment, not quite sure what to do with myself. So I did what I would have done before. I grabbed my stuff, and walked to my room, like it was just any normal day.

5 minutes into reality

There were just as many balloons, stuffed animals, and cards in my small room as there were in the living room. I couldn't even put my bags on my double sized bed, it was covered with so much stuff.

I normally liked to keep my room clean, but I didn't mind that it was messed up with support.

Dropping my bags onto the floor in the corner, I gathered a handful of the cards and dropped them onto the dresser. Pushing some of the bears, lions, and ducks to the side, I flopped down on my back, arms crossed behind my head. That's when I noticed the t-post, stood up against the wall. Someone had attached a sign to the top of it, just a simple white square of wood. Printed in neat, black letters, it read: *"The only way of finding the limits of the possible is by going beyond them into the impossible." -Arthur C. Clarke.* I didn't have to inspect the post further to know it was the post that had changed my life forever.

It was sickening to think that thing had been inside of my body.

Adjusting my position, I forced myself to look away from it and stare up at the ceiling.

I had a decision to make in that moment. I could let this accident, this insane thing that had happened to me ruin my life. It wouldn't be hard to let it consume me. It would be really easy to get mad at life and to just give up.

It would be a heck of a lot harder to keep doing what I had always been doing. It wouldn't be easy to go back to school in a few days. It wouldn't be easy to walk around the island, to have every single person know what had happened to me. Because that was the way it was going to be.

So I had a decision then.

Was I going to take the easy way out, or take the hard, high road?

I must have fallen asleep because when I opened my eyes it was pretty dark out. I heard muffled voices outside my door.

"Mom, don't let them wake Jake up," Jordan said from the hallway.

"He'd want to see his friends," she insisted. I faintly heard my doorknob jostle as someone's hand rested on it.

"Yeah, Jordan," Rain teased her. "Jake needs his posse right now."

"Posse?" Jordan mocked him. I could just see her crossing her arms over her chest and giving him "the look" girls were so good at.

I pulled myself up and made my way through the mess that was my room and opened the door. Their eyes jumped to my face, their expressions surprised and guilty.

"Oh, hey, Jake," Carter said. "You're awake."

I just nodded.

Having no voice kind of felt like being a prisoner in my own body. I couldn't even say *hey* in return.

"We're glad you're back," Rain said, wrapping his arms around me, pounding on my back in a very "manly" hug. "School hasn't been the same without you."

"You okay, Jake?" Jordan asked. "I'll make them leave if you want me to."

A smile cracked my lips and I shook my head.

Jordan eyed them for a long moment and finally turned and walked away with Mom.

The guys shuffled into my room and I closed the door behind them and flipped the light on.

"So how's it feel to be back on the rock?" Carter asked, picking up a very pink teddy bear and sitting on my bed.

I shifted through my backpack until I found one of the notebooks Mom had bought. Finding a pen took a while longer. Frustration made my face hot when I couldn't find one.

I finally found it at the very bottom of my bag.

Opening the notebook, I glanced at my friends. I felt like an idiot. *Feelin' the spotlight, that's for sure,* I wrote.

"The whole island hasn't been able to stop talking about you," Rain said, flipping through the cards on my dresser. "A bunch of the old ladies put together a fund raiser to help pay for everything. I think I heard they raised something like six thousand dollars."

My eyebrows rose, surprised. That was a lot of money.

"I think Mr. Carol donated about half of that," Carter added a little more quietly.

I honestly hadn't even thought about Mr. Carol since all of this had happened. Would I still continue to work for him? Ninety percent of my pay had been the use of Mr. Carol's plane. And I couldn't fly anymore.

I couldn't fly anymore…

I hadn't realized I'd been too quiet for too long until I saw the perplexed expressions on my friend's faces.

"Everything's going to be okay, isn't it?" Rain asked. "I mean, you're going to be alright physically, and everything?"

I swallowed hard, my eyes falling to the floor for a second.

This was that moment again, where I had to decide.

My insides felt like a bunch of lizards biting and snapping at each other. I nodded.

Yeah, I wrote. *Everything's going to be okay.*

"It's just going to take some time," Carter said, a sad half-smile on his face. I nodded and tried to smile too.

So, I wrote. *You think Samantha missed me much?* Time for a change of subject.

That brought a chuckle out of both of them. "She's actually been talking to my dad a bunch about rearranging your schedule," Carter said, tossing the small bear from one hand to the other. "Don't ask me why she's been involved."

My brow furrowed, giving a small nod.

Think I got a shot with her anymore?

"Hey, you never know. Some chicks like the sick and the helpless."

I chucked my pen at Carter's face, shaking my head.

"What?" he continued, throwing the pen back at me. "It's true."

I wondered how it was possible, for things to go back to normal so easily. I may have been writing my words instead of saying them. But these two were still my best friends, and they were still going on like nothing was wrong with me.

The family, Dr. Calvin, and my psychologist all decided that I would go back to school as soon as I could eat solids again, and that meant Thursday. So the days between when I got home and then should have seemed peaceful.

They were the total opposite.

Mom hounded me about watching the sign-language videos I'd been sent home with for three hours a day. On top of that she still expected me to stay caught up on my school work.

And the phone wouldn't stop ringing.

It seemed every hour on the hour someone else would call, talk to Mom for about thirty minutes, and ask how I was doing, what was going to happen in the future, and what they could do to help.

A lot of people would just show up at the house too, wanting to see how I was doing. Jordan got very good at being the door guard. Any time the doorbell rang I would slide into my room and close the blinds. Jordan would simply tell them that I was sleeping or studying and couldn't be disturbed.

I never appreciated my sister as much as I did in those few days.

My cracked cell phone wouldn't stop vibrating on the dresser, text messages from half the student body at OHS saying they couldn't wait to see me.

To say I was overwhelmed was an understatement.

I was terrified to go back to school on Thursday.

Because I knew everyone was going to be staring at my neck, every single one of them knew what had happened to me. And they were all going to feel sorry for me.

I didn't want anyone feeling sorry for me.

I continued to receive all nourishment by IV, my esophagus still not healed enough to eat solids. I never thought I'd miss food so much.

By Wednesday night, Mom was trying to force me to sign as much as I possibly could. But it was a disaster. My eyes may have been watching that woman on the sign language videos, but I wasn't absorbing any of it.

Mom was getting way better at sign language than I was.

I kind of felt bad for not making a bigger effort when she was trying so hard.

2 years ago
8 months into sophomore year

It was slim pickings.

I should have guessed it would be, seeing as it was the day before Mother's Day. Had I thought about it earlier, I would have gotten Mom something nice when the family had gone off-island last weekend. Now I was stuck browsing the tiny aisles of Ray's Pharmacy.

Picking up a silver photo frame that had JOY engraved into it in cheesy font, I wondered if Mom would like something like that. Probably not. Mom wasn't into cheesy.

"Mother's Day is just a day asking for people like us to get into trouble," a familiar voice said as it approached from

64

behind. I turned to see Samantha browsing through a rack of cards, each of them equally cheesy to the JOY frame.

"If you don't get something for Mom, she'll be offended," Sam said as she continued to look through the cards. "But if you get something she doesn't like, she has to go through the painful experience of pretending like she loves it. My mom's a terrible actress, so I always know."

"I thought moms were supposed to love whatever you get them," I said, browsing through some photo albums. "Isn't that part of being a mom?"

"It is," she said as she picked up a card. After reading what was printed in it, she closed it and put it back. "But you know they're secretly hoping for something really good."

I chuckled and considered the small selection of scented candles. Mom wasn't really a candle person. "Why are mom's so hard to shop for?"

"Seriously," Sam said, leaving the card rack and joining my side. I felt my heartbeat pick up just a little bit. "Okay, who really wants a fresh cut grass scented candle?"

"I don't know," I said seriously, picking the green candle up and giving it a whiff. Sure enough, it smelled just like grass. "It might bring back good memories to someone who worked on a golf course."

Sam burst out laughing, covering her mouth when she got strange looks from other shoppers. I couldn't help laughing too as I put the candle back.

"Okay, so I have an idea," Sam said, swishing her hair over her shoulder. "How about I pick out something for your mom, and you pick out something for mine? That way if our moms hate what we got, which they won't say if they do, we can push the blame off on each other."

"A twisted but genius idea," I said, a smile spreading again on my face as I looked at Sam's proud smirk. I couldn't help but smile when I was around Sam.

"I have been told I'm the smartest girl in school," she said seriously. She couldn't hold it though and a smile cracked on her face a moment later.

"Did... did your head just get a little bigger?" I said, my brow furrowed.

Sam just laughed again and punched my shoulder. "Get shopping, boy! Get my mother something nice! She deserves it."

First day back at school

Thursday morning dawned brilliant and irritatingly bright. It would have been easier to talk myself, and Mom, out of me going to school if it had been just miserable and wet outside. But I'd kept myself cooped up in that house for days and I couldn't deny I wanted to get out and soak up some vitamin D.

"You're going to do great today," Mom said as she scooped up a mountain of pancakes and set them on a plate. She'd also cooked a huge pan of eggs, toasted an entire loaf of bread, and had bacon cooking on the stove. Mom was going all out. She had a tendency to do that when she was nervous or unsure about a situation. To her, food cured all.

"We called Principle Hill last night and let him know you were coming back today," Dad said from where he sat at the table reading the newspaper. "He said for you to go straight to his office this morning."

I nodded, barely listening to him as I bit into my first solid bite of food since the accident.

Bacon had never, *never* tasted so good. It burned a bit as it went down, but it was totally worth it.

Real food was so much better than food pumped directly into your system.

After school, I was going to the family doctor here on the island to get the stitches and my IV line removed.

"Joshua, James!" Mom suddenly yelled, making me jump and nearly slop orange juice down my front. "Get down here! You're going to be late for school!"

Their footsteps thundered down the stairs. James tripped down the last two and landed flat on his face.

Nice! I quickly wrote, shaking my head at them.

"Shut up," James glared as he walked to the bar and grabbed a piece of toast. "I mean..." he stuttered, flushing red.

I just shook my head, and tried to laugh.

"You look like a mime or something when you do that," James said, his tone totally serious. "Your body tries to laugh, but nothing comes out."

I just tussled his hair and grabbed another handful of bacon. I went to retrieve my backpack from my room. Loading my books back into it, I then stuffed two blank notebooks in it as well. I zipped it up and stood there, staring at it there on the floor for a long moment.

This was the final step back to reality.

Taking a deep breath, I picked it up and slung it over my shoulder.

Joshua, James, Jamie, and Jordan were already shuffling out to the family's eleven-passenger van, piling in, backpacks slamming into each other, irritated morning voices yelling.

I'd never yell at any of them again.

I'd never yell about anything again.

The pity of my siblings was obvious as I climbed into the front passenger seat. It was normally a race to get there. They never would have left it for me if they didn't feel sorry for me.

I stared longingly at my beat-down, red and grey Bronco sitting in the driveway as I buckled. The deal was Mom could drive me to school the first few days, just to make sure

I was okay, and then I could go back to driving. At least one thing would go back to normal then. It was embarrassing to have my mom drive me to school.

Mom expertly backed the massive van out of the driveway and started rolling down the road toward the school.

"You got your notebooks?" Mom asked. She kept glancing over at me, her eyes flicking to my throat. I nodded. "You got your cell phone?" I nodded again. "You can call me any time today if you need me. I can come pick you up any time."

mom! I wrote in black ink on the palm of my hand, flashing it at her with annoyed eyes.

"Sorry," she apologized, completely ignoring Joshua and James' fighting in the back seat. "I'm just... worried about you today."

"He'll be fine today, Mom," Jordan said from behind me, reaching up to squeeze my shoulder. I placed my hand over hers, giving it an appreciative squeeze.

"I know," Mom said, though it sounded like it was mostly to herself. "I know."

The elementary, middle school, and high school on Orcas were all located right next to each other. Mom pulled into the parking lot of the middle school, in the center of them all. I sat there for a moment, as my siblings piled out, just watching all the people went their different ways.

I knew as soon as I stepped out of that van the whole world was going to be looking at me.

"It'll be okay, Jake," Mom said again, pressing a quick kiss to my cheek. "Principle Hill will be waiting for you."

I glanced at her, seeing the worried lines creeping out from around her eyes and mouth. It seemed unfair of me to make her look so scared after everything she'd done for me the last few weeks. So I finally nodded, kissed her cheek, and climbed out of the van.

The sun was blinding as it reflected off of the white high school in the distance. I squinted as I pulled my backpack over my shoulders and took in everything around me.

One advantage to getting out at the middle school parking lot was that the crowd around me was younger, so they weren't all looking for me. I managed to get half way to the high school before I started seeing the glances.

"Hayes!" Blake Shaw bellowed from across the lawn, pounding his fist to his chest before pumping it in the air. I lifted my chin to him, trying to smile.

Thanks to Blake, I'd been spotted.

"Jake!" my insides turned cold when I heard Norah Hamilton's voice from behind me. "Jake, wait up!"

I barely slowed as I continued toward the front doors.

"Jake!" she called as she came up to my side. "I'm so glad that you're back! I was so worried about you." She twirled her hair around one of her fingers.

Well, at least the ugly scar wasn't scaring the girls away. At least not Norah the Whora.

"So are you all better now? Oh wait, how are you going to answer that question?"

I tried really, really hard not to roll my eyes at her.

I pulled the small notebook out of my pocket and flipped to a well-worn page that read I'm fine.

"Oh, got it," she laughed. It was seriously annoying. "Well, if you're doing okay..."

She was thankfully cut off as Rain wedged himself between her and I. "Thanks for the concern Norah," Rain interrupted. She gave him the look of death, one of those other looks girls are really good at. "But I'm sure what Jake really needs is his posse."

"Whatever," Norah said as she rolled her eyes and walked back to her own group of friends.

"Welcome back, bro," Carter said, suddenly appearing. He clapped his hand on my shoulder. I winced just a little. "You ready for this?"

No, I simply wrote, flashing it to the both of them.

"Don't worry," Rain said, squeezing my shoulders. "We'll be with you the whole time. Well, at least until you get to Principle Hill's office."

I just shook my head and gave a silent chuckle.

"'K, that really is a little weird when you do that," Carter laughed, eying me. I just swung a fist at him, which he too easily dodged.

We were finally at the front doors, a whole herd of students following and staring. Pretending like I wasn't terrified, I stepped through the front doors and into the commons.

Everyone slowed just a little when they saw the three of us, their eyes jumping to my face. Through the mass of people I spotted Samantha, standing in the hall, her books clutched to her chest. She gave me a small smile, her eyes watching me with an expression that was hard to read.

71

"Jake," Principal Hill drew my eyes from Sam. "Glad to see you." He stuck out his hand like I was supposed to shake it. It felt awkward as I did. I glanced at Carter who just gave me a quizzical look, his brows furrowed together.

"We've got a lot to go over this morning so why don't you join me in my office?" he said.

I took a deep breath. Squeezing my hands into fists, I finally nodded my head. Rain and Carter patted my shoulders and muttered good-byes.

"We're really happy to have you back, Jake," Principal Hill said as he draped an arm across my shoulders. It felt unusually heavy. But then, Principal Hill was a very fit, very muscled man. At least I was going to pretend I wasn't physically weakened by the accident. "The entire school has really missed you."

I nodded again.

The man's office was small and crowded with stacks of papers, books, trophies, and more than a few discarded ties. I sank into the only available chair, pushing aside a few books. Principle Hill sat in his seat across the desk from me, unbuttoning his suit jacket and pulling his tie loose. He never looked comfortable in a suit. I had a sinking feeling that I knew why he was wearing it.

"So, how you feeling?" he asked, his eyes automatically going to my throat. That was just something that I was going to have to get used to. It was the first thing people were going to notice about me for the rest of my life.

I zipped my backpack open and slid out one of my new notebooks. Rummaging around for a pen, I clicked it open.

Oh how these slow motion conversations were going to drive me insane.

Fine, I simply wrote.

"You ready to get back into regular school life?" Principal Hill asked, shuffling through a few papers on his desk. I saw flashes of my name on a few of them.

I guess, I wrote. *I can't really sit at home anymore and do nothing.*

"I would guess that would be hard for an active guy like yourself," he said with a smile. "Well, I'm hoping we can make things as easy as possible for you. I've been reviewing your class schedule and there are a few adjustments I'd like to discuss with you if that's okay?"

I didn't want anything to change. I just wanted things to go back to the way they had been, back when my world was boring and made sense, back when the most agonizing part of my life was wondering when Samantha Shay was going to realize how crazy I was about her.

I nodded.

"Most of your classes won't really require any change. But I wanted to see if you were still wanting to stay in your Woods and Weight Training classes? Oh yeah, by the way, you've been kicked off the football team if you didn't guess." He gave me one of those looks that teachers were good at.

I figured, I wrote, giving him a sheepish look.

"I'm not going to lecture you about what a stupid thing you all did, I figure you've been punished enough to learn your lesson," Principal Hill said, resting his elbows on his desk and clasping his fingers together.

Thank you, I wrote.

"Anyway, back to my question. Would you still like to stay enrolled in your Woods and Weight Training classes? They're a little more physically demanding and I don't know how you're feeling in that way."

I considered for a moment, gauging my physical state, what I felt like I could do. The whole incident had left me physically weaker than I would ever admit. But this was part of that whole decision thing I had to face. I could use this all as an excuse to get lazy. Or I could take control again and get myself back in every way I could.

I'd like to stay in them, I answered. And I'd like to be back with my team members.

"I figured you'd say that," he said, a smile cracking on his face. "Just thought I'd better ask." He wrote a few things down on a paper, some kind of form. "Now, there's one class that's going to have to change. I don't want to dance around this Jake and make things awkward for both of us so I'm just going to say it. You're obviously going to have to drop your Spanish three class."

I honestly hadn't thought about that until then. I didn't realize that I hadn't been given any of my Spanish homework until then.

I'd never speak Spanish again.

Not that I was ever that good at it.

"One of our students has actually been taking American Sign Language through independent study for just over a year now and I'm highly recommending that you enroll in the class as well. Given your circumstances, I think it makes sense that we just go ahead and replace your Spanish class with that."

74

Independent study. In a school as small as Orcas High, that kind of class wouldn't be taught, but I'd never thought about that option. I wondered who the student was that was taking it.

"Does that sound okay?" the principal asked, giving me a cautious look. I hoped people wouldn't always look at me like that for the rest of my life. Like I might break or have a meltdown at any moment.

Sounds good, I wrote.

"Great," Principal Hill replied, looking a little relieved. He wrote a few more things down. "I'll be right back." He walked out and into the other administrative offices.

I slouched back in the seat when Principal Hill left, feeling like I was finally breathing for the first time since I had woken that morning. Everything was happening so fast, there was so much going on, it felt like I hadn't had time to actually process everything, to figure out where my life was going to go. But here I was, already thrown back into it all, feeling like I hadn't even gotten to bob my head above water.

Reality hadn't really sunk in yet, I knew that.

I didn't want to know what life was going to feel like when it finally did.

"Here you go, Jake," Principal Hill said, reentering the room. He handed me a sheet of paper. My new class schedule. "A few of your classes have switched hours, to adjust for that independent study class, but a lot of them are still the same."

Well, about half of them were. Physics, AP English and US Government were all different hours. And I no longer had a single class with Rain and Carter besides Weight Training. *Great.*

"So do you think you're feeling up to your first class today?" he glanced at my schedule. "Calculus?"

I clicked my pen again. *If that's okay, sir, I think I'll wait 'til next period. People are going to be staring enough without me walking in on the middle of a class.*

I watched Principal Hill's face as he read my sloppy handwriting.

"Understandable," he said with a nod. "I'll let Mr. Sue know you're excused from first period today."

I nodded. *Thanks.*

"If you need anything, you're always welcome to come and see me," Principal Hill said, standing and walking me out the door.

I just nodded.

It felt weird to be talking to Principal Hill like that. Troy had been like another dad to me all my life, Carter and I having been best friends for forever.

My muteness had changed every relationship in my life in one way or another.

That was the first time I'd thought that word about myself.

I tried not to pair the word "mute" with "broken".

The halls of the high school were long silent as I worked my way toward my locker. It rattled deafeningly loud when I pulled it open. A single sheet of white lined paper fell onto the ground. It must have been folded up and slid between the vent slats.

I bent down and picked it up off the cold tile floor and unfolded it.

See you third period, was all it read.

It was a girl's handwriting, that was for sure. Neat and organized looking.

Third period was my new independent ASL class.

Wondering who my new classmate was going to be, I stashed my books for my later classes and swung the locker closed. Heading toward the stairs to the upper level, I heard someone call out behind me.

"Jake, wait up!" I turned to see River jogging up behind me, coming from the direction of the girl's bathroom. She smiled when she saw me, only briefly glancing at my beautiful scar. "Rain said you might be coming back to school today."

I just nodded, trying to manage a smile.

"Must be kind of awful, huh?" she said, her nose scrunching just a little. "Talk about attention."

Seriously, I wrote on my pocket notebook.

"Hey, look," she smiled. To my surprise, she started signing, her hands moving slowly and cautiously. "I learned that on the internet a few days ago."

I gave a silent chuckle. Sorry, I have no idea what that means.

She laughed at me, giving me a disbelieving look. "It means *you're a jerk*."

I gave her a puzzled look and a hard glare. Jerk? Excuse me?

"For leaving me hanging about the Homecoming dance," she said in a very girl tone. It only took me a second to realize she was joking. She laughed all the harder. "You really thought I was serious for a minute there, didn't you?"

I just shook my head, rolling my eyes at her.

"Hey, I'll see you at lunch or something," she said, turning in the opposite direction. "I've got to get back to class. And Jake, just be prepared for sixth period."

Before I could ask her to explain, she took off down the hall.

With nothing else to do, I made my way to the upper floor, toward second period, Physics. Dropping my backpack on the ground, I sank to the floor next to it. I fished my cell phone out of my pocket, barely getting one bar of service on this middle-of-nowhere island. There were two text messages, one from Mom and one from Jordan. Mom was going to kill Jordan for texting during class.

How's things going? Mom's first text read. *You doing okay?* the second said.

Jordan's said practically the same thing.

I had just finished texting them both that things were fine when the bell rang, signaling the end of first period. I pulled the hood of my jacket up over my head and tried to sink into the floor as much as I could as students came pouring out of class rooms and into the hall. As soon as I was sure the classroom was empty, I slipped into Physics.

Mr. Roy didn't even glance up at me as I settled into a seat near the back of the classroom, grateful that he didn't assign seats. Hopefully I wasn't stealing anyone's regular seat. I couldn't be sure since this was one of my rearranged classes. I pulled my book out and started rummaging through my notes, attempting to look busy and keeping to myself beneath the protective cover of my hood.

I heard someone slide into the seat next to me as the warning bell rang, other bodies shuffling through the door. I stole a sideways glance. My heart jumped into my throat when I saw Samantha was the one sitting right next to me. She did a little double take, her eyes locking with mine.

"Jake?" she said, leaning forward. She pushed her bangs out of her eyes in that adorably annoying way of hers. "Hey, I didn't realize you were switching into this class."

I tried to manage a smile and pressed a finger to my lips, glancing around to see if anyone had heard her. Eyes had flashed to my face, including Mr. Roy's. I glanced back at Sam and saw her mouth "sorry" and give an apologetic smile.

"Mr. Hayes," Mr. Roy said as he rose from his seat and started walking toward me as students continued to fill the classroom. "Glad to have you back. Principal Hill called me just a few minutes ago to let me know you were transferring to this hour."

I could only nod.

"If you need any help getting caught up with everything we've gone over since you've been gone, just let me know. Your homework has all looked fine."

Thanks, I scratched on the notebook in front of me.

Mr. Roy looked at my page contemplatively for a moment, and then glanced at my face. He gave a little grunt that I didn't quite understand, and then sauntered back toward the front of the classroom as the tardy bell sounded.

As Mr. Roy started rattling off about stuff that I really didn't understand, a folded piece of paper was flicked onto my desk from the right. I glanced over at Sam as I reached for it. She stared intently at what the teacher was scrawling on the whiteboard.

Sorry, it read. I didn't mean to expose you.

I read it twice, glancing back over at Samantha once. My chest broke out into a weird little sprint.

No worries, I replied. They're all going to see me eventually. I flicked the note back onto her desk. She very stealthily wrapped her fingers around it and opened the page under her desk.

A small, sad smile spread on her face as she turned her attention back to the lecture.

I had no idea what we were supposed to be learning about that day.

3 hours since stepping into the spotlight

The bell finally rang, ending second period. I couldn't decide if the hour had gone by too fast, or not nearly fast enough. Samantha gave me a little sideways smile as she left the room, her books gathered up into her chest.

I sighed and shook my head as I slid my things back into my backpack, and pulled my hood over my head again.

Man, I'm pathetic. What am I? Some love struck girl?

Somehow I made it to my next classroom without anyone seeing me, or at least I didn't see them seeing me. My independent study class was located at the far end of the high school, in a room that was only used to teach ancient world history one period a day.

Whoever my fellow independent studier was, they weren't there when I got to the room. I flipped the light on, the fluorescent bulbs buzzing to life above me. Pulling my hood down, I dropped my bag onto one of the dozen desks and sank into it. Rummaging through my backpack, I pulled out a fresh notebook, one with a red cover.

I remembered then how the psychologist had advised me to write in a journal frequently. Something about how I couldn't voice what I had to say, and sometimes I would have things to say that I didn't want anyone else to hear.

It seemed like the normal mumbo-jumbo crap psychologists always spouted off. But for some reason I wanted to say something about this crazy weird day, and the unexpected benefit that came from my new class schedule.

The door squeaked as it swung open and my eyes jumped from the notebook to it.

The last person I expected or wanted to be standing in that doorway was Samantha Shay.

"Hi Jake," she said with a small smile, giving a little side wave, even though we were less than ten feet apart.

Out of pure instinct, I tried to say *Hi* back, but instead just felt like an idiot when no sound came out. I could only give a little awkward wave back.

She was at least kind enough not to smile or laugh at my attempt at talking. She closed the door behind her and walked to the desk next to mine. She dropped her messenger bag on the floor as she sank into her seat.

"'K, this feels too weird, sitting side by side like this when it's just us," she kind of laughed. "Let's turn these so they're facing each other."

I felt awkward and weird as we both stood, grabbed our desk/chair combo's and shuffled them until they were touching each other at the front. As we sat back down, our knees accidently bumped. I hoped I wasn't blushing, or something embarrassing like that.

"So," she said with a bright smile, glancing at me as she pulled her books out of her bag. The half dozen rings she wore on her fingers flashed in the light. She produced a book that looked like it weighed about ten pounds. Easily. "You glad to be back in school?"

I gave a shrug, feeling like my stomach was filled with acid or something. Everything inside of me felt like it was squirming.

Why did my tutor have to be Sam? I was glad I had more classes with her, but I didn't want her to be with me, constantly seeing the effects of that stupid drunk night.

"I'm really glad you're okay," she said, her eyes suddenly growing more serious. I thought I saw something flicker behind them, but didn't know what it was, or if I even really saw it. "The whole school was totally devastated when we found out what happened."

And just like that, she put me back in my distant place.

Guess that will teach me a lesson for drinking, I wrote with shakier hands than I would have liked.

"It's a pretty harsh lesson," she said, her eyes on mine. They reminded me of melted chocolate. "But I guess a lesson none the less."

I just shrugged, my eyes dropping from her face. In that moment I wasn't sure if I was going to make it through third period without dying or shriveling up from humiliation.

"Okay," Sam said, taking a deep breath and sitting up straighter. "So I've been doing ASL for just over a year now. Obviously with how small our school is, we don't have any teachers who actually teach it, or enough interest for them to get someone."

Why'd you decide to take ASL on your own anyway? I wrote, turning the notebook so she could read it.

"Uh," she stumbled over her words, her eyes suddenly dropping from mine. "A family member of mine suddenly lost their hearing. I thought it would be a nice thing to do."

I didn't quite believe what she said. Pretty much everyone on the island knew Samantha didn't have any family besides her single mom, who traveled for business

83

frequently, leaving Samantha at home by herself most of the time.

"How much sign language have you learned?" she asked, expertly changing the subject. "I know you probably haven't had much time to pick up on it, with everything that you've probably been through since the..." she trailed off, the same way a lot of people did when they referenced what had happened to me.

Accident? I wrote out for her.

"Yeah, that," she said, tucking a long lock of hair behind her ear uncomfortably. "Is it okay if I call it that? I don't... want to offend you or anything."

Don't know what else you'd call it, I wrote. I could tell I was being a bit of jerk but I wasn't sure how to stop myself. *My idiotic night of self-destruction?*

"Accident it is then," Sam said, her eyes falling to the book in front of her. From the tone of her voice I could tell I'd offended her.

I should have apologized, but I felt stupid enough already.

Instead I started signing my name, followed by the one phrase I knew. *I'm mute.*

That's it, I wrote when I was done.

"Okay," she said, her tone even and natural again. "That's a start. Do you know the whole alphabet?"

I shook my head and reached for my pen. *Not really. Just the letters in my name.*

"We'll start there then," Sam said, mercifully giving me a little smile.

And this was why I had been in love with Samantha Shay since the first day I saw her. Because even though I was being a jerk to her, she was still being nice to me. Sam was one of the nicest people I'd ever known.

1 year ago
4 months into junior year

"Nice game Kelly," Carter called as a few of the girls from the basketball team walked outside. She waved, flashing him a brief smile. Carter looked a little defeated she didn't stop to flirt with him or something.

I stuffed my hands into my pockets, pretending like I wasn't looking around for Sam. Carter and Rain had been relentless with their jabs and jokes lately. Not seeing her, I watched as three other girls from the team walked out of the locker room and headed for the doors to the parking lot.

"Man, Karina seriously needs to learn how to use some lotion," Carter said quietly, raising an eyebrow as she walked by with her friends. "We may have to stick her in the tank with Charlie soon." Charlie was Carter's gigantic iguana he'd had since he was twelve.

"Karina has a skin condition that's getting worse, you jerk." Sam had suddenly appeared, her duffle bag slung over her shoulder. She was still sweaty from the game, her jersey clinging to her skin. I might have had a hard time not staring if she hadn't looked so mad. "She can't help it."

Carter face instantly turned red, unable to meet Samantha's eyes. He didn't say anything, just stood there awkwardly.

"You might think twice next time before judging someone like that," Sam said, giving Carter a hard look. "Maybe think about what people say about you behind your back."

"Oh! Burned!" Rain said, pressing his fist to his lips, laughing.

Samantha just gave the tiniest of smiles, then turned and walked out of the commons with her mom.

6 hours since stepping into the spotlight
10 minutes 'til it got a whole lot worse

I felt like I was on Samantha-overload that day. Normally I couldn't see Sam enough, but with her in my second, third, fourth, and fifth periods, I felt like her eyes would never leave me and my brokenness. Had this happened three weeks ago I would have been beyond thrilled. But I really didn't want her seeing me like this.

I had to give it to her though. She wasn't staring at my throat. She wasn't really giving me special treatment.

Really, she was acting like a friend.

River had been right to warn me about something coming sixth period. As soon as Mr. Donnor took attendance, the Woodshop class was told to head down to the gym for an assembly. My stomach immediately sank into my feet.

They wouldn't really have an assembly for me, would they?

I tried asking Carter and Rain about it as we headed toward the gym, but they weren't exactly being helpful. I figured they thought they were being funny by not telling me what was going on, but it was just pissing me off.

I spotted Sam walking in front of me and stepped up my pace.

Any idea what's going on? I quickly wrote. I gently grabbed her arm to get her attention and held up my pocket notebook for her to read.

She looked up at me, with an expression like she wasn't sure if she should say anything. "It's not totally about you," she said. "But yeah, you're going to be getting a lot of attention."

I must have blanched white or something, because her expression was suddenly sympathetic. "Do you want to sit by me?" she asked, bumping her arm against mine.

I glanced once back at Carter and Rain. They both gave me a wink and encouraging, smug nods, so I figured that I was good to go.

Thanks, I wrote.

Everyone bottlenecked into the gym, the volume of everyone's voices seeming to double as they echoed off the wood floor. I followed Sam through the crowd and we sat on the second row from the floor, right in the middle of the bleachers. I gave her an unsure look.

"This will make things easier," she said, giving me an apologetic smile. She twisted one of the rings on her thumb.

I just shook my head and turned to watch Principal Hill and a few other teachers walk to the middle of the gym. There was a microphone sitting on a table there, as well as a stack of colorful papers.

My palms started sweating and I suddenly itched everywhere.

"Sit down, please," Principal Hill said into the microphone, standing just in front of the folding table. The one hundred and sixty or so students of Orcas High made their way onto the bleachers. "Let's get started."

I felt like a hundred pairs of eyes were burning into the back of my head. I fought the urge to pull my hood back up.

"You okay?" Sam whispered, her shoulder brushing mine as she leaned towards me.

I swallowed hard and nodded.

"I wanted to welcome you all to this special assembly," Principal Hill said, walking back and forth on the floor of the basketball court. "And we especially welcome Jake Hayes back. We've all missed you."

The gym suddenly broke out in clapping, my name being shouted from several of the students. I turned slightly and waved at them, feeling like I might die from the embarrassment.

"Our school suffered a great tragedy, you all know that," Principal Hill said, pausing in front of the table and leaning against it. "Some poor choices were made and unfortunately there are some permanent consequences due to those choices."

Oh gosh.

I thought I was going to dic.

"Jake," Principal Hill addressed me directly. "This is actually the second assembly we've had in two weeks. The whole student body directed the last one. I'd ask our student body president, Norah Hamilton, to come up and fill you in on what the last one was about."

Oh no...

I really *was* going to die.

Norah tromped down the stairs, her high heels clanging with each step she took. She flashed a bright smile as she walked passed me and Sam, and took the microphone from Principal Hill.

"Jake," she said, looking directly at me. "What happened to you is beyond tragic. And really, we are all to blame for what happened to you. As a student body, we all admitted we have a problem. Living on such a small island with, let's face it, basically nothing to do this time of year, we too often turn to alcohol to keep us entertained."

I heard a lot of people squirming as Norah spoke. I wondered if everyone at Rain's party had admitted to being there. Practically everyone at the school drank from time to time at parties.

"But with everything that's happened to you Jake, we've realized we have a problem. And we don't want to see this escalate until something worse happens. With how horrible your accident was, it could have been so much worse."

I glanced over my shoulder to the students behind me. I was surprised to see that several girls had reddened eyes, a bunch of guys were nodding their heads, leaning forward, hanging on every word Norah said.

"We've all talked, and we're ready to give it up. All the booze, all the alcohol," Norah continued, her eyes shifting over the whole student body. I was surprised their faces reflected what she said. "We're ready to make a pledge not to drink again, ever, this whole school year."

Norah grabbed one of the colorful papers off of the table and held it up. "I'm asking all of you to sign with me. To not drink again, and to not let another tragedy like this happen ever again at our school. There are pens up here and some tape. We're going to make them into a mural in the commons as a reminder of our commitment."

No one moved for a second, everyone waiting for someone else to take the first step. And then Samantha rose to her feet and walked to the table. She grabbed a bright green pledge and wrote her first name across it in big, bold letters. Grabbing a piece of tape, she turned back and looked at me.

I climbed to my feet and crossed to the table. Barely glancing at Norah, I grabbed a blue paper, scratched my name across it, and grabbed a piece of tape. I heard a mass of feet behind me and turned to see the entire student body climbing down the bleachers.

I stood to the side with Samantha and watched as each and every one of them signed their name on the pledge. They all looked up at me when they were done. Many of them said things like, "Sorry this happened," "Glad to have you back," and "Thanks for the reality call." And then as a student body, we all filed out of the gym and into the commons. The US Government teacher, Mr. Crow stood at the top of a ladder. One by one, each of the students handed him their pledges and he taped them to the side of the walkway that overlooked the commons area. With Norah directing where to put them, he taped them up. They would be the first thing everyone would see when they walked through the front doors every day.

As I looked around at my fellow students, I was surprised to see that each of them meant it when they signed that pledge. I saw it in each of their faces. They really were sorry for what happened to me.

I knew a lot of them wouldn't really keep that pledge the entire year. But this was a step. They really were willing to try. At least for a while.

Out of all the bad that had happened the last few weeks, at least one good thing had come around. Maybe with what had happened to me, I could keep something worse from happening to someone else.

I caught a ride home with Carter after school. How he'd managed to get a new car already I didn't know. It kind of bugged me if I was being honest. But it felt nice to get back to normal just a little, riding home from school with one of my best friends.

Carter dropped me off at my house, Mom's gargantuan van already parked back in the driveway. I noticed a beat up bike with a trailer attached to the back of it parked next to it. I'd seen that bike before.

I opened the front door and walked in to see Mom talking to a familiar face.

"Jake," Mom said, jumping as if she'd been caught doing something bad. "You're home. You remember Kali?"

I wouldn't say I remembered him. Everyone always saw Kali riding around town on his bike with his trailer hooked up. Kali had ink dark skin, and a headful of some serious dreadlocks. Kali was hard to miss.

I just nodded.

"Well," Mom said, looking slightly uncomfortable. "Kali has known sign language since he was a child and when he heard what happened to you, he volunteered to help teach you."

A hard knot formed in my stomach.

"My mother was born deaf, as was my younger sister," Kali said. He had a Haitian accent that made some of his words difficult to understand. "I was lucky enough to be born hearing but with just the three of us, I knew sign language better than I knew how to speak. I thought maybe I could help."

I was already getting so sick of all this attention. I wanted nothing more than for life to just go back to normal, back to the days when I spent afternoons practicing football and procrastinating my homework. Not days of freaking out around Sam and having the town crazy man offering me his help.

"Is that okay, Jake?" Mom asked.

How was I supposed to say no? That would have been rude and uncomfortable.

I gave just the smallest of nods.

"Great," Mom said, her shoulders relaxing noticeably. "I'll leave you two to it then."

And just like that, Mom walked out of the room and into the kitchen, leaving just the two of us alone.

Awkward.

"You want to shoot some hoops?" Kali said, a small smile on his dark face.

I furrowed my brow at Kali, not sure I'd heard him right. I thought we were supposed to be going over how to talk with our hands, not using them to throw a ball around.

"I haven't played in a long time," he said, heading for the front door. "I figure you probably haven't either."

I glanced in the direction of the kitchen, catching a glimpse of Mom spying. She just nodded her head and waved me away. So I dropped my backpack on the floor and followed Kali outside.

Dad had installed a heavy duty basketball hoop over our driveway just after we had moved to the island fourteen years ago. It was pretty beat up and was in need of a new net, but it had held up pretty good considering how much use it had gotten over the years.

Kali grabbed a ball that sat at the base of the hoop and started dribbling. He shot and it made a quiet swoosh as it dropped through the net. Kali flashed me a blinding smile and pumped his fists in the air. I couldn't help but smile back as I chased after the ball.

I turned back to the hoop, about to shoot when Kali caught my attention. He made a motion with his hands, repeating it three times. "That's the sign for score," he said, nodding for me to go ahead and shoot. I tossed it up. It circled around the rim twice before dropping through the net.

"And this," Kali said, making another motion. "Means basketball."

I made another shot, letting the ball bounce into the side of the van harmlessly as I repeated the motions Kali made.

"Good," Kali said, smiling as he nodded. "And this," he made another motion. "Means to play. You put them together to say 'to play basketball.'" He put the two signs together. I watched his hands closely, making sure I would get it right when I tried it.

Much more slowly, I repeated Kali's hand motions.

"You got it!" Kali said encouragingly. "Won't be too long and we'll be having this entire conversation in sign."

I tried to give him a small smile, grabbing the ball again. I threw it up, watching as it fell through the net. Basketball season would be starting again in about a month. Would I be able to play?

As we continued to play basketball for the next hour, Kali taught me other sports terms in sign, laughing and joking the entire time.

It wasn't too long before I was silently laughing along with him.

Maybe Kali wasn't as crazy as everyone thought.

Maybe sometimes I was as guilty as anyone else of placing judgments too quickly.

The psychologist told me to write, so here I am.

I'm not exactly sure what I'm supposed to say. I think she wanted me to write about how I'm so angry with the world, or maybe angry with myself. I think I'm supposed to spill all my feelings out on this page, the one's I don't feel like I say to anyone else.

But I don't really know what to say.

Not being able to talk sucks. There's no doubt about that. There's a lot of times when I almost feel like I'm trapped inside of myself. Like if I don't talk or yell or scream or laugh I'm going to explode. A lot of the time it almost feels like I'm suffocating.

And when I think about the fact that I won't be able to talk for the rest of my life... that feels like too long to even comprehend. I can deal with not being able to talk for the next week, the next month. But forever...?

Of course I regret that night we all got drunk. So many times I just think, well, **what was I thinking**? Mom was right. All the grown-ups were right. About staying away from drugs and alcohol. And the stupid thing is that I think every teenager knows that. We all know we aren't supposed to do the things our parents tell us not to do. But that's why we do them. Cause they tell us not to.

How stupid is it that my biggest regret about all of this is what I didn't say to Sam? I just keep thinking about it, over and over, every hour of every day, how I was such a chicken. I've wanted to tell Samantha that I loved her for how many years now? And now I'll never get the chance to tell her.

My biggest regret is what I didn't say...

Guess that should teach me a lesson about procrastination or something, right? About not putting the really important things in life off?

Life can be pretty cruel sometimes.

My leg bounced up and down as I sat in Physics. It had been three weeks since I'd gone back to school. Norah had finally backed off, she and Blake getting hot and heavy. Eyes still stared at the hole in my neck, but they didn't linger like they used to. I wasn't quite the spectacle I'd been before. I wasn't picking up on the sign language very quickly, but I wasn't going to complain, at least I was getting to spend a lot of time with Samantha.

It seemed weird that she wasn't in class that day. Samantha never missed classes. Ever. But we were half way through Physics, and she hadn't shown up. What was I going to do in our independent study class during third hour? I wasn't exactly great at turning the pictures in our books into actual hand motions.

I sat with my forehead resting against the palm of my hand, pretending to be working through the worksheet Mr. Roy had given us when someone slid into the seat next to me. My head jerked up to see Samantha settle into her chair.

She looked tired. Her hair was a mess, her clothes wrinkled.

You okay? I wrote in the notebook with the red cover, the one I only ever used to write to her in. I stealthily slid it across to her desk.

Samantha glanced at me once, something like fear or the look of being caught flashing in her eyes. She turned her attention to the notebook and pulled out a pencil.

I had never noticed until then, how Samantha's physical appearance had gotten a little rougher every day since the first day of school. Her clothes always looked wrinkled and worn. There were always bags under her eyes these days it seemed. She looked thinner than she did at the end of last year.

Maybe I had just dismissed it as stress from the school year, or that her mom was gone for work and Sam had to take care of herself. I really hoped that was all it was.

Samantha pushed the notebook back onto my desk and turned her attention to her work.

Yeah, she wrote. Just tired. The power went out at our house last night and I didn't sleep very well. Got kinda cold.

I glanced over at her, though she didn't meet my eyes as she worked. Somehow I thought that was a lie. The power didn't just go out at one house on the island unless there was a serious problem, right at the house. When the power went out, it went out for most of the entire island.

For the rest of the class period, I couldn't help but wonder if something serious was going on with Sam. It actually felt kind of nice, worrying about someone else, instead of being the one that was being worried about all the time.

The bell rang and Sam and I went separate ways to our lockers. Carter and Rain gathered around my locker between classes, griping about being bored since the football season had been canceled. They were actually seriously talking about going hiking that weekend.

We hadn't gone hiking since about sixth grade.

I suggested the lake instead. With Halloween only one week away it was going to be freezing, but at least it was something to do.

As the warning bell rang, I finally headed to the far end of the building.

Samantha was already there, reading through one of the books we'd been assigned in AP English. She didn't even notice me as I walked in and turned my desk towards hers. I watched her as she read, chewing on her lower lip, making it red and slightly swollen. Her face looked totally engaged. She used her thumb on her free hand to twist the ring on her index finger in a slow circle. Her feet were propped up on her desk, making her looked crammed and wedged in her seat.

Deciding not to bother her, I pulled out the notebook she'd written in earlier and set it and my ASL book on the desk. Opening to the section we were in, I set to studying the pictures, attempting to make my three-dimensional hands look like the flat, two-dimensional ones. A book was a ridiculous way to learn sign language.

I hadn't noticed that Sam had taken my notebook until she pushed it in front of me again, more of her handwriting scrawled below what she'd written the period before.

So I wanted to try something different today, she'd written. I'm not going to talk the entire period either. So it's either writing or signing. Maybe that will help you to pick up on it faster.

I looked up at her, giving her a doubtful look. She just smiled at me innocently, resting her chin in her hands, and batted her eyes at me in a teasing way. A small smile spread on my face as I shook my head at her.

This ought to be interesting, I wrote beneath her neat handwriting.

She reached for the notebook. *I have to admit, I've been curious what it's been like for you, not being able to talk. Maybe someday I'll try it for a whole day.*

Ooo, a whole day, I taunted her on the page.

"Hey!" she said defensively. Realizing her mistake, she covered her mouth with her hands, her eyes growing wide. I just silently laughed and shook my head. I scratched "whole day" out on the page and replaced it with minute.

Okay, she wrote. *This might be a little harder than I thought.*

Hey, it's kind of nice, I wrote. *Not to be the only silent one.*

I can't even imagine. It must feel pretty lonely.

It could be worse, I wrote. I watched her face closely as she read it. Her eyes lingered there for longer than it would have taken to read them, making me wonder what was going through her head.

Ready to get started? she wrote, sitting up a little straighter. She looked slightly uncomfortable.

Nice going, I thought to myself. *Way to ruin whatever we had going on.*

The plans for the lake that weekend were getting more elaborate as the week went on. It really helped that the weather was supposed to get to seventy degrees. Considering it didn't get much hotter than that in the middle of the summer, it was practically a heat wave. From what Carter and Rain said, at least half the school was planning to go Saturday.

Even Samantha was coming.

I tried not to imagine too much what Sam looked like in a swimming suit.

By the end of the week, things were starting to feel... almost normal. Principal Hill had allowed most of the guys that were at the party the night of my accident to get back onto the basketball team. Practices would be starting on Monday. I had met with most of the guys every day after school in the weight room for extra workouts in preparation.

Kali and I had gotten into a routine over the past few weeks. He'd come over in the evenings on Tuesdays and Thursdays. We'd go for walks, or play basketball, or once we even went on a bike ride. And he'd teach me signs, always applicable to whatever we were doing that day. I felt pretty stupid for not catching on very fast. But Kali was patient with me, always easy going. Other times he didn't even really do any sign, he'd just tell stories about when he was a kid in Haiti.

I didn't feel as sorry for myself after hearing about Kali's childhood.

By the time Saturday came around, I could officially introduce myself in sign, explain that I was mute, and could tell someone what I liked to do in my spare time.

For some reason I felt bad that I was learning more sign with Kali than I was with Samantha. I could tell she was getting frustrated that we weren't making very fast progress. I guessed that would be frustrating for the smartest girl in the school.

When Saturday rolled around Rain hitchhiked his way to my house and the two of us headed toward Moran State Park.

As we drove in silence, I could feel that something was changing between me and my two best friends. Carter, Rain, and I hadn't hung out much since the accident. I could tell they were trying hard to act like everything was normal, like nothing had changed between the three of us. But they'd pulled away a bit. And there was always this little bug in the back of my brain, one that reminded me that if it hadn't been for them, I might still be able to talk.

I hated that I couldn't entirely blame them though for pulling away. It had to be awkward for them. It was hard to talk to a person who couldn't talk.

With all the tourists gone, I was actually able to find parking at the lake for once. With no public swimming pool on the island, that's what the lake became. I'd spent more than half my summer there, lounging out in just my swimming trunks on the grass next to the lake, or jumping off the bridge or the cliffs.

It really did look like half the school was out that day. Already I could tell there wasn't much area left to claim on the leveled, grass shore.

Just as I climbed out of the Bronco, I saw a car stop in the middle of the road. From out of the passenger door, climbed Samantha. She thanked the driver, who took off as soon as she shut the door.

Hitchhiking would seem pretty dangerous anywhere else in the country. But on Orcas it seemed weird if you drove from your house to town without seeing someone looking for a ride.

"Hey," she said with a bright smile as she walked up to my side. Rain gave a smug side look, and stealthily snuck away. "That was probably the scariest ride I've ever gotten on this island. I think I'm a little high just from riding in that guy's car for the last five minutes."

I gave a silent laugh, offering to carry her bag. She gave me a little smile and handed it over.

"Such a gentleman," she teased. I just bumped her with my shoulder, knocking her slightly off balance.

We walked through the trees to the edge of the lake. There really wasn't a whole lot of room to lie out. Half naked teenagers were everywhere, spread out on blankets or spread out on each other. Carter sat in the middle of a swarm of girls, shirtless, playing his guitar and singing. He may have been a good guitar player, but he definitely couldn't sing. The girls didn't seem to mind though.

Sam waved to two of her friends, Marina and Summer, but to my surprise she didn't go sit with them, just stayed at my side, looking for a place to settle.

A small flicker of hope jumped to life inside of me.

Pretty crowded, I wrote on my pocket notebook.

"Yeah, this is crazy," she said, blocking the sun from her eyes with her hand. "I think the whole school's here." She suddenly looked over at me, a mischievous grin on her face. "Follow me."

I couldn't help but smile too as she took off down the trail that went around the entire lake. She bounded in front of me, picking up speed as her sandaled feet jogged down the trail. I shifted Sam's bag and my towel over my shoulder, sliding my notebook into my pocket as I jogged after her.

We didn't run far before she slowed. I knew where she was headed before we even got there.

There was a bridge that crossed over a section of the lake where it bottled into a small lagoon. I had gone skinny dipping here more than once, as had the rest of the school at one time or another. I was surprised that there was no one else around. It was a popular spot for jumping, or even just hanging out.

Sam stopped when she got to the middle of the bridge. She kicked her sandals off and scaled the rail of the bridge until she stood on top of it. I could only watch her in wonder as she closed her eyes, raising her arms to her side, and just stood there.

She looked... free, standing there. Like she always carried the weight of her future on her shoulders, but standing there, above the water and in the sun, she looked different.

She looked beautiful.

But I couldn't tell her that.

Sam suddenly gave a laugh, her eyes flashing to my face. I jumped, getting caught staring. "You going to jump with me?" she asked with a smile. She suddenly pulled her tank top over her head and shimmied out of her denim shorts, tossing them back on the bridge. She stood there in just her swimming suit.

I laughed and pulled out my pocket notebook. *It's going to be freezing,* I wrote.

"So," she taunted. "You afraid of a little cold water?"

I chuckled again and shook my head. Setting our stuff down, I pulled my shirt over my head. Maybe I just imagined that Sam stared for just a moment too long, the same as I had done with her. Pushing that thought aside, I climbed the railing until I was balanced beside her.

"You should know I'm not a very good swimmer," she said very seriously, her eyes glued to the water.

And before I could react, Sam grabbed my hand and pulled me off the railing with her and into the water.

The water felt like ice as it enveloped my skin, sucking me into its depths. My head surfaced, and I gasped for air. As Sam's head popped out of the water, I realized she was still clinging to my hand.

Her arms flailed, and she gasped as her head started to sink back under the water.

Crap.

Sam wasn't lying when she said she wasn't a very good swimmer.

Gripping her hand tighter, I pulled her upwards. Maneuvering her so she was behind me, I pulled her arms around my neck. She coughed violently, squeezing tight

106

around me. Thankfully I *was* a good swimmer and I slowly made our way to the rocks at the end of the bridge.

"Wasn't that fun?" Sam said, coughing violently as we climbed back up to the bridge.

I just looked at her like *seriously...?* as we walked back toward our things. I grabbed my notebook and furiously wrote.

What was that about? Were you trying to kill yourself?!

She gave me this sheepish look that was so irritatingly cute it virtually washed away my frustration. "I've never jumped off the bridge before," she said as she dried herself off with her towel. "There's always been too many people around and I didn't want to embarrass myself in front of them all. I just... I just wanted to try it."

I just stood there, almost not believing what she had said. Sam was unwilling to try a bridge jump in front of everyone else. Everyone but me.

A chuckle suddenly shook my chest, a smile breaking free on my lips. I just shook my head at her. Sam laughed too.

We both spread our towels out on the bridge, each of us lying down on our stomachs.

"Oh yeah, I brought something for you," Sam said, shifting so she could reach her bag. She pulled out my red notebook, the one I only used to talk to her. "You left it on my desk after AP English yesterday."

I smiled, taking it from her extended hand, and set it to the side.

Sam folded her arms in front of her and rested her head on them, letting her eyes slide closed. "This is nice," she said, her voice relaxed. "All warm and quiet."

I nodded, letting my head rest in my own arms.

We didn't say or write anything for a long time. Normally silence like that was uncomfortable and awkward. Like you needed to say something to fill the empty space in the air. But it didn't feel like that with Samantha. Maybe it was because I *couldn't* say anything and fill the quiet, but I thought it was more about two people just being with each other, enjoying the slowdown and the rare sunshine.

I lifted my head to turn it the other direction when my neck started hurting and realized Sam was lying with her chin resting on her arms, staring at me. I froze there, my eyes locked on hers, just looking at her.

Even though Sam had lost so much weight lately, she was still beautiful. I had thought so the very first day I saw her, just after she and her mom moved to the island. Sam had been a little different then. She was always the smartest in our class, outshining everyone by a long shot. But back then she used to be more... involved, in everything. She'd been on the girls' basketball team. She used to go out with friends all the time. She had seemed a little more... alive.

But Sam was different this year. She wasn't going out for sports. I didn't see her interact with anyone very often, besides Summer and Marina occasionally. She seemed so much more reserved. She seemed so much older.

"I think my back is getting sunburned." I jumped violently when she spoke, causing her to laugh. Mercifully, she just rolled over onto her back, letting one of her arms fall across her eyes to block out the sun.

I tried not to overthink the moment we'd just shared, just staring at each other, and rolled over onto my back as well.

We were quiet again for a while, just soaking up the sun. But I could tell there was something on Samantha's mind.

"Will you ever be able to fly again, Jake?" she asked quietly, as if on cue.

Something sank inside of me as I considered her question. I thought about the powerful feeling of controlling a plane, of the rush I felt knowing I was thousands of feet above the Earth, the only thing keeping me from falling to my death being two aluminum wings.

I held up my hand and made the sign for *no* when I faintly heard her slide her arm off of her eyes.

"I'm sorry you can't anymore," she said, her voice filled with thought. "I know how much you loved to fly."

I just stared up at the perfectly blue sky, trying to not let myself feel too much. I'd been doing that a lot since the accident, like I'd set up a screen over myself that wouldn't allow all my emotions to drip through and drown me.

"I always meant to ask you to take me flying sometime," she said. I was surprised when her hand reached up and she linked her fingers with mine, the backs of our hands resting against the wooden planks of the bridge. "I've never been in a small plane before."

With everything in me, I wanted to tell her that I wished I could have taken her flying. But writing it down and showing her would have broken the moment. And an even bigger part of me didn't want to have to let go of Sam's hand. Ever.

So instead I just squeezed her hand tighter.

There was a lot about my life that was crappy, now that I couldn't talk. But if I hadn't gotten drunk that night, if I hadn't gotten in that accident, would I have ever had this moment? Lying there in the sun, holding Sam's hand like time didn't exist and the real world couldn't touch us?

Somehow I didn't think so.

5 hours since... what **was** that with Sam?

I lay down gingerly on my bed that night. After spending four hours at the lake and not bothering to use sunscreen, not that I ever did, I was pretty fried. Living in the Pacific Northwest, one didn't get a whole lot of sun exposure. My skin wasn't used to it.

Having showered and said good-night to my family, each of them signing it to me, I hunkered down into bed, two of my notebooks in one hand, a pen in the other. One was my journal, the other was me and Sam's notebook.

I smiled, recalling the events of the day as I flipped through the pages of the red notebook. Me and Sam's handwriting alternated throughout the pages, her handwriting neat and careful, mine always rushed and messy.

I was about to set it aside when I noticed some writing at the very end of the notebook, upside down. Folding back the back cover, I flipped it over. It was an entire page of Sam's handwriting.

I saw that you left your notebook at the end of class today. I put it in my bag and meant to give it to you after school, but I didn't see you. I figured you'd already left.

Sitting here by myself at home sucks. Mom's out of town again, as usual, for work. She's gone more than she is at home these days. You never expect you'll miss your parent until they're gone all the time. Do you think you'd miss your mom if she were always away? I bet you would. Your mom's got such a big personality, she'd leave a big hole if she was gone.

I keep thinking that maybe I should have kept up with sports this year. I see you, and know how badly you still want to be playing football, but can't anymore, and I feel bad that I'm not doing it when I could. School just feels so overwhelming this year, I don't think I could keep up with it all.

Jake, I'm really sorry about what happened to you. It's awful. But... don't hate me for saying this, okay? Maybe I shouldn't. What the heck, if I change my mind I guess I can just rip this page out and throw it away. You'll never have to see it. But... I'm kind of glad it did happen. There are not a whole lot of people I feel like I can talk to lately. Things have... changed for me recently. But I feel like I can talk to you, Jake. You listen, and I feel like you actually see me for more than just the super smart girl at school.

Thanks for being my friend, Jake. I really need you.

I re-read the entire page three times, feeling like I couldn't entirely absorb everything she had said. A small knot formed in my chest as I read Sam's words.

Samantha was so alone.

I'd seen it happening since the beginning of the school year, how she'd been pulling away from her friends. Just earlier today I'd noticed how she seemed so much older. It was kind of scary to see what was happening.

That night I made a resolution. I wasn't going to let Sam keep slipping into her solitude.

Thanks for returning this. I guess I didn't even realize I'd left it. My mind feels so distracted every day after every class, trying to think of how to take the least crowded ways to class, so the least amount of people will stare at the hole in my neck. Sometimes it feels like it has a beacon in it, flashing for the entire world to see, except it's not cool like the Bat signal.

I'm sorry your mom is gone so much these days. That must be hard, being home by yourself all the time. I've always thought it would be nice to have the house to myself for a while. This place gets so loud all the time and there are always so many people in it. But I guess I'm grateful for all the noise and chaos. I don't know if I want to be alone in the quiet with my thoughts these days.

Until just now, I haven't realized how everyone at school except you doesn't get it, how crappy this is. Carter and Rain just joke about my not being able to talk. I go along with it, but honestly, I wish they'd lay off a bit. They're just making it worse. Like they won't ever let me forget what happened. They're good guys and my best friends but...

So I'm grateful that with how bad everything's been, you've been the way you have. I think I need you too, Sam.

My chest was pounding as I wrote the letters. I fought with myself for a full five minutes, debating if I should just rip the page out and pretend I never wrote any of it. Pretend that I'd never seen Sam's note either. I could just throw the entire notebook away, pretend I lost it, and force everything to go back to the way it was.

That seemed the least dangerous thing to do.

But I kind of wanted a little risk. I wanted to see what was down the end of this tunnel.

The tunnel eventually had to lead to light, right?

2 days since whatever that was...

The weekend was agonizing, even though there was only Sunday left until I could go back to school on Monday. I'd never been as eager to go back to school as I had been when Monday finally rolled around. I parked my car in the parking lot and Jordan bounded away to join her friends. I walked through the halls, my heart hammering in my throat as I made my way to Sam's locker.

To my relief and panic, she was standing there, digging through something at the bottom of her locker. Picking up my pace, I slipped the notebook onto the top shelf, reaching over her. I glanced back just once as I walked away, her eyes catching mine. She looked up to see the spiraled pages sticking just over the ledge of the shelf. She glanced back at me, a smile spreading on her face.

I couldn't help but smile too as I turned my head back in the direction I was walking and made my way to Calculus.

My good mood was brought down a bit when Sam returned the notebook during Physics and she had only drawn a smiley face. I wasn't quite sure how to take that.

Nothing seemed different between the two of us for a few weeks after that day at the lake and after I read her note. We were friends. I was sure about that. But she never tried to hold my hand again, not that I had really expected her to.

It was stupid of me, and I never should have done it, but one day, before I slipped our notebook into Sam's backpack, I wrote: Do you really not believe in love?

I really wished I never would have asked.

No, she had written back. I believe people become infatuated; maybe they even really like each other. But I don't believe in love. Those kinds of feelings just don't last. You feel them for a while, maybe even a few years, but eventually the feeling goes away.

That's what happened to my parents.

My mom was only nineteen when she met Mike and "fell in love" with him. He was only twenty. They were head over heels and my dad "wanted to give her everything in the world." I guess they were happy for a year or so. Happy enough to decide to have a kid.

And eventually that man called my "dad" stopped loving my mom, stopped loving me. Maybe love is real, cause he sure loved his alcohol. He stopped coming home, stopped being around. And finally he just left. I haven't seen him since I was six.

If a man can't love his own offspring, what can anyone love?

So my mom and I did what we had to do. We changed our last names to her maiden name after the divorce finalized, and we moved on with our lives.

Love doesn't last. It's a fantasy.

That crushed me. Any hope, any fantasy I'd ever had about telling Sam how I felt, about the slim possibility of her ever feeling the same, was demolished.

I was thankful for the distraction of basketball drills. Practice had been underway for two weeks and our first game was going to be a week from Friday. I had started feeling just a little off a week and a half before the game, but I was brushing it off as nothing more than a cold. Sam kept asking me if I felt okay and I always told her I was. But by Wednesday I had a fever of 105 and I was feeling so out of it that I didn't even realize Mom had loaded me into the van and we were at the ferry landing.

I was headed back to Seattle Children's Hospital.

The aches I had brushed off as just being sore from working out so much made me curl into a ball on the seat and groan in pain. My clothes stuck to my skin I was sweating so bad. Everything in my body hurt.

With the ferry ride and the drive from Anacortes to Seattle, it was about three hours of travel. But it felt like days until we pulled into the hospital. Mom put her arm under me and helped me walk through the doors of the emergency room. My feet felt like lead and my body screamed in pain as I moved.

Dr. Calvin was waiting for us when we walked through the doors. I didn't even remember going from the doors into a hospital bed. They started hooking tubes up to my arm, taking my temperature, and all those other kinds of things doctors did.

It didn't take long for the lights to go out.

I had gotten an infection. Due to my weakened immune system, some small virus had gotten inside of me, getting into my bloodstream and embedding itself in my lungs and snaking out into the rest of my body. No wonder it started getting so hard to breathe during practice and whenever I got too close to Samantha.

They put me on antibiotics, but it was going to take nearly a week for my system to recover.

Dr. Calvin said if I hadn't been pushing myself so hard at basketball practice I wouldn't have gotten so bad. He ordered me to sit out the rest of the season.

That was it for sports for me for the rest of my high school life.

I started blocking it all out, shutting down as the days in the hospital rolled by. No one came to visit that time, being too in the middle of things and too busy with life. I was glad they didn't. I just wanted to be alone and zone out the entire world.

Seven days before Thanksgiving I was finally released. Mom had been given a handful of prescriptions for me, had been the only one that paid enough attention to know what to do with them. My psychologist had come to visit three times since I was readmitted. I didn't say much, just the things I knew I would need to say to not be kept there longer for psychological evaluation.

I went straight to my room when we got home and didn't talk to a single one of my brothers or sisters.

It felt like this was never going to end. The world wasn't going to stop crashing down until there was nothing left of me but dust.

Something snapped inside of me after my last hospital visit. That screen I'd placed over my head disappeared and I let myself drown. I let myself wallow, let me feel sorry for myself, let me hate myself. I let myself hate Carter for crashing the truck, hated Rain for convincing me to go tell Sam I loved her that night. Let myself hate Sam for the fact that I did love her.

Everyone backed off those slow two days of school before Thanksgiving break. Carter and Rain ignored me after the first day. River had even tried talking to me once, but I didn't think I'd even responded to her. Sam kept trying to persist, to tell me things weren't that bad. But I didn't listen to her.

How could life be worse?

I sat across from Sam during our ASL class, staring off into nothing. She was pretending I was listening, showing me some new sign we hadn't gone over before. Our red notebook sat between us, untouched for nearly two weeks. I was thinking about how if we hadn't all gotten caught for drinking the night of my accident, if the accident never would have happened, the football team might have had the chance to be playing at state that weekend.

If my body didn't have the weakness of a five-year-old, I would still be able to play on the basketball team.

"Jake!" Sam finally yelled. "Did you lose your ability to hear too?"

My eyes suddenly jumped to her face. I'd never heard Sam sound so mad and she'd only spoken a single sentence.

"What is wrong with you?" she demanded, her eyes blazing. She looked pissed. "You've been acting like a total douche since you got out of the hospital. I understand life kind of sucks for you right now, but you need to get over yourself and stop feeling so sorry for yourself."

My insides hardened as I glared at her.

You don't say stuff like that to people like me.

I just grabbed my stuff, shoved it back into my backpack and walked out of the room. I stalked through the silent, empty halls, straight out the front doors and into my car. I threw my backpack into the back seat, my books exploding out of it. Slamming the door behind me, I started the car and went peeling out of the parking lot.

Not having anywhere in mind that I wanted to go, I just drove. The slow speeds pissed me off as I went down the narrow winding roads. Forty just wasn't fast enough. I tore passed the Corner Store, rocketed past the lake in Moran State Park. Soon I was passing Café Olga and the Doe Bay resort. I pulled off onto a dirt road. I didn't care that I was trespassing on private property. I lucked out, the dirt driveway dead ended just before the water, at an empty lot. The land sloped toward the water before breaking away to the ocean.

I climbed out of the car, leaving the keys in the off position in the ignition, and walked out to the dock that stretched out over the water.

Fall had returned in full force, the sky cloudy, mist sitting on the top of the ocean water. Off in the distance I could just make out the other islands that blocked the view to the mainland.

I wanted to scream as I stood there, my toes hanging over the edge of the dock. I wanted to let a gut wrenching howl rip from my disfigured throat toward those clouded skies. I wanted to say every swear word my mother had ever taught me not to say.

I would have settled for a cut off whimper, just as long as some kind of sound came from my lips.

I sank to my knees, my pants instantly growing moist from the dock. I fell forward onto my palms and eventually sank my forehead to my knees, clutching my hair with enough force I was surprised I wasn't ripping it out.

Tomorrow was Thanksgiving. Tomorrow my Hayes grandparents would come up from Tacoma, my dad's sister, Aunt Tally would bring her three kids. Our house would be filled with the scent of a million dishes, we'd all sit around our gigantic dining table, and before we'd eat we'd each say just one thing we were grateful for.

Sitting there on that dock by myself, I didn't feel like I had anything to be grateful for that year. Or ever.

Still nothing...
Will there ever be anything ever again...?

I didn't go home until after eleven that night. My parents were totally freaking out, on the verge of calling the police to come look for me. Dad really ripped me a new one. I had just stood there emptily and taken it.

Thanksgiving morning dawned gray and dark, threatening to rain at any moment. I just lay on my bed for a long time, looking out the window, not thinking or feeling anything.

The door creaked open and Mom popped her head inside. I could hear the sound of Grandma and Grandpa outside, along with Aunt Tally and the kids.

"Jake?" she said cautiously, not fully coming into the room. "I forgot to grab a few things for dinner tonight, would you mind running down to The Market for me and grabbing them? If not I could send Jordan."

I sat up, rubbing a hand over my hair that was sticking up in all directions. I shook my head and reached for a notebook.

No, I wrote. *I'll go.*

"Thanks sweetie," she said, her face breaking out into a relieved smile. I was surprised when her eyes suddenly started watering, turning red. Before I could write *what's wrong?* she crossed the room and wrapped her arms around me.

"We have a lot to be grateful for this year, Jake," she said, her voice filled with emotion. "I know it's hard, but don't forget that."

She stepped away from me, a few loose tears rolling down her cheeks. She placed a kiss on my forehead and I tried to return the smile. I didn't think I managed it though. Mom handed me a list and then walked back out.

I pulled clothes on in a weird slow motion, not really feeling like I was in my body. Someone else's legs were sliding into those jeans. Someone else was pulling on that jacket and putting on those shoes.

Not even really thinking about it, I slid the window open and climbed through it. I didn't really feel like seeing everyone at the moment. Closing the window behind me, I crossed the dewy grass to my car.

Island Market was a small grocery store and you couldn't help running into people you knew there, even on Thanksgiving morning. Or maybe especially on Thanksgiving morning. I ran into Officer Ryan, the police officer who found Carter, Rain, and me after the accident. I ran into Ms. Sue. I even caught a glimpse of Kali from across the store at the checkout, though I didn't actually talk to him.

I got the things from Mom's list and loaded them into the backseat of the car. I was just headed out of the parking lot when I saw Sam walking around the corner. By that point it had started to misty rain and no one would be walking around without an umbrella, but for some reason Sam was, her hair growing damp.

I turned left instead of right to follow her. It didn't take long to find her as she walked down the sidewalk. I slowed down as I drove along side of her and rolled down the window. She walked with a brown paper bag in one hand, a book in the other that her nose was glued to.

Looking around for something to get her attention, I settled on a pen and threw it at her. It hit the brown paper bag she was carrying and made her jump in surprise. Looking around, she finally saw me through the window. I waved her over, pulling over half-way into a parking lot.

She looked over at me, glancing back the way she had come. I could tell she was debating on just walking away. I couldn't blame her after the way I had been acting for the last week. Finally she crossed the street and walked around the car. She opened the passenger door and sank into the seat, her bag dropping to the floor by her feet.

"What do you want Jake?" she practically spat. "Shouldn't you be at home with your family right now?"

I pointed to the shopping bags in the backseat and fished around for a notebook and a pen. I unearthed a pen, but without finding even a single notebook, I settled for my arm.

Shouldn't you? I wrote.

Sam's eyes lingered on my words for a long moment, her entire frame stiffening. I thought I saw her eyes redden just a little bit.

Sad realization hit me.

Your mom's gone again, I wrote. Isn't she?

Samantha looked out the window away from me. I wondered if she'd looked away so she could wipe tears away without me seeing.

"She's snowed in at an airport back east," she said, her voice stiff. "She won't be able to get home until the weather clears up." She turned her face back toward the front of the car. I could see the moisture pooled in her eyes. "I was just walking to the store to get something to eat for myself."

I sat there looking at Samantha for a long minute. Finally, I just put the Bronco back into drive and flipped around on the street.

"Uh, where are you taking me?" Sam asked, her voice a mix of annoyance and uncertainty. I thought I picked up on the smallest trace of hope. "I'm going the opposite direction."

I didn't bother responding to her, just kept driving.

Sam didn't say anything else. She sat there stiff for a minute, as if she wasn't sure if she should demand to be let out of the car, or maybe even jump if I didn't allow her to get out. But by the time I passed the airport she finally relaxed into her seat, watching the scenery as it went by.

I parked the car in the driveway and pushing up my sleeves again, wrote, *Come on in.*

"Jake, I don't want to impose or anything," Sam tried to protest, though it sounded pretty halfhearted. "I mean, I'm pretty set with my wheat thins, banana, and frozen pizza."

I just rolled my eyes and shook my head. *Get inside,* I wrote on my skin.

She gave an appreciative smile, keeping my eyes for a minute. "Okay fine," she said finally. "But I'm helping you carry these bags inside."

And she did. We both paused in front of the door, our hands full. I gave her a look that I hoped said *you ready for this craziness?*

Samantha took a deep breath, squeezed her eyes closed for a moment, and then nodded.

The house was complete chaos. Joshua, James, and Tally's two youngest kids ran like maniacs throughout the house, chasing each other with a mix of plastic swords, light sabers, and Nerf guns. Mom, Jordan, Jenny, Grandma, and Aunt Tally were in the kitchen, talking to each other in raised voices. Anyone outside of the family would have thought it was a heated fight. I knew it was just the way they talked to each other when they were discussing how best to bake a pie or dress a turkey. Grandpa, Dad, and John sat looking at something on one of their laptops. Jamie lay in the window seat reading one of the half dozen books she read a week.

There was so much going on that no one even realized I was back and had brought a guest with me.

"Are you sure it's okay that I'm here?" Sam asked nervously. "I won't stay if there's not going to be enough food, or make it awkward for anyone."

And then through the kitchen we both noticed Kali helping out.

I looked back at Sam with a look on my face like, *are you kidding me?*

Sam just smiled. My mom's reputation for having the ability to feed armies at any given moment was well known.

I gave a nod of my head, *come on,* and cautiously, Sam followed me into the kitchen.

125

"Finally," Mom said as she glanced up at me from something that was cooking on the stove. Her eyes then caught sight of Sam. "Well hi there, Samantha," Mom said with a bright smile, just as I had expected her to. "Glad you could join us." That was just the way Jackie Hayes was. The more the merrier. Just look at our family of seven kids.

"Thank you, Mrs. Hayes," Samantha said, offering Mom the bag of groceries she was carrying. "I really appreciate you letting me stay."

"Well, someone needs to eat all this food," she said as she glanced back at the stove. All four burners had something going on them. "Will your mom be joining us?"

Samantha stiffened, her eyes dropping from Mom's face. "My mom's been traveling, as usual, the last little bit. She was supposed to fly home last night but her flight's grounded, for snow. She won't be able to get home until tomorrow, at the earliest."

"I heard about that snow storm," Mom said as she grabbed for some spice from her cluttered drawer of bottles and baggies. "I'm so sorry she's stuck all by herself. But I'm glad Jake brought you home so you're not alone."

"Thanks Mrs. Hayes," Sam said again.

"Mrs. Hayes," Mom chuckled. "Half the kids on this island call me Mom."

Sam just gave a smile and a nod. I thought I saw her eyes redden again, just a little bit.

Kali seemed to have noticed I was standing in the kitchen and joyfully greeted me. I couldn't help but smile back as I returned Kali's embrace. Kali always hugged.

With most men that would have been awkward, but with Kali it would have seemed weird if he didn't hug to greet you.

And as easy as anything in the world, Sam flowed right into the kitchen, helping out where she could, chatting with Mom, switching to Jordan, talking with Jenny. Just like she belonged there. I smiled a little as I watched her from the living room, pretending to pay attention to whatever Dad, Grandpa, and John were talking about.

Sam didn't look lonely anymore.

It took another two hours before dinner was ready but having a meal for sixteen people ready by one o'clock was pretty impressive. The Hayes dining table had been extended to its biggest, both extensions placed in the middle of it, as well as a folding table placed at the end of it. It stretched halfway into the living room, but per Mom's instructions, we would all be able to sit together. Sam, Jamie, and I helped bring everything to the table when it was ready. Sam looked a bit unsure of where to sit, so I sank into a seat and patted the one next to me. Joshua sat next to her and Aunt Tally sank into the chair on the other side of me.

"Quiet down everyone," Mom shouted above all the chatter. "Continuing with tradition, I would ask each of you to say one thing you're grateful for."

Giving Dad one of those warm looks that assured me they'd always be together, she took his hand in hers. Dad took Jamie's hand on his other side. I glanced at Sam, giving a small smile as I took her hand, and took Tally's hand in my other. Looking unsure if she was doing things right, Sam took Joshua's hand in her other.

Mom started, as usual, saying she was grateful for her family, that everyone was together and that everyone was healthy. Dad, Grandpa, and Grandma pretty much said the exact same thing. Jenny mumbled something about being grateful to be in college, James joked about his Xbox. When it came my turn, I just shook my head. There was an awkward moment where everyone just stared at me. It felt like there was a big dark cloud growing in the room that was going to suffocate us all.

"I'm grateful for life," Sam said, breaking the cloud. "It slips away too easily."

I did my best not to look over at Sam when she was finished and Joshua said something I didn't even hear.

When everyone finished, Mom asked Dad to say prayer over the food.

Dad waited a second for everyone to quiet back down. Everyone still holding hands, we each closed our eyes and bowed our heads.

"Our Father," Dad began. "We have much to be grateful for this year. We are grateful for our home, for the chance we have to live on this beautiful island. We are grateful for family, and especially grateful for Jacob this year." I felt Sam give my hand a small squeeze. "We are grateful for our friends, that Kali and Samantha could be with us this year." It was my turn to squeeze Sam's hand this time. "We ask a blessing on this food and say these things, amen."

"Amen," everyone but me echoed.

And just like that, the table became a flurry of arms grabbing, spoons dishing, and drinks pouring. Sam just sat back for a moment, a chuckle escaping out of her throat. I just looked at her and smiled. I reached around her to accept the gigantic bowl of mashed potatoes Joshua was passing without looking. Taking a heaping scoop, I plopped it down on Samantha's plate, and then placed an even bigger one on my own.

I could hardly even see the edges of my plate by the time I was done serving up my first round of food. I made extra sure that Sam couldn't either. She needed to put a little more meat on her bones.

"So," Joshua said to Sam around a mouthful of turkey. "Are you Jake's girlfriend or something?"

Sam laughed, glancing once back at me. "Jake's my friend," she answered little Joshua, ruffling his hair. "He invited me so I didn't have to be by myself today."

"Too bad," he said swallowing his bite before he shoved another in. He'd taken an entire turkey leg. "You're sure pretty."

I couldn't help but laugh too as half the table busted up into chuckles. Sam blushed bright red.

The rest of the meal passed in similar fashion: relaxed, joyful chaos. By the time everyone was finished, there was still about a third of the food on the table. I knew Mom would be running around plates of food to different people on the island later that night, determined to feed half of Orcas.

As everyone waited for their stomach's to digest enough room for pie, we cleared the table and started three different sets of games. A round of domino's started on one end with everyone under the age of thirteen playing. Another round of a card game I didn't really understand how to play started at the other end with Tally, Grandma, Jamie, Jenny, and Jordan.

Mom, Dad, Grandpa, Sam and I played some new game that consisted of cards, a board with plastic pieces, and dice that I'd never played before. I was losing badly, only half paying attention to the game. Of course Samantha was winning, too smart for the game to really be fair to the rest of us.

I felt like I should have been happier that day. Life was pretty good. I had my family all together, everyone was getting along. I had a warm house, good food. The girl of my dreams was with me and my family like she was one of us.

But I couldn't seem to shake the self-pity from my head.

I couldn't join in any of their conversation. I kept catching my extended family staring at my throat. I couldn't even laugh along with them all. Everything just felt wrong.

Eventually as it started to get dark outside, which it did at close to 4:30 that time of year, Sam, Jenny, and Mom went back into the kitchen to serve up pie for everyone. I didn't realize Sam knew me so well when she brought me a plate of all four different kinds of pie. She just gave me a little smirk as she walked back into the kitchen.

Everyone was pretty quiet as we sat in the living or dining room, savoring the pie. I sat in the window seat, Sam right next to me, so close our shoulders kept brushing each other. I knew the entire family was watching us, looking for signs that we were something more than friends. I knew how happy that would make most of the girls in the room. They'd never say it and it wouldn't be a big deal for a few years, but I knew it worried at least Mom that I'd never get a girlfriend who could be understanding enough about my inability to talk.

But I wasn't really thinking about that then. I was trying pretty hard to not think about anything at all, cause my thoughts kept trying to turn dark on what should have been a pretty freaking good day.

Sometime around 5:30 the grandparents and Tally headed back toward the ferry to go home. Sam and I offered to do the dishes which we did in the comfortable silence we had experienced that day at the lake. But on that Thanksgiving day, the day at the lake didn't seem real anymore.

"Well," Sam said as she dried her hands, all the dishes done. "I guess I'll start walking home."

I made the sign for laughing, getting the message of *very funny* across.

"Really, it's fine," she said. She suddenly sounded nervous. "I don't mind walking."

Having found a pen in my pocket, I grabbed a paper towel and scrawled, Its pitch black outside, and raining.

My face must have looked pretty annoyed, cause Sam's suddenly hardened, her eyes narrowing. "Fine," she said, her voice sharp and cold.

Rolling my eyes at her, I turned and walked toward the door. The entire family called good-bye to Sam as the two of us walked outside, she returning their good-bye's warmly. These days it felt like their smiles were never quite that real when they looked at me.

Neither of us said anything as we got into the Bronco, each of us slamming the doors as we got in. I could tell there was something on Sam's mind again as I backed out of the driveway. I hadn't even put it into drive before she exploded.

"What is your problem, Jake Hayes?" she practically yelled. I looked over at her as I started to pull forward, my brows knitting together. "Besides your stupid accident, you have the perfect life and you're moping around like... I don't know, but like a spoiled, little baby!"

I wanted to yell back at her, to ask her *how dare she*, but I could only glare at her, glancing back and forth from her to the road.

"You have a family, one who loves you!" she continued, her face growing red. "You have a roof over your head and more than enough food to eat. Your friends might not 'get it'," she made little quote marks in the air. "But they're still trying to be there for you. And all you can do is shut out the world and feel sorry for yourself."

There was nothing like getting yelled at and not being able to defend yourself. I turned on my blinker, about to turn down Enchanted Forest Road.

"No," Sam suddenly said, shaking her head. "I don't live down there anymore. Cut through town and start out toward the lake."

I hadn't realized Samantha had moved.

I kept my eyes forward, trying really hard not to look at Sam as I made my way toward town. But I could tell Sam's eyes were on me. I could feel anger rolling off of her.

"There's something I want to show you," she suddenly said, looking back out the windshield and slumping into the seat. "I think it's something you need to see."

I followed Samantha's directions, through town, turning right at the Corner Store, and out toward the lake. We hadn't gotten much further than a mile from the Corner Store though when she told me to take a left down a dirt driveway.

Like a lot of driveways on Orcas, this one was overgrown, all the trees pushing back in on man's cut through its territory. Ferns were sprouting up between the tire tracks and the gravel looked washed out in more than one place. We drove in hard silence for a full minute down that driveway until a small house came into view. I started to pull in front of it.

"No," Sam said, shaking her head. "Pull around back."

I gave her a quizzical look but did as she said, pulling around the side of the house to the back.

There was an old motorhome parked just behind the house, out of view from the driveway. A green garden hose ran from the house to the motorhome, and another orange line I assumed was a power cord. The motorhome was covered in moss, the same moss that claimed everything on the island that wasn't kept up.

"Come on," Sam said, getting out of the car. Her demeanor was still cold as I climbed out after her. She walked up to the motorhome and climbed up the shaky stairs. She opened the door and stepped inside, me following right behind her, our notebook in hand.

The inside was cleaner than the outside, but it was still dark and old. A small kitchen consisted of a tiny cluttered counter and sink. The dining table was covered in school books and pages from notebooks. Toward the back there was a door that opened to what looked like a bedroom and a broom closet of a bathroom.

I looked at Sam, searching for an explanation as to what we were doing out here instead of going into the house.

"This is where I live, Jake," she said, her eyes holding mine firmly. "All by myself."

Not sure I was doing it correctly, I made the signs for *where* and *Mom*.

Sam didn't respond immediately. Her eyes reddened and a little moisture pooled in them, but they never left mine.

"My mom died in August," she said, her voice cracking.

I just kept looking at Samantha, my brain not quite processing the heavy words she had just spoken. Kids our age didn't have to say sentences like that.

Dropping her eyes from my face, Sam sniffed, wiping at a tear that had broken free onto her cheek. She walked back toward the bedroom, me numbly following her. She sank onto the messy bed and I sat next to her.

Opening our notebook and pulling a pen from my pocket, I wrote. I don't understand.

Sam read my writing, sniffing again, looking completely exhausted. Finally, she raised her eyes to meet mine.

"My mom quit her job in June," Sam started. "She was getting tired of all the traveling and I didn't want to travel with her anymore; it was just getting too hard with school. She didn't want to leave me alone all the time. The same week she quit, she went to the doctor because she wasn't feeling very well. A week later we found out she had stage-four brain cancer. She'd always written her headaches off as just stress from work. She'd joke around and say her diminishing hearing was because she was getting old."

And that was the real reason Sam started taking sign language.

I let out a long, slow breath, leaning back on my hands, like I needed to give some space to the huge *thing* that had just been revealed. This was much, much bigger than I ever would have expected.

"Only a few people on the island knew," Sam moved forward. "Mom didn't want people feeling sorry for her, you know?" I did. "So she kept it quiet. It wasn't that hard, not a lot of people on the island really knew Mom because she was always gone.

"Not many people survive stage-four brain cancer. By that point it's too late. It was for my mom. They said she could start treatments, but it was only going to slow it down for a few weeks and it was just going to make her feel sick all the time," Sam's lower lip quivered a little bit. "She only had ten weeks after we found out. We had some money saved up after she quit her job, but it wasn't anywhere near enough to pay for all the hospital bills. We put the house up for sale the beginning of August, hoping we could keep her in the hospital for just a little longer, give her another week or so. The house sold just eight days before she died. She signed all the papers for it in the hospital. We got the money for it the day she died."

Tears were freely slipping down Sam's face now. I reached a hand out and brushed a stream of them from her right cheek. She squeezed her eyes closed, pressing her hand against mine, trapping my hand against her face.

"No one ever came to get me, Jake," she said in a hoarse whisper, her eyes still closed. "I talked to people, thought

136

my grandparents were coming, or Mike, my father. Child services kept going back and forth on who would take custody. But no one ever came for me.

"Finally I caught a bus after Mom had been buried in Everett, and came back to the island. By then I realized I was on my own. So I took what money we had left, after we sold the house and paid Mom's bills, and bought this crappy motorhome. That house is just a summer home so I figure I'm good to stay here until they come back in June."

I brought my other hand up to the other side of Samantha's face. Her eyes opened to look at mine, so uncertain looking. I could only stare at her.

This explained everything. Why Sam had withdrawn from everyone so much this year. Why she had lost so much weight. She had no money for food. And her mom hadn't been stuck in an airport, today on Thanksgiving. She'd been long gone.

Sam was lonelier than I ever could have imagined.

"So you understand why I was so pissed earlier," she said, holding my eyes. "Maybe you can't talk anymore, and that sucks. But you still have family. You still have a house. You still have *food*," her breathing was coming out heavy and tired. "You still have everything Jake, and you just didn't see it."

I felt something behind my eyes prickle and was surprised when a tear rolled down my own cheek. I wanted to tell her I was sorry. I wanted to take back the entire last seven days. I wanted to crawl into a hole and disappear.

There were a lot worse things that could happen to you than losing your voice.

Opening the notebook again, I set to scribbling a confession. I had to tell her now.

The night I had my accident, I wrote. *I was coming to see you. I was drunk, but the guys talked me into it. I was coming to tell you...*

Samantha ripped the page out of my hands, her eyes reading along as I wrote. I looked up into her face, confused, on the verge of being hurt that she wouldn't let me write it.

"Don't say it," she whispered, her eyes locked on my face, her eyes misty. She shook her head. "Don't say that."

Everything within me wanted to say *but it's true.* My hand rose to the side of her face again. Sam's eyes studied my lips and I studied hers. We each leaned in closer until our foreheads were touching. It felt like currents of electricity were running through the two of us, making me feel like I was going to melt from the intensity.

I wanted to whisper a million things to Sam, all the things I didn't say, but I couldn't. So instead I leaned forward and let my lips show her.

Sam's lips were hesitant at first, as if over-thinking if she was going to regret doing this. And then they softened under mine. Her hand came to the back of my neck, as my hands pressed into her back.

There was a lot of pain in that kiss. There was so much hurt and so much fear in it. I felt tears rolling down the both of our faces. But, in that kiss, there was even more want. We both wanted to smother out that pain, to not have so many horrible things in the all too recent past, to just be normal, to do the types of things we were supposed to be dealing with besides death and disability.

Sam shifted on top of me, pressing me back against the bed. Her lips moved with mine in a way that was so familiar I could have sworn we had done this a thousand times before. And yet it was so new, I never wanted to stop cause I was afraid if we did, I would realize none of this was real.

Sam's lips tasted like strawberries and bananas.

Sam leaned back away from me, her eyes studying mine. She had that look again, like there was something on her mind.

As if she could read *what?* on my face, she answered.

"I've liked you for a while, Jake," she said. "I meant to do something about it this summer, but then Mom got sick and I couldn't be worrying about the boy I liked when my mother was dying." She stopped for a second, studying my eyes again. "I just wanted you to know that."

I brushed the back of my hand against her cheek, my eyes still locked on hers.

She hadn't told me she loved me. I believed Sam when she had written about not believing in love. But she had said that she at least liked me.

In that moment, that meant everything.

I lifted my head off the bed and pressed my lips to hers briefly. She smiled in a way I'd never seen her smile before. I committed to making her smile like that as much as I possibly could.

I reached over on the bed for our notebook and the pen.

This changes things, I wrote, turning it so she could see it.

"Yeah," she smiled, kissing my lips again. "It does."

We spent the next two hours talking, filling a full ten sheets of paper. I asked how she survived, where she got money from. I was surprised when she told me she made money from some girl who went to a prep school down in Seattle, doing homework for her and sending it online.

She told me how she was afraid someone would eventually realize she was still here and try to come and take her away. The plan was always to go to UW after graduation and get her teaching degree, but to secure her scholarship she needed to make sure she kept her Valedictorian status, and she couldn't do that unless she stayed here at Orcas High School.

She just had to stay hidden for the next nineteen weeks until she turned eighteen.

About three weeks ago she'd moved the motorhome to this house from somewhere just passed the golf course when the owners moved back into their house. And a few weeks back, she'd looked so terrible because she'd gone three days without power. Some rodents had chewed through her wires. I was impressed she'd fixed them herself.

I couldn't feel sorry for myself anymore, I knew that. Seeing what Sam had to live with, how she'd kept going after she'd lost everything, *everything,* made me feel like a criminal. I did have everything, except a voice. I wasn't going to waste any more time acting like an idiot and letting my life go unlived.

I vowed to live every second of it after that day in Sam's motorhome.

There had never been a better Thanksgiving break than the one senior year. Mom, Jamie, Jenny, and Jordan went off-island early on Black Friday, not expecting to get much, just going off. Dad, John, James, and Joshua went off as well to do I didn't know what. I pretended to be unawakable when they came in to get me in the morning, and thankfully, they left me alone with a note. As soon as I knew they were gone, I pulled my clothes on, and went to Teazer's for cinnamon rolls and strawberry milk. I got to Sam's trailer at eight, just as the sun was starting to come up. I knocked three times, careful not to drop our breakfast on the ground.

I heard something hit the ground with force, followed by a curse. I smiled, silently chuckling. Finally, Sam opened the door, her eyes wide with fear.

"Jake!" she said, surprise and relief washing over her. "Oh my... Geesh! You scared me! I thought you must have been the owners or the cops. What are you doing here so early?"

I held up the bag and the cups. I couldn't help but stare at Sam's legs. They stuck out of a thin red bathrobe that clung to her tiny frame. Sam really did need to put on about fifteen pounds. I'd have to start bringing her to dinner as often as Mom would allow.

"Aww," she said, that smile spreading on her face. "You brought me breakfast?"

I nodded and stepped inside. It wasn't freezing in the motorhome, but it wasn't terribly warm either. I noticed one little space heater back in the bedroom. I made a mental note to look through our storage for a more powerful one.

Sam scarfed down her cinnamon roll faster than I ever could have, and after some insistence, I gave her half of mine too. She licked her fingers clean when she was finished.

"Thank you," she said, wiping her mouth with a napkin. "You'd think after that huge meal your family fed me yesterday I wouldn't be this hungry."

I suddenly stood and walked to Sam's tiny fridge and pulled it open. I found a half gallon of milk, a small brick of cheese, and a few apples. A half a loaf of bread sat on the tiny counter along with the crackers and banana that had been intended to be Sam's Thanksgiving dinner. Her frozen pizza had sat out too long yesterday and we'd thrown it out. I glanced back at Sam. She watched me, shame in her eyes.

Why don't you get dressed, I wrote. *We'll go to my house for a while. Family's off island today.*

It didn't take much more than that. In less than three minutes Sam walked out of her bedroom wearing the same jean's she'd worn the day before and a sweater that looked like it had been worn once before as well. Not waiting for her to protest, I walked past her into her bedroom. Looking around, it didn't take long to find her laundry basket wedged into the corner. Grabbing it, I walked right past Sam, who looked rather embarassed. Not saying anything, Sam grabbed our notebook off the table and followed me out to the Bronco.

Sam seemed relaxed in a way I hadn't ever seen her before as we drove through town and to my house. She was quiet as we rolled along, watching the trees and small shops around us. It was one of the rare times she didn't seem to have something on her mind, just enjoying the moment and being.

The house was unusually quiet when we walked inside. Quiet was about as rare in that house as snowfall on the island. It happened, but it seemed like something just short of a miracle when it did.

Sam followed me to the laundry room just off the kitchen. There were piles of everyone's clothes in the room and I found a load of Jamie's things still in the washer. It smelled just a little off, like it'd been in there for a day or so. I shoved the clothes into the dryer anyway and started it.

Putting some detergent in the machine, I then poured Sam's clothes in, pretending like I wasn't seeing all of her underwear and bras. Closing the lid, I turned back to Sam, finding her watching me closely.

"I'm impressed," she said, nodding her head. "I didn't think too many guys knew how to do laundry."

I just smiled. When there were seven kids in the house, you taught your kids pretty early on how to do their own laundry. It saved Mom hours of work every week. Joshua was the only one who didn't do his own laundry.

Next I went to the pantry, which was the size of a small bedroom. When Mom went off-island she came back with the entire van loaded with as much food as she could possibly manage. With so many people, shopping off-island was way cheaper than shopping on. Finding an empty box on the floor, I started filling it with stuff. Crackers, cereal, canned soups. Anything I could fit in the box.

"Jake," Sam said, horror filling her face. "That had better not be for me. I can't take all that. That's like stealing."

I shook my head, walking out of the pantry, Sam's box full. I grabbed the notebook. *Trust me,* I wrote. *Mom won't notice. And if she does, I'll just tell her I got extra hungry today.*

"Jake," she protested, shaking her head. "I can't."

Look, I wrote, rolling my eyes at her as I glanced up. *I'll get Mom and Dad an extra nice Christmas present this year to repay them.*

She stared at me for a long time, and I could see the internal debate she was having. Finally she just shook her head, a small smile spreading. Her stomach won out.

Digging up a small cooler, I filled it with a bag of leftover turkey, a couple bags of frozen vegetables, and a few pieces of frozen chicken. Setting it next to the box of non-cold stuff, I went out to the garage, Sam trailing behind me.

It didn't take long to find a pretty good sized space heater. It would work a lot better than the one Sam was currently using. She'd tried protesting against that too as I carried everything out to my car, but I just waved her off.

Is there anything else you need? I wrote when we got back inside.

"Really, Jake," she said. "This is all too much."

I pointed at my writing again, turning my eyes on her.

A small smile spread on her lips and she closed the space between us. She wrapped her arms behind my neck, burrowing her face in my chest. "I'm okay. Thank you."

I kissed her cheek. She turned her face to mine and my lips found hers, warm and soft.

Today they tasted like grape juice.

We turned the TV on and watched some bad comedy while we waited for Sam's laundry to finish. I couldn't help but smile and lick my lips every so often, the flavor of grape still lingering.

It felt good to be helping someone else out, someone who really needed it. Better than good. I hadn't felt like this in a long, long time.

For some reason I was nervous for school to start again on Monday. Sam and I had both said that things had changed, but I really wasn't sure what they had changed into. We'd kissed a few times, grown a whole lot closer, I finally knew her secret. But did that make her my girlfriend? Would she consider me her boyfriend now?

The uncertainty was killing me.

Mom said she was feeling under the weather on Monday so I offered to drive everyone to school. Jordan called shotgun, Jamie wedged herself in the backseat with James and Joshua. I couldn't help but notice the little smile that spread on Jordan's face as we got closer and closer to the school. She didn't say anything but I knew she knew.

My palms were sweating like they had that first day I'd gone back to school after the accident.

What's going to happen today?

I stopped in front of the elementary school and Joshua and James hopped out and scampered toward the old red-brick building. Jamie headed toward the middle school and I pulled into the parking lot of the high school.

I hadn't thought of how Sam got to school these days. She certainly wasn't driving the motorhome. I hoped there was a school bus that stopped close to where she lived.

"Hey Jake?" Jordan said, just as I was about to get out of the car. I glanced back at her, already knowing what she was going to say. "I'm really happy for you," she said, giving a smile. "Samantha seems perfect for you."

I simply returned her smile and gave a little nod before climbing out of the car. Jordan dashed ahead to join her friends. I watched her as she went, feeling incredibly appreciative of everything she'd done for me. Even though she was eleven months younger than me, Jordan had always felt like more of a big sister, even more so than Jenny ever had.

Jordan always had my back, she always looked out for me.

I was disappointed when I didn't see Samantha before school started. Calculus felt like it took forever, as if the subject wasn't bad enough. My heart jumped into my throat when the bell finally rang for second period.

But Samantha wasn't in class. And she wasn't in our ASL class or AP English. I tried not to let myself have a total panic attack when I didn't see her at all before lunch break. Had I scared her away? It would take some major scaring for Sam to skip school.

As I wandered in the direction of Sam's locker just after lunch period started, I felt a hand clamp down on my shoulder. I turned to see Rain and Carter.

"Hey, how was your Thanksgiving break?" Carter asked, shifting his books from one hand to the other. "Feels like I haven't seen you in forever."

I nodded, pulling out my pocket notebook. Fine, I wrote. Yours?

"Boring," Carter said. "Just went up to Bellingham to my grandparent's. There was only six of us there."

I nodded in Rain's direction.

"Well, let's see," he said as we started for the parking lot. No one at the high school really ate the food from the cafeteria. It was a mass migration at lunch time to the deli at Island Market. "I think every one of Mom and Dad's hippy friends showed up. It's not quite a real Thanksgiving dinner when everything's all organic, or raw, or vegan."

Carter and I both laughed. As much of a circus Thanksgiving was at my house, I couldn't even imagine what it must be like at Rain's.

We all loaded into the Bronco and headed for the Market.

"So Blake's putting this party together, out somewhere in Olga this weekend," Carter said from the backseat as he flipped through some of my notebooks. I was grateful that mine and Sam's was tucked safely in my backpack. "Sounds like a lot of people are going. You going to be able to make it, Jake? Promise there'll be no booze. Everyone's sticking to those pledges."

My stomach clenched a bit at the mention of a party. Especially one that sounded a lot like the one that changed my entire life. And there were other things I had wanted to do that weekend, all of them involving Sam. But maybe this would be the perfect time to make something public.

If there was anything to actually make public.

Finally I nodded, letting them know I was up for it.

"Awesome" Carter said as we pulled into the parking lot.

"Think you could invite Jordan?" Rain asked as he hopped out of the car.

I just gave a silent chuckle, shaking my head at Rain. Rain was every bit as much of a chicken as I had been about Sam.

I'll think about it, I wrote, flashing the page at him.

"Thanks, man," he said, punching me in the arm.

The Market was insane during lunch hour, being flooded by the high school students. We all loaded up on chicken strips, Jojo's, corn dogs, and burritos. I glanced around the store briefly when we got inside with dim hope that I might run into Sam. But she wasn't there.

I went back to school after lunch with a heavy weight in my stomach. School just seemed boring and dull without Sam around. I didn't absorb a single word Mr. Crow said in Government, I nearly chopped my finger off in Woodshop, and I almost got Carter's chest crushed in weight training when I was supposed to be spotting him. I just kept wondering where Sam was.

Everything in me was afraid she was avoiding me.

Maybe everything had been ruined.

It hadn't felt like anything had been ruined over the weekend though. Everything had felt like it was going great. But sometimes girls were complicated like that. You never could read them.

My heart leapt into my throat as I walked out to my car after school. I saw Sam leaning against the driver's door of the Bronco, her backpack resting at her feet.

"Hey stranger," she said with a small smile as I walked up to her. I smiled back, my chest doing weird things.

Really hoping I was doing it correctly, I signed something like *where were you?*

149

"Yeah," she said, dragging the word out. "The owners of the house called someone out to work on the front deck. It was a lot of fun trying to get the motorhome out of there without being seen."

By then I had dug our red notebook out of my backpack.

Crap, I wrote. *Where'd you move it to?*

"There's a small cabin just off of the road that goes out to Raccoon Point," she said. She looked tired, her nerves strung out. I couldn't imagine the stress that must have been her life. "It looks like the owner's left a few weeks ago."

I wished I could have offered to let her put the motorhome in our backyard. But that would send up the red flag to my parents, and then social services would have to get involved. And then she'd be gone.

Wish I would have known. I would have come and helped you.

"Don't think that would have been a good idea," she said, though an appreciative smile spread on her face. "With as much school as you've missed this year. I've got a lot to catch up on what I missed just today. I told all my teachers my mom was sick today so I had to help her out."

I gave a sad smile. What happened to me was bad, but at least I didn't have to lie out of necessity all the time.

You want to come over to my place and work on homework? I wrote. *Mom's making enchiladas tonight.*

She laughed as she read it, throwing her arms around me. It felt like my entire body finally relaxed, relief flooding through me. Maybe everything hadn't been ruined.

"I'd love to," she said. I was surprised when she looked at me again to see there were tears pooled in her eyes. My brow furrowed to ask her *what was wrong?* She just gave a cut off laugh, a few tears breaking free from her eyes. She wiped at them with the back of her hand. "It was just a stressful day, you know? I feel like I can't ever relax, always afraid I'm going to get caught. And I can't afford to miss school and let my grades slip."

I pulled Sam into my arms again, hugging her tightly. I could feel all the pain she was in, as if it clung to her like a heavy, itchy wool sweater. She relaxed in my arms, almost as if she was relieved to have me holding her together for just a few moments and not have to do it herself.

I stepped away from her. *Come on,* I wrote. *Let's go.*

I set our backpacks in the back seat and we both climbed in. As soon as I started pulling out of the parking lot, Sam slid her hand into mine, our fingers intertwining. She squeezed my hand tightly, as if she were afraid if she let go, she'd crumble.

It was amazing, how easily Sam fit in with my family. I'd brought her home with me and everyone went out of their way to say hi to her. And everything just felt so... normal. Sam talked with Jordan for a second, and then she and I went into my room and worked on homework. And we did actually work. There was no pressure in the air to have to do anything physical; it didn't feel weird that we were in my room alone together.

It felt like something we'd done a hundred times before.

Just like she was a part of the family, Mom set a place for her at the dinner table and she ate with the lot of us.

I took her home that night and kissed her good-bye just once. Her lips tasted like cherry.

But something felt... off at school the next day. Sam was still friendly, she still smiled that smile she only smiled at me. We still sat next to each other during class. But she never did slip her hand into mine. She never came with me to The Market for lunch. She'd just quietly say she needed to do some homework in the library.

Sam was just... distant.

And I honestly wasn't sure how to react. I felt like I was being whiplashed. Any time we were alone or at my house, she was the sweet girl who felt like my girlfriend, who held my hand and kissed me, and ran her fingers through my hair absentmindedly. But at school, she felt like nothing more than a really nice girl who was my friend.

Considering what she was currently dealing with, I didn't dare push her about it. She was already trying to balance so much in her life, I wasn't going to make things worse. And I could make it through the agonizing school Sam for the intoxicating after-school Sam.

She didn't come over to my house on Tuesday and Thursday since Kali always came over on those days. He was already at the house when I arrived at home. He suggested a walk and together we set out down our road.

The very-end-of-November chill bit at my skin, all the moisture in the air making it feel colder than it actually was. The last of the fall leaves barely clung to the non-evergreen trees, a prelude to their dead winter skeletal selves. The island felt different in the winter. Things slowed down, more so than normal island time. All the tourists left, all the snow bird residents went to warmer places. The people who stayed were true islanders, appreciating Orcas' beauty even when it was dark sixteen hours of the day.

Already as Kali and I walked down the road, at only quarter to four, it was starting to get dark through the overcast clouds above us. There was actually a chance of snow that night if it got cold enough.

How was school today? Kali signed. I actually understood everything Kali's hands said.

Okay, I signed back. *How was your day?*

Cold, he signed with a chuckle. *The bike isn't very warm in the winter.*

I chuckled too, watching Kali's dark, smiling face. I couldn't help but wonder at Kali whenever I was around him. I didn't think I'd ever met a person who had so little, but was so happy at the same time. I had never heard him complain; never saw his face without the hints of a smile.

Where do you live? I suddenly signed, not even thinking about what I was asking.

Kali's eyes grew sad for a moment, falling away from my hands and face. He was quiet for a long time and I realized he wasn't going to answer.

Tell me more about your sister, I signed, not really sure I even did half of it right.

I must not have done too bad, cause Kali started talking about her non-stop.

8 months 'til graduation
18 weeks 'til Sam's birthday

After dinner that night, I lagged behind in the kitchen with Mom, watching from the bar as she did dishes. I was only half seeing her, my eyes glazed over as I thought about the conversation I'd had with Kali earlier.

"Something on your mind, sweetie?" Mom asked, her arms covered up to her elbows in bubbles as she washed a pan.

I shrugged, and reached for one of the dozens of notebooks I left lying around the house.

Just thinking about Kali, I wrote, holding it up for Mom to see.

"Oh yeah?" she said, her eyes turning back to her work. "What about Kali?"

I don't think he has anywhere to live, I scribbled. *I'm pretty sure he sleeps in a tent. I saw it in his bike trailer today as he left.*

Mom was quiet for a while, her eyes focusing on something outside the window above the sink.

"It's getting awfully cold out there these days," she said, sounding far away.

I'm worried about him, I wrote. I had to wait almost a full minute for Mom to look over and read what I had written.

Slow-mo conversations.

Mom's eyes lingered on my words for a long time, like she was considering something very serious.

Finally, when she still didn't say anything, I clicked open my pen again.

Our loft is pretty big.

Mom's eyes lingered on my words again, slowly going from them to my face, and back again. And then a small smile spread on her face as she rinsed the pan.

"I'll have to talk to your dad about it," she said, drying her hands off and walking over to the bar. She rested her elbows on the countertop and placed her chin in her balled up fists. "But I think that's a really good idea. Just until spring though."

I leaned across the counter and gave Mom an awkward hug, as best I could manage with a three-foot counter between us.

"I'm really proud of you, Jake," Mom said, squeezing me tightly. "You could have taken life so differently after everything you've been through. But you're becoming a man. You amaze me every day."

Mom backed away from me slightly, looking me in the eye, a smile spreading on her face. I smiled back as she pressed a brief kiss to my forehead. "I'm going to go talk to your father," she said quietly. Giving me one more brief smile, she turned and headed up to their bedroom.

I had to admit to myself, having Kali live in our house would be weird. But how could I feel okay about myself, knowing there was someone out there that needed our help, and not try and offer it?

18 weeks 'til Sam's birthday

3 days 'til the party

Per Rain's request, I invited Jordan to the beach party on Saturday. She'd been reluctant at first, but I had a feeling most of that was because she remembered what the last school party had resulted in. But to my surprise, she agreed to it when she found out Rain was going to be there.

It was easy to tell there wasn't much to do on our little island that time of year. All anyone could talk about was the party on Saturday. Normally a chance of snow might kill plans for an outdoor party, but not on Orcas. It almost guaranteed that everyone would be there.

So do you want to go to the party on Saturday? I wrote in our notebook during ASL.

It's been a long time since I've been to a party, Sam wrote back. I suddenly missed our letters back and forth in the back of the notebook. It had been a while since we'd written any. I was still trying not to push Sam.

You should come, I said. *It will be fun.*

From what I hear, everyone is sticking to their 'no drinking' pledges, she wrote. *Should be semi-safe to go.*

So is that a yes?

Sam's eyes met mine, and finally, a small smile spread on her face. She nodded. I couldn't help but smile back.

Yet a hard ball settled into my stomach. Was I going to get the standoff-ish school Sam, or the after-school Sam that I loved?

Well, Kali is all moved in. We sectioned off a small part of the loft by moving the entertainment center out from the wall, and then shifted some other stuff around too so there's this little space back there for Kali to sleep and put some of his stuff. Kali isn't around too much, mostly just comes back to sleep and sometimes he stays for dinner. Then he helps Mom and Dad out whenever he can.

It's kind of weird, but it feels good to be helping out someone who needs it. Guess it took Mom and Dad quite a while to convince him to move in.

The other day Kali asked me what I wanted to do with my life, what I wanted to do after high school. The answer had always been pretty simple before. I was going into the Air Force. I was going to be a pilot and serve my country.

I don't really know now. It would be easy to get pissed off at the universe for changing my plans, but what good is that going to do me?

Maybe I'll do something with computers, that doesn't require much talking. Or maybe I'll work with animals. They won't mind or think I'm broken. I really have no idea. Guess I should start thinking about that. I am a senior, people expect you to start having an answer to the future question.

I'd like to say Sam's going to be in my future, but honestly I just can't see that far. I'm just hoping Sam is in my three month future, or even just the two week future. Lately it feels like everything with Sam is a big question mark.

I shouldn't complain. At least she's with me now. I think.

Guess that's the problem though. I don't **know**.

I picked Sam up at four on Saturday. The new house she was at wasn't as nice as the last one. Out of fear of a replay of what happened at the last house, she'd set up the motorhome a ways away from the house, running a long hose and extension cord into the trees where she was hidden away. It would make it easier if she had to make a last minute escape again.

Sam looked tired when I picked her up. Of course she looked tired all the time those days.

We drove out toward Olga in silence, as seemed usual for us when we were in the car. But I had a sick feeling in the pit of my stomach. It felt like things had come to a stop, as if the two of us weren't going to go beyond pecks and a few scattered hand holds at my house and occasionally at hers. I had been pretending that it would be enough for me, that I could live with it, as long as Sam was part of my life in some way.

But I had to admit to myself that I wanted more.

The feeling of dead weight inside of me kept growing heavier and heavier as we made our way down the slow, winding roads. I was suddenly dreading the party, even dreading spending time with Sam. I just wanted to hunker down in my room and blast my ear buds too loud.

There were only a few places to park at the beach so it was pretty obvious we were only the second group to show up. I saw Blake and two girls, one of them Norah, stacking wood on the beach to start the fire as I put the car into park. Despite all their public fights, Norah and Blake were still together.

Sam and I both sat there, just staring out the window at nothing. It felt like there was a big suffocating cloud filling the car that wouldn't dissipate until one of us said something.

"Just say it, Jake," Sam finally said, keeping her eyes glued forward.

I felt everything seize up inside of me, dread filling every corner of my body. But I had to get it out, or it was going to kill me.

Grabbing our notebook from the back seat, I clicked a pen open.

What's going on with us, Sam? I wrote. I tried to not let my hands shake, whether from frustration, anger, or fear, I wasn't sure. *What are we?* I underlined the last sentence.

Samantha's eyes stayed glued to the page for a long time, her jaw clenched tight. I could feel the defensiveness building up in her.

"I don't know what you want me to say, Jake," she said, turning her eyes forward again. "I like you, I like being with you. But you know how I feel about... about that L word. So don't expect me to proclaim my undying love for you. I've got a lot to deal with these days and I'm sorry if I'm not paying enough attention to you or fawning all over you all day, every day."

It would have been better if Samantha had raised her voice, if she had started getting mad. But she didn't. She kept her voice calm and even, just a little too quiet.

161

She clenched her jaw once more, her gloved hands balling into fists. Suddenly, without saying anything more, she climbed out of the car and shut the door behind her.

Great.

As if things hadn't been bad and weird enough, I had just made them worse.

Seeing another half dozen cars pull up, I climbed out. Rain, River, and Jordan pulled up in one car. Carter and seven other people climbed out of his car. Within about two minutes, pretty much the entire school piled out of various vehicles and flooded down toward the beach.

I hung back by the Bronco as I watched them go. I suddenly envied them. Their lives seemed so uncomplicated. The biggest worry for most of them that day had probably been what to wear, or thinking of tactics to dodge snowballs. I had a girlfriend, well, maybe-girlfriend, who was homeless and three words I wanted to say more than anything, but the person I wanted to say them to wouldn't let me. And I literally couldn't say those three words.

Finally, as the sky started to grow dark, shadows dancing on the sand, I made my way down to the party. Trying to pretend like I wasn't really looking, I noticed Sam seated on a large log, talking with Summer and Marina.

It was stupid that I felt almost betrayed that she was talking to her old friends. I didn't want to be the jealous type of guy. I should have been glad she was socializing.

Carter found me before too long, Rain having successfully engaged my sister in conversation. Carter was moping too, River more into talking to some girl named Ashley than him. I felt kind of bad for him. It would seem

162

fairer to tell him he wasn't her "type" rather than to let him suffer. The guy needed to move on. But I had promised River I'd keep her secret.

So us loser guys sat by ourselves on a log by the fire, and Carter pretended to be interested in sign language and I taught him a few signs.

This sucks.

When I pictured the party that night, I hadn't imagined I'd be spending it with Carter, teaching him stuff I could barely manage to remember.

I kept catching Samantha's eye from across the fire. We were each pretending not to see one another, knowing it was a lie. My pride wouldn't let me feel sorry for her and hers wouldn't let her do anything but pretend nothing had changed between the two of us.

Trying to ignore her, I watched my classmates around me. I was impressed that I didn't see one brown bottle or red plastic cup. They'd taken that pledge seriously. Here we were, nine weeks later, and they were sticking to it. I hadn't expected them to take it so seriously.

And they were still having a good time. They were still laughing, throwing snow balls that were closer to slush and ice than snow. They were still singing idiotic songs and doing stupid things.

But even that couldn't cheer me up.

It was obvious this party was going to last half the night. I debated leaving but then I'd have to figure out how Samantha was going to get home, or make her come with me.

Again, there was my pride.

So I just sat down in the sand, a ways back from the fire, by myself, and pulled my hood up over my head. My butt was slowly getting wet, the melted snow in the sand soaking into my pants. I didn't care though. I was trying not to care about anything then.

A few minutes later, a crunch in the sand from behind me caught my attention. Considering that it was probably just some couple trying to sneak away from the crowd to make out, I just ignored it. But then a pair of skinny legs settled on either side of me as someone sat on the log behind my back, and a pair of arms wrapped around my shoulders.

I didn't have to look up to know it was Sam.

She pulled my hood down and pressed her cheek against mine, giving me a squeeze around my chest and shoulders. I faintly detected the scent of kiwi coming from her lips.

"I'm sorry," she said quietly. Her lips brushed my cheek as she spoke. "I was a really big jerk earlier. What I said was really mean."

I turned my head slightly, so I was looking at her face. She really did look sorry, her eyes downfallen, more tired than usual.

"I have been pushing you away this whole time," she said. "When we're at your house, I just feel... safe. But when we're at school, it just reminds me how fast my whole life could fall apart. I've worked so hard these last few months and it could all crumble if anyone were to ever find out I'm only seventeen and living on my own.

"You're a part of all that," she said, her eyes growing serious. She placed a hand on my cheek. I placed my hand over hers. "While I can't say that word, the thought of letting you in, really letting you in, just to have you ripped away..." she trailed off, closing her eyes. "If my own dad could walk away from me so easily, what's to keep you from getting tired of me too?"

I turned so I was kneeling in front of her. Her eyes still closed, I pressed my lips softly to hers.

I'd been right earlier. Kiwi. I loved how her lips tasted different every time hers met mine.

I placed a hand on either side of her face. Slowly, she let her eyes open. Reaching into my pocket, I pulled out my small notebook and a pen.

I'm not going anywhere, I wrote. *So don't keep pushing me out.*

A smile cracked in the corner of her mouth. A small gleam came back into her eyes and she took my hands in hers. "I'm sorry," she said. "I've never had a boyfriend before. Guess I don't really know how to treat one."

The smile that spread on my face must have looked ridiculous.

Boyfriend.

I was Samantha Shay's boyfriend.

I kissed her kiwi lips again before. Holding my hand out, I caught her eye, testing her to see if she was really ready to do this.

She looked at me for a long moment, her smile faltering and strengthening. I could see the fear in her eyes. If we walked back to the party together, her hand in mine, it would change things again. It wouldn't just be us anymore. It would be us and the whole island knowing there was an us.

It meant she had to take a risk.

165

The smile finally spreading to show her white teeth, she placed her hand in mine. Our gloved fingers wrapped around each other. And finally, our shoulders bumping in the dark, we walked back to the fire.

As soon as Carter saw the two of us walking toward everyone, he started clapping, his hands above his head, and gave a huge whoop. Heads automatically turned, and more clapping and cheering broke out. Norah just glared at the two of us.

A laugh bubbled out of Sam's lips, her face instantly blushing as every face turned to us.

"Finally!" a few cheers rang out through the crowd.

Pressing my lips to Sam's temple, I felt like maybe, just maybe, everything in the world was going to be okay.

15 weeks 'til Sam's birthday

I felt like I was in one of those cheesy teen romance movies, maybe one from the nineties, after that night on the beach. After all the hardship and trial, the boy and the girl finally get together. They move past the things that are fighting against them, and love conquers all. Happily ever after.

After my accident I didn't expect there to be a happily ever after for me. I'd resolved with myself that life was just going to suck. But there I was every day, walking through the halls holding hands with the most beautiful, and smartest girl in school. I spent my afternoons wrapped in blankets with Samantha Shay, on my bed in my room, or in hers in the motorhome. I spent chilly winter weekends walking around town like a tourist with her by my side.

The only thing that was missing from my happily ever after was the "I love you" part. It sucked that she wouldn't say it, and that she wouldn't let me say it, but I knew I could wait. Maybe forever if I had to.

The Monday before Christmas, I collapsed onto my bed after dinner. Kali and I had been signing to each other most of the night, a lot of the family catching onto it as well since Kali was now living with us full time. Flipping on the lamp next to my bed, I pulled the red notebook out of my backpack.

I'd left it with Sam after ASL, in hopes that she'd write another letter. There were a few pieces of paper stuck to the spiral binding, like she'd ripped a page out that I wondered at, but I wasn't let down.

My mom started traveling a lot when I was about ten. We'd been really poor for a long time, after Mike left. She'd been going to school part-time and working full-time. Finally when she finished school, she got this new job. She had to travel for a few days every other week and so I'd stay with my grandparents when she was gone.

I hated it. My mom's parents are the most un-grandparent type of people you've ever met. Grandma only cared about impressing and outdoing her fancy "friends." Grandpa was absorbed in his stock trading world, or whatever the crap it was he did.

Mom knew I didn't like staying with them when she was gone. I tried not to make it hard on her, but she knew. Guess that's just part of being a mom. One time she came back and gave me a present. It was this package of six lip glosses, flavored, and totally little kid. When I was ten it seemed so cool that they were all the way from New York, even though you could have gotten them anywhere.

I'd wear that lip gloss all the time when she was gone. Even though they were all different, each one reminded me of her. After that, whenever she went away, she'd always bring me back some new kind of lip gloss or Chapstick. One time when she had to travel to Paris for work, she bought me this fancy make-up bag for me to put them all in. Over the years I've filled the whole bag. It's a pretty big bag.

Seems silly, doesn't it? That just Chapstick makes me feel like Mom's here again. Sometimes when I put it on, certain smells make me think of what she looked like when she was making breakfast, or drinking her coffee out on the back deck.

It kind of scares me though, to keep wearing it every day like I do. What happens when I run out of it? Will I forget what she looked like? What it looked like when the sun reflected on her hair? The way her pillow always smelled like her? Will my memory of her run out too?

I let the notebook rest on my chest when I was done reading, my head filled with a lot of rambled thoughts. I almost felt worse and worse about every time I had felt sorry for myself these past few months. Really, for ever feeling sorry for myself.

It seemed so simple, Chapstick and lip gloss. I certainly enjoyed the million flavors that were Sam's lips. But it was so much more for her. Those flavors and smells were someone who she cared for, who had meant more to her than anyone else.

I had this airplane when I was little. Guess I shouldn't say had. It's still sitting on my bookshelf. You've probably seen it before and not even noticed it. My grandpa gave it to me when I was like five, my mom's dad. I don't even really remember him, he died when I was seven, I think. But he was this old, shriveled up guy, who couldn't even stand up straight, and always looked like he was scowling. But I remember that he told stories about when he was in the Air Force. I don't really even remember any specific stories, but I remembered him telling them. And then he gave me that old metal airplane on my fifth birthday.

It was pretty roughed up. But I loved that crappy old thing. When I was eight, one of the wings broke off and I bawled my eyes out until Dad finally found someone who could weld it back.

Guess that's where I decided I wanted to get my pilots license. I wanted to test out the skies, to see how the world looked from above. I took that stupid metal plane up in the air with me the first day I flew solo. I was so scared I thought I was going to crap my pants. But for some reason I felt a bit better having that little plane there with me. Maybe my grandpa was flying with me that day.

Some days I miss flying so much it makes my entire chest hurt, feels like I can't breathe sometimes. I try not to think about the fact that I'll never have thousands of feet of air between me and the ground again. But it's those times that I have to remind myself that at least I got the chance to do it sometime in my life. A couple dozen solo flights are better than having never done it at all.

15 weeks 'til Sam's birthday

The weather took a turn for the worse the next day. Tuesday dawned with a fresh blanket of snow. And six inches of snow meant school was definitely canceled. If Orcas got more than two inches, the entire island pretty much shut down.

Normally I would have been stoked, but considering the circumstances I knew Sam was living under, I felt pretty panicked and worried. With everything in me, I wished Sam had a cell phone so I could call her and make sure her pipes didn't freeze. Or that she hadn't frozen. Instead I had to wait until almost eleven when the roads were semi-cleared to take as many extra blankets as I could steal without Mom noticing. I told her I was going to spend the day at Sam's. She'd just told me to be home before ten so I didn't get stuck somewhere in the snow.

Sam's driveway was covered in a perfect, fresh blanket of white snow and for a minute I didn't know if I was going to make it all the way into her place. I wasn't so sure I was getting out unless the snow started to melt.

I shivered at the sight of the motorhome. It definitely didn't look warm. I could only hope the small trail of steam coming through a vent on the side of it meant it was warm enough on the inside.

I knocked on the door just once before I let myself in.

Everything inside was covered with a thin film of dew, the warmth from the space heater battling the cold outside.

The motorhome was a mess, and there was no sign of an alive Sam.

Walking back toward her bedroom, I found her still zonked out in bed, buried beneath a pile of blankets. She lay there with her mouth slightly open, her hair stuck to her forehead, which looked slightly damp.

My guess was that Sam was sick. She wouldn't have slept in like this otherwise, especially considering it was supposed to be a school day.

Deciding to let her keep sleeping, I closed her bedroom door quietly behind me. Turning to her tiny sink, I set to doing her few dishes. The water at least hadn't frozen.

I slowly worked my way through the motorhome, straightening the kitchen, discarding wrappers, sweeping the floor. It was humbling to fully immerse myself in Samantha's new way of living. She really had nothing.

"Jake?" I heard a croaky voice call from the bedroom.

Leaning the broom against the wall, I walked back towards her, grabbing our notebook from the table. She had propped herself up on one elbow, squinting in my general direction. She looked terrible.

"What time is it?" she asked, her eyes squinting, looking for the clock. "What are you doing here before school?"

I held up one finger on one hand and two on the other, hoping it would look like twelve instead of three. I could never remember the signs for any numbers above five.

"Crap!" she shouted, jumping out of bed. She groaned as she did, her face looking pained as she searched around for clothes.

There's six inches of snow outside, I wrote. No school today.

172

"Oh," she said, her frame instantly relaxing. She slumped back into bed, pulling her pile of blankets around her.

You okay?

She kind of shrugged her shoulders. "I don't feel real great today," she said, nuzzling further into her blankets. "I feel kind of achy. I really hope I'm not coming down with something."

I shifted on the bed, grabbing one of Sam's legs from inside the blanket and pulling it towards me. Pressing my thumbs into the sole of her foot, I started working firm circles into it.

"That feels really good," she said, her eyes sliding closed, her whole body relaxing into her worn out bed.

I glanced around Sam's room. Her clothes were everywhere, mixed with notebooks, textbooks, and random sheets of paper. Sam was messier than I was. I didn't think girls were allowed to be sloppy.

On the tiny nightstand next to her bed, I spotted a golden colored bag with dark red, intricate stitching and beading. It was unzipped a little bit, and inside I could see colorful tubes, the entire bag full of them.

The lip glosses from Sam's mom.

It took me a minute to notice that Sam's leg and foot had gone totally limp in my hand. She'd fallen back asleep. Setting her foot down gently, I lay next to her, a pile of blankets underneath me. Resting my head on my arm, I just lay there and studied Sam's face.

Her lashes fanned out on her cheek, long and perfect. Yesterday's make-up still clung to them. Her nose was

173

slender and rounded, it almost reminded me of a little kids nose. All kids had cute noses; Sam never lost hers. Her lips were perfect and pink. For once it looked like there was nothing on them.

She gave a little sigh, rolling towards me just a bit. Her arm rolled off of her and onto my chest. Careful not to wake her, I took her hand in mine, resting my lips against her skin just lightly.

I thought about Christmas coming up. Only four days away. I'd never had a girlfriend before so I didn't know what I was supposed to get Sam. I wanted it to be something special, not just some stupid thing she'd say thanks for and never really look at again. It was going to be all the harder to get something good since I didn't have a job.

Sam slept for another hour, her eyes finally fluttering open and locking with mine.

"Hey," she said, a small smile spreading on her lips. I had never seen such a perfect sight.

I smiled back, tucking a lock of hair behind her ear.

"I could get used to waking up next to you."

I was surprised at such a serious comment from Sam. I didn't get to hear things like that from her very often.

But I'd take what I could get.

Me too.

"I feel gross," she said, breaking the spell that had been weaving between us as fast as it had formed. "Though I feel a little better. Not quite so much like I'm cooking from the inside out. I think I'm going to jump in the shower, if you don't mind?"

I shook my head, trying to keep out thoughts of joining her.

Sam closed the door to the pocket-sized bathroom behind her and I heard the water sputter on. I shoved a pair of her underwear with the toe of my shoe, trying not to imagine what she looked like in them.

"So what do you want to do today?" Sam called from the shower. I sat there for an awkward moment, unable to respond. A little more quietly, I heard Sam mutter "Duh," to herself. I just chuckled and shook my head.

I couldn't blame Sam for forgetting sometimes. There were endless times when I found words forming on my lips, taking the short, un-thought about breath before the words came out. But they didn't. They stayed trapped inside of me, eventually having to find their way out through my fingers and onto the page if they ever wanted to come out.

Sam and I ended up spending the entire day outside, romping through the snow. She got creative with a piece of hard plastic and some rope, turning it into a sled. Her energy seemed to come back as we threw snow balls at each other, rolled an entire family of snowmen, and created a pretty impressive-sized igloo. I kept worrying about Sam and her wet hair while we were outside. The ends of her dark auburn strands became icicles. Sam teased me relentlessly about worrying over it, asking when I'd become such a girl.

It had been dark for well over an hour before we tromped back into the motorhome. Our clothes were soaked, neither of us having any real snow clothes.

Sam's teeth chattered as she peeled her coat off in the tiny kitchen/dining area. My toes and fingers were completely numb. I clumsily pried off my soaked tennis shoes. We stood there awkwardly for a moment, both of us realizing we were soaked completely through, and I didn't have anything to change into.

A smile started forming on Sam's face, so slow I didn't even realize it was there for a while. There was a look that formed in her eyes that I'd never seen before. It was the look of wanting something, and not wanting to fight against wanting that something.

My entire body seemed to jump to life as she crossed the tiny kitchen toward me. Her hand came to the back of my neck, her skin feeling like ice against mine. But I didn't care one little bit.

Sam's other hand pushed my coat the rest of the way off my shoulders as our lips met. As my coat dropped to the floor with a wet slop, Sam's lips became more urgent, her lips parting. Her lips tasted like cotton candy today.

Electricity ran through my blood as Sam's hands slid down to the hem of my shirt. Very slowly, she raised the soaking fabric, making goosebumps flash across my skin as she lifted it up and over my head, our lips parting for just a brief moment as it came off.

It scared me that I hadn't even noticed my hands slipping under Sam's shirt until I'd lifted it over her head. I didn't want to think that I could lose control like that, but I didn't want to stop. Apparently, neither did Sam. She'd slipped out of her wet jeans before I could even let my eyes trail to what she was wearing beneath those wet things.

The world never seemed more real or bright as it did when I saw Sam standing there in next to nothing. The dark blue fabric clung to her skin in ways that made my head spin and my breath catch in my chest.

My eyes met hers and I saw another thing there that I'd never seen before. Being with Sam was all about dancing around walls and searching for invisible doors. But in that moment, there were no walls up, there were just her chocolate brown eyes, watching to see what I thought of her.

I held her eyes as my hand rose to her cheek. Her skin was cool against mine. I hoped she could see how beautiful I thought she was in that moment. It was painful that I couldn't make the words form, my chest actually ached from holding them in. But I saw the softness in her eyes, and knew that she knew I loved her, even if she wouldn't let me say the words.

"Come warm up with me," she breathed, her lips brushing against mine as she spoke against my skin. Reaching down, she unbuttoned the top button of my pants. It didn't take me longer than a second to slip out of them. Hooking her index finger into the waistband of my boxers, she pulled me toward the bathroom with her. Turning the hot water on, she pulled me in after her.

The water burned my skin but I didn't even notice as my eyes ran over Sam again, wearing nothing but a bra and panties. Sam bit her lower lip, looking at me from under those perfect dark lashes.

We stayed in that shower until the hot water ran out, our lips locked together, our hands exploring each other's skin. Sam held all the important stuff back, but just barely. I felt light headed and my knees weak by the time Sam let out a half giggle, half scream as the water poured over us, ice cold.

We both stumbled out of the shower, wrapping ourselves in towels. We tumbled into her bed, burying ourselves into the blankets and pillows. We lay facing each other, our noses only a half inch apart.

"This has been the best day I've had in a really long time," Sam said, a happy, lazy smile on her face. "It feels nice to just be... me. Just be me with you."

I smiled, pressing my lips to hers briefly. The excitement of the day was settling down, leaving my body feeling heavy and sluggish.

Sam's eyes drifted down, resting on my throat. She studied the scars there, the gaping hole that was never going to go away. Her warm fingers rose to touch the skin there.

"You've been amazing to me, Jake," she said quietly, her eyes still on my scars. She was quiet for a second. Finally, her eyes met mine again. "Thank you."

I clumsily made the sign for *your welcome*. The words of *I love you* wanted to break free from my lips so bad in that moment. But they stayed trapped in my throat, safe, where they wouldn't ruin anything.

8 hours since falling asleep
15 weeks 'til Sam's birthday

The sound of my phone vibrating pulled me from dreams of flying. I searched for my clock, wondering who was calling me in the middle of the night. But nothing looked familiar. My clock wasn't where it was supposed to be. These blankets weren't familiar.

The sound of someone else sleeping next to me in the bed sure wasn't familiar.

Crap.

Stumbling through the dark, I scrambled to pick up my phone before the call went to my voicemail. My stomach sank into my knees when I saw it was 3:12 AM and it was Mom calling.

Ending the call, I set to texting Mom. *I'm soooo sorry. Fell asleep at Sam's. Heading home now.*

I checked my phone after I hit send. Mom had called four times, Dad had called twice, and Jordan had called once. There were two voicemail's from Mom, one of them yelling and seething for me to come home immediately, the other worried sick, saying if I didn't come home soon she was sending the police to look for me in a ditch.

Realizing I was still more naked then clothed, I frantically set to pulling on my still damp things. My stomach felt sick as I searched around for my keys. I was so busted.

I went back into Sam's room, leaning over the bed and pressing a kiss to her forehead. Through the dim light I saw her eyelashes flutter open. She looked confused for just a second, and then a smile spread over her face.

For a second I considered just letting Mom call the cops. Going home was the last thing I wanted to do.

"Oh no," Sam said, her face growing serious, almost as fast as she had smiled. "You're probably in a ton of trouble, huh?"

I nodded, giving her a lopsided smile that said *it was worth it.* I kissed her lips, lingering briefly. She muttered good-bye and I slipped out the door.

The snow had started to melt on the roads by afternoon, but when the temperatures dropped back to freezing that night, it just made all the melted snow on the roads turn to ice. I slipped and slid on the road the entire drive. As I drove past the airport, I saw an older blue car half sitting in the ditch. After slowing down to make sure there wasn't anyone still in it, I continued on my way home.

But the crappy drive home was nothing compared to what I knew was waiting for me when I walked through the front door.

Pulling into the driveway, I saw that the light was on in the living room. They were waiting for me.

It felt like my heart was trying to hammer its way out of my chest as I walked up the sidewalk. I pushed the door open. Mom sat in an overstuffed chair in the corner, her arms folded over her chest. Dad paced the floor, rubbing a hand over his chin. He froze when I closed the door behind me with a small click.

We all just stood there for a silent second. Glancing at the clock on the wall, I saw it was 3:38.

I was *so* dead.

"You know you're grounded, right?" Mom said, her voice tight. I saw her hands shaking just slightly where they were pinned against her body with her arms.

I just nodded.

"You know you just about gave me a stroke, worrying that I'd get a call that you'd been found in a ditch again, right?"

I glanced at Dad, nodding my head. I wasn't sure if I wanted Dad to say anything or not. He just stared at me with blank eyes.

"I thought I was going to go crazy," Mom said, her voice and body relaxing slightly. "I called Rain's parents, I called Principal Hill. I tried calling Samantha's house but their number is unlisted."

My stomach instantly tightened. Samantha just didn't have a house for anyone to call.

Mom squeezed her eyes closed, taking a deep breath. I could almost see her plotting out my punishment behind her eyelids.

"Okay," she said, letting her eyes slowly slide open. "You're grounded for a week. That means no Samantha, Jake," she said, her eyes growing serious. I wanted to protest, yet I knew I deserved it. "Do I have to give you an actual curfew?"

I shook my head. Mom had never given any of us kids an official curfew, it was just the unspoken rule that nights like this never happen.

"Okay," Mom said, her eyes suddenly growing tired.

I glanced over at Dad. I was surprised his expression wasn't harder than it was. "Go get some sleep," he said, nodding in the direction of my bedroom.

As I walked back toward my room, the teenager in me wanted to protest, to defend myself. It's not like I'd done anything really *bad*. I'd just fallen asleep, that's why I'd gotten home so late. And yet I knew they had every right to be worried. Considering my past, I was surprised they hadn't already called the cops.

As I stripped out of my wet clothes, turned out the lights, and climbed into bed, my tongue ran over my lips. Cotton candy.

Yeah, I was in serious trouble.

But it had been worth it.

I scoured the beach for hours, more than one beach actually. By the end of the day on Thursday, I was exhausted and frozen, but I had a handful of blue and green sea glass. With Mom's help I fashioned it into a bracelet. Mom even let me see Sam for all of five minutes on Christmas Day to give it to her.

Sam had gotten me these incredibly cool vintage pilot's goggles she'd found at The Exchange, which was kind of like a never-ending, open-air garage sale. It was like what a flea market would be like if the world came to an end. You would be hard pressed to find places like The Exchange anywhere but on Orcas.

Mom stuck to the grounding. Five minutes was all I got with Sam for a week. She'd even sent Rain and Carter away when they showed up the day after Christmas.

But by New Years I was forgiven and un-grounded, and Sam spent the entire night at our house, sleeping in Jordan's room when we all finally went to bed. I couldn't have been happier, having my whole family there, all seven kids, Kali, and the girl I loved. It was the best New Year's ever.

School started back up and things went about as usual. But when you live on a weird, little island like Orcas, things can't really stay normal for long.

The second to last week of January was predicted to be the coldest weather we'd had in nine years. Even though the island didn't get any snow, which also meant school would not be canceled, we got wicked winds from our too-close neighbor, Canada.

The second day of the storm, the entire island lost power.

It happened during Woods class, just after the bell had rung to start the period. As soon as it went out, a cheer could be heard throughout the entire school. No power meant we all got to go home.

After we were dismissed, we all filed out into the halls and I immediately began searching for Samantha. Finally, I found her heading for her locker, her eyes wide, her expression something like a mix of worry and fear.

You okay? I wrote and flashed to her as I joined at her side.

"The power's out," she said quietly as she pulled open her locker in the dim light.

I nodded in agreement, resting my back against the locker next to hers.

"I wonder how long it's going to be out for," she said as she grabbed a few books from her locker and slid them into her messenger bag.

I just shrugged. *Want a ride home?* I wrote.

Sam just nodded absentmindedly and twisted one of her rings around her finger.

She didn't say much as I drove her back to the motorhome. The car wiggled and shook on the road as the wicked northern winds tore into us. When I finally parked at Sam's place, we both ran inside, pulling our hoods up to keep the icy cold out.

I felt like an idiot as soon as we got inside.

The power being out meant Sam's space heaters wouldn't work.

It was already ice cold inside.

Crap.

Sam hesitated in the kitchen, wrapping her arms around herself, her teeth already starting to chatter. Her eyes met mine and I could see she didn't know what to do.

So I did the only thing there was to do.

Telling her to pack clothes to last a few days, I then went outside and shut off the hose that lead from the cabin to the motorhome. It took me a bit to figure out how to drain the water from the hose and the trailer, but I was fairly confident her pipes weren't going to freeze and break during the cold weather.

Ten minutes later, we were back in the car, the heat blasting.

"Jake," Sam said. "There's no way your mom's going to let me stay. Not now that we're together. New Year's was one thing. She'll probably suspect something fishy is going on."

She doesn't have to know you're spending the night, I quickly wrote when we got to a stop sign.

"I hate lying to your mom," Sam said. "It's a lot harder to lie to people you like."

I glanced over at Sam. She looked like she had the weight of the world on her shoulders again. She twisted one of her rings round and round. I considered that maybe I should tell Mom and Dad about what had happened to Sam. Maybe they'd understand and not tell social services. Maybe they'd let her move in with us until she turned eighteen.

185

But something within me suspected that wasn't what would really happen. This was one of those big situations that even when you felt you knew what the right thing to do was, the state would disagree. And I didn't want to put them into that difficult situation.

The two of us walked into the house together, leaving Sam's bag of stuff in the car. It felt like walking into a furnace.

When Dad built the house he had put in an enormous wood burning stove in the living room. The pipe ran up into the vaulted ceiling which opened up into the loft and the hallway upstairs.

We wouldn't be getting cold with that thing.

"Sam!" Joshua said excitedly as soon as we walked inside. He ran over and put his arms around her. "Mom's making hot chocolate on the fireplace! You want some? She put real chocolate chips in it too!"

Sam chuckled, ruffling Joshua's hair. "I'd love some."

"Mom!" Joshua yelled as he started for the kitchen. "Sam wants some hot chocolate too!"

Sam chuckled as she looked back at me. She had one of those gleams in her eyes, like she knew where she belonged.

Mom invited Sam to stay for dinner, as I knew she would, and the entire family, Sam, and Kali spent the rest of the day doing homework by candle light and playing board games at the kitchen table.

I slipped a note to Sam under the table during the family's third round of Uno at Joshua's request.

My window's the second on the end. No screen in it. I'll head to bed as soon as you leave and let you back in.

186

Sam stealthily read it under the table. She glanced at me, her eyes nervous and unsure. I just reached for her hand and gave it a squeeze.

As if she'd been planning it the whole night, at exactly ten, Mom said it was time for everyone to go to bed. Sam took that as her cue to leave, lying and saying a friend was coming to pick her up.

See you soon, I mouthed to Sam as I pretended to say good-bye to her at the front door. She gave me a sly smile and pretended to walk down the driveway.

As soon as I closed the door, I said good-night to everyone, took two seconds to brush my teeth, and headed straight for my room. Lighting a candle and setting it on my dresser, I then crawled onto the bed and as quietly as I could, slid the window open.

Sam stood hidden in the shadows, already shivering, holding her bag of things. I waved her over and helped her climb through.

"What if we get caught?" she whispered, looking at the door like it might burst open at any second.

I took Sam's bag from her and set it at the foot of the bed. A smile spreading on my face, I pulled her into my arms. Our bodies melted together, like they were made for each other. All the worry and fear disappeared from Sam's face as she looked up at me. I loved it when she smiled the Jake smile.

I love you, I said in my head for the millionth time.

There was something perfect and sweet about the way Sam's body folded into mine. We both slid into the sheets after we'd gotten ready for bed. She'd laid her head on my chest, every inch of her body tucking into me. I rested my chin on the top of her head, wrapping my arms around her.

"How'd I get so lucky to have you?" she whispered against my chest. "You always take care of me."

I pressed my lips into her hair, squeezing her tighter.

I'm the lucky one.

17 hours since the power went out

11 weeks 'til Sam's birthday

"Oh my gosh!" someone suddenly yelled. I jerked awake to see Mom shielding her eyes and stepping back out the door. Sam suddenly sprang awake as well, her eyes wide and terrified.

"Jake!" Mom was trying really hard to keep her voice under control. "What is Samantha doing in your bed?"

"Oh shi..." Sam said, climbing out of the bed. I blinked my eyes hard, trying to clear the sleep from my head. "Mrs. Hayes, I'm so sorry," Sam started hurriedly explaining. "My Mom's out of town again, and the power's out, and we don't have a wood stove at our house. It was really cold and I was scared to be home by myself last night. I'm so, so sorry."

I wanted to butt in and blurt out an explanation too, but well, I couldn't... So I just grabbed the nearest notebook and pen.

SORRY! I wrote in big letters, underlining them. I flipped the page. *I didn't want her to freeze to death!*

Mom just shook her head, clenching her jaw tightly. I could see the wheels turning in her head, debating whether to be the good Samaritan or kick Sam out right then and there.

"Breakfast is ready," she finally said. Without anything else, she turned and walked out the door, closing it behind her.

Sam looked back at me, almost in slow motion. Her eyes were comically wide, her face flushed completely red. I instantly burst out into a silent laugh.

"Jake Hayes!" she nearly yelled at me. "This *so* isn't funny!"

Which only made me laugh all the harder.

"Stop it!" she shouted, a laugh bubbling out of her lips as she launched herself at me. She started beating me with pillows and trying to suffocate me with a blanket.

Samantha was beyond embarrassed to walk out into the dining room and sit down to eat hash-browns, eggs, and bacon, all cooked on the wood stove. But hardly any of the family seemed to notice this was out of the usual, besides Jordan, who just gave Sam that little sly smile that girls frequently give each other.

With no indicators that the power was going to come back on any time soon, and the Canadian winds still raging, we all hung out at home, drinking hot chocolate again, stocking the fire, playing games, reading, relaxing.

I kissed Sam at the bottom of the stairs that night, just before she went up with Jordan for bed.

I smiled to myself as I lay on my bed by myself that night, feeling like maybe there was someone watching over me.

My screwed up little life felt pretty perfect.

11 weeks 'til Sam's birthday

School resumed one day later, when the power finally got back up and running. I had been dreading it like nothing else. It was nice to have Sam living under the same roof for a while.

Mysteriously, after Sam went back home, I found another page had been torn out of our notebook.

What had Sam written that she didn't want me to see?

I sat down in Calculus for first period a few days after school started up again and pulled my book and a notebook out. I hadn't noticed anyone had sat next to me until a hand suddenly touched my arm.

"How's it going, Jake?" a voice practically dripping with sexual innuendo's said. I looked over to see Norah sitting in the desk next to me. I couldn't help my eyes jumping to her mile long legs that stuck out from beneath a skirt what wasn't more than a short piece of fabric. The top she wore under her jacket dipped low enough on her chest that I could see the middle of her pink lacy bra.

I gave a hard swallow, my eyes quickly jumping away from her. I hoped my face didn't flush red.

So it seemed the rumors that she and Blake had broken up were true.

Fine, I managed to scrawl. You?

"Oh," she said with a dramatic sigh, tossing her hair over one shoulder. "Fine. Lonely."

I gave a small nod, trying my best not to look at her without being rude.

"So how's... Sam... doing?" she said. The way she said Sam's name you'd think she was a rotting banana peel at the bottom of the garbage can. I instantly felt my inside's harden.

Great, I wrote. She's been staying at my house while the power's been out.

There. That ought to put a damper on Norah's smoldering.

"Too bad," she said, her voice turning bored as she pulled out a notebook. "Can't imagine she's a lot of fun. All she ever does is study."

My jaw clenched and so did my fists.

I was grateful Ms. Sue showed up then and started class.

I couldn't concentrate as the lesson got underway. Norah kept giving me all these seductive side glances. Then she'd turn towards me, crossing her bare legs so she was practically touching my leg with the toe of her high-heeled shoes.

Had she done this last year, I might have gotten a little excited. Even though I'd been in love with Sam for forever, any guy got excited when he caught the eye of Norah. Even if she had been dubbed Norah the Whora.

I practically ran for the door when the bell rang, and didn't look back.

I'd seen Norah's eyes stalking me off and on the last few weeks. It was surprising that my whole accident and the scars didn't turn her off. Was that admirable? But I knew this was a game to her. She was trying her hardest to make Blake jealous, and what better way to make him jealous than by flirting with the town cripple?

I breathed a sigh of relief when I got to physics and saw Sam sitting in her usual desk. I walked straight over to her and planted a kiss on her lips, right in front of the class.

"Well, hello," Sam said with a smile as I sank into the seat next to her. "You're in a friendly mood today."

I rolled my eyes as I pulled our notebook out and clicked a pen open.

Norah, I simply wrote, flashing it in her direction.

"Oh," Sam said, her eyes falling slightly. "Norah."

You okay? I wrote, touching her arm to catch her attention again. She gave me a slightly sad look, just as Mr. Roy started class. Reaching for our notebook, Sam set to writing.

I didn't like the look that suddenly filled Sam's perfect face. I knew Sam and Norah had never been friends, but was there something more going on between them?

When Mr. Roy had his back turned to the class, Sam slid the notebook back onto my desk. Tucking it next to my notes, I read Sam's handwriting.

Norah's never been exactly nice to me, but she's been a total witch lately. Always making comments about my worn out clothes and how I look. She's been spreading rumors that I have an eating disorder.

She's a tramp though. Just trying to ignore her. She'll get bored eventually. Though if she keeps looking at you like you're a freaking lollipop I may end up clawing her eyes out...

I chuckled as I read Sam's words. I instantly felt better.

No worries, I wrote back. *Norah the Whora's got nothing on you.*

Sam just glanced at the notebook to read my response. A small smile worked its way back onto her face. While Mr.

193

Roy wrote on the whiteboard, she reached for my hand and gave it a quick squeeze.

Norah's approaches got more and more aggressive over the next few weeks. And her clothes grew smaller and smaller. It got to the point where it wasn't attractive anymore. I didn't understand how she thought I'd leave Sam for that. She looked like a freaking prostitute. One day she was even sent home cause Principal Hill deemed she was wearing too little. Her position as student body president was in serious danger.

And her jabs at Sam got worse. The entire school soon believed Sam had a major eating disorder and Sam had even been called into the school guidance counselor's office. She'd nearly had a panic attack when the counselor wanted to meet with Sam's mom. Samantha did the only thing she could: lied and said her Mom was out of town again for three weeks.

I started stealing more food to bring to Sam. I hoped Mom just suspected it was Kali or James, putting on some winter weight.

By the end of January, Sam couldn't even walk through the halls without hearing people whisper about how ragged she was looking, about how she was starving herself.

It pissed me off. I wanted to punch each and every one of them in the face for saying anything bad about Sam. If only they knew what was really going on.

They deserved to feel horrible about what they were saying, for helping to spread the toxic rumors. I wanted to tell them the truth, to make them feel guilty. But I could never betray Sam's secret. And as soon as anyone found out, Sam would be gone.

8 weeks 'til Sam's birthday

"Now step up," Sam directed. I stubbed my toe on something hard and nearly landed on my face. "Sorry," she tried to hold back a laugh, her hands still fixed over my eyes. "A bigger step up. Just one more."

I managed to step up without killing myself, a smile spreading on my face as I placed my hands over Sam's.

"'K," she said, sounding slightly nervous, which made me all the more curious about what was going on. "Sit... here," she directed me onto some surface. "For just a second, and keep your eyes covered. No peeking! I'll be back in just a minute."

I squeezed my eyes closed and made a saluting motion. I heard Sam scamper off.

I was in the motorhome, I knew that for sure. Sam had walked over to my house a few hours after school. For the first time in the history of our relationship, Sam had insisted on driving.

"Keep your eyes covered," Sam had said as we slid into the Bronco. She had the Jake smile all over her face. She leaned across the center console and pressed a kiss to my lips that made my entire body feel warm. "I've got a surprise for you."

I had driven to the motorhome enough times to know the route, even if I couldn't see. I'd also recognized those rickety metal pull-out steps that led into it.

Something inside smelled... good. Had Sam cooked?

"Okay," I heard her say. There was that nervous tone in her voice again. "You can open your eyes."

My eyes instantly locked in on Samantha.

She'd changed and done her hair different. She'd teased it up or something toward the back and had placed a wide, white headband in her hair. She was wearing a knee length baby blue dress that had white polka-dots on it. She also wore these shiny white high heels.

She totally looked like a fifties housewife.

It was freaking hot.

She was cast in a soft glow from the dozen candles sitting on the dining table. In one hand she balanced a small birthday cake I could tell she'd gotten from The Market. It said *Happy 18th Birthday, Jake!* in tiny red letters. In the other hand, she held a hanger, from it hung a white button up shirt and suit jacket I recognized from my closet. There was also a baby blue tie that matched her dress.

I let out a silent laugh. Rising to my feet, I crossed the tiny space and kissed her. I could tell she was still nervous about everything she'd set up, but she was beaming.

That for me to wear? I asked by raising my eyebrows and pointing at the items on the hanger.

"You'd better believe it," she said with a crooked smile and handed me the hanger.

I couldn't help but smile back as I draped the shirt and jacket over the back of the dining seat. Keeping Sam's eyes the whole time, I slid my jacket off. I then pulled my long sleeved t-shirt over my head.

"Umm," Sam said, her eyes trailing over my bare chest. "Must be my birthday too."

Giving a silent chuckle, I pulled on the button up shirt and the jacket. It took the two of us a minute, but somehow we got the tie on, even if it didn't look quite right.

"Well look at us," Sam said, beaming as she held my tie in one hand, pulling me a step closer to her. "All couple-like and matching."

Pulling my phone out of the pocket of my jeans, I wrapped my arm around Sam's shoulders. Extending my other arm as far away from us as I could, I snapped a picture.

"I hope you're hungry, Mr. Hayes," Sam said when I was done, turning toward the tiny oven. She pulled it open, and with some pot holders, pulled out a casserole dish that took up the entire space. "I've been working on this since lunch time."

I wondered where you disappeared to, I wrote in our notebook, which I found on the dining table. Yet again I noticed another torn out page. I'd forgotten about the others, but wasn't going to ruin Sam's plans by asking her about them.

"So it had better be good." Sam's face suddenly didn't look so sure.

She pulled back the aluminum foil that covered the dish and I knew without a doubt that I'd love her forever.

She'd made a perfect pot roast, covered in potatoes, carrots, and onions. Next she pulled out a bag of rolls.

"Your mom said it was your favorite meal," Sam said as she checked the center of the meat. "I drilled her with questions on how to make it, and then made her write it all out for me." She nodded at a piece of lined, yellow paper on the tiny counter.

I placed my hands on Sam's hips, hugging my body to hers. She paused, placing her hands over mine. Letting her eyes slide closed, she leaned back into me.

I didn't think about the distant future too often, didn't fantasize about Sam and me in five or ten years. But I did then. I imagined us in a tiny, crappy apartment, poor as dirt, struggling to scrape by as we worked our way through college, married and in love. No matter what life brought us, we'd always have each other.

I suddenly wanted to hold onto the hope of that future.

I pressed a kiss to her cheek and she instructed me to sit down and let her work.

Where did you get that dress? I wrote as I watched her.

"It was my mom's," she said. "Some old costume from before I was even born."

The food was perfect. The entire night was perfect as we sat at Sam's crappy dining table in her crappy motorhome. We turned out all the lights and just ate by candlelight, not saying a word, only writing in the notebook occasionally.

Just before we cut the cake, Sam wrote HAPPY 18th BIRTHDAY, WITH MANY MORE TO COME, in big bold letters over two entire pages.

I hoped maybe Sam had thought about being there for every one of those birthdays to come.

I sat watching TV the night after my birthday, some show about vampires Jordan had convinced me to watch with her, though she'd fallen asleep half way through it.

"Jake," Mom said as she walked into the room. "Can I talk to you for a second?"

I glanced down at Jordan whose head was resting on my thigh and managed to wiggle out from under her without waking her up. Thankfully Jordan slept like the dead. Following Mom into the kitchen, I suddenly felt nervous. When a mom asks if they can talk to you like that, it usually isn't about something good.

She rested her elbows on the bar, cupping her chin in her palm, and I settled onto a stool. It kind of felt like I was stepping into Mom's office.

"I'm a little worried about Sam," she said, her eyes concerned. "The whole island's been talking about her. Is she okay?"

I grabbed a notebook that was sitting on the counter. *You're not going to fall for island gossip, are you?*

"I don't want to," she said, her face serious. "I see Sam eat all the time when she's at our house. I try to fatten her up as best I can when she's here. But Jake, everyone's saying she has an eating disorder, and I can't help but wonder. Just look at how skinny she is this year."

I was about to write "she's fine." But I had to think about it. Sam had maybe gained back five pounds since we'd got together, but she was still probably right around one hundred pounds. The lifestyle Sam was living really wasn't healthy for her.

She doesn't have an eating disorder, I wrote. *Trust me. I see her eat all the time. And she's not throwing it all back up. I'd notice...*

Mom chuckled, her eyes lightening somewhat. "Well, I'm glad to hear it. Eating disorders are scary. Is she doing okay, other than that? She always looks so tired. And she doesn't exactly dress great. Did... did her mom lose her job? Do they need some financial help?"

My heart started beating faster as the subject of Sam's mom surfaced. It was nice that Mom was asking if they needed help with money, yet I knew my parents couldn't really give it.

They're going through a hard time, I wrote. Lie. *Things will be okay.*

Seeming to have satisfied Mom, she let me go back to watching TV. But I had a sick feeling in the pit of my stomach as I settled back into the couch. Was that another lie, saying that things would be okay? Sam's life could crumble at any moment. Sam only had a few pieces of her life left. She couldn't afford for those few pieces to fall apart.

There were only eight weeks left. We just had to keep everything quiet and under the rug for eight more weeks. Somehow I was going to have to find a way to help Sam more. She couldn't keep being so skinny and ragged looking. For her health, and to keep the ugly truth hidden.

The next day I contacted Mr. Carol. While I'd always worked in trade for flying time before, he was more than willing to let me start working for just good old regular money. He said I could come by that afternoon and work on some projects.

Sam asked if I wanted to come over to the motorhome after school that day, but I told her I had some stuff I had to take care of. I didn't like lying to her, but I didn't really want to tell her that I'd gotten a job just to help her out.

It wasn't too hard dodging her every afternoon the rest of the week. She was swamped with homework and she had to keep up her perfect grades. And I knew I was a distraction.

It was kind of nice, working for Mr. Carol again, even if it was only temporarily. He'd always felt kind of like an uncle. A very rich and powerful uncle. The man had a lot of money and a very big house. He also had endless projects around that big house that he'd start and then get too busy working on some new case to finish. That's where I came in.

I'd done a ton of landscaping in Mr. Carol's yard. I'd helped him retile his bathroom. I had even painted his kitchen cabinets, though I never did understand why he wanted them painted black. They'd been really nice before.

It was weird little projects like that I would do for him. And he paid me pretty well for it.

By the time Friday rolled around, I had changed all of Mr. Carol's light bulbs in the entire house to more energy efficient ones. It was a big house and there were a *lot* of bulbs to change. I had painted his theater room dark red, and fixed the baseboards in two of the bedrooms. By the weekend I had earned almost three hundred dollars to take Sam to buy some new clothes. I told her I had a surprise for her on Saturday and that she needed to be ready to be gone the entire day.

I picked Sam up around eight on Saturday and we headed for the ferry. She looked tired, as usual. She'd been up until two, doing homework for that rich girl for a few bucks. I hated that she had to do what she was doing, but respected that she was taking care of herself.

We pulled into the ferry landing just a few minutes before the boat glided into the dock. There wasn't a whole lot that was nice about Orcas in the winter, but the lack of tourists trying to get on the boat was a definite plus. In the summer you had to show up at least an hour before boarding time to make sure you got on. Getting overloaded and bumped to the next ferry hours later sucked.

"Where are you taking me?" Sam asked with a chuckle after we parked on the ferry and walked up to the passenger deck. We settled into a seat right by the window so we could look out over the chilly water. The sky was overcast, as it was most of the time in the winter.

Surprise, I signed. Slowly, very slowly, I was getting better at sign language. It felt a little pointless at times though. It only did me any good if the person I was signing to actually understood sign language, and that wasn't anyone outside my family, Kali, or Samantha.

"I don't usually like surprises," she said with a sly smile, taking my hand into hers. "But I'll make an exception for you."

I pressed a kiss to her temple, a smile spreading on her face. The Jake smile.

Sam laid her head on my shoulder, snuggling into my side. She launched into stories about her mom. About how she always made cinnamon rolls Christmas morning. About how they went to Disneyland once when she was eight, just the two of them. They'd saved for months to afford to go. The two of them really had been best friends. They were all each other had.

I didn't think I'd ever admired anyone as much as I did Sam. A lot of people wouldn't be able to go on living life after losing their only family like that. A lot of people probably would have given up. They would have just gone back to their dad and lived a crappy life until they turned eighteen. Instead Sam was taking charge, living the life she had always planned to live.

There was so much more I wished I could do for her, more than just get a few bucks to take her shopping. But I had to take things one step at a time. I'd do what I could do.

We just needed to keep her secret hidden for another eight weeks, and then we wouldn't have to worry about it anymore.

The closest mall from the ferry landing was about a half an hour away. The Burlington Mall wasn't exactly big, but it would do. Sam gave me a cautious look as we pulled in.

"Jake," she said, shaking her head. "I don't have any money to go shopping."

Grabbing the notebook, I wrote, *My treat.*

"Jake," she said with a pained sounding sigh. "I can't just let you go around buying me things. It's not your job to take care of me."

But I like taking care of you.

She kept looking at me, her eyes serious and sad. Finally I saw them soften. A smile spreading on my face, I leaned forward and pressed my lips to hers.

I kept watching Samantha's face as we slowly made our way through the stores. She considered everything so carefully, like she knew whatever she got that day had to last her for who knew how long. She'd run her fingers over the fabric, seeming to appreciate how crisp and new everything was.

It made me sad to see her like that. She was just one step above what homeless Kali was. Yet I knew this was one of those experiences for me that made you grow as a person. This was one of those times that made you put things in perspective and appreciate everything you had.

Hand in hand, the two of us walked between the stores. We passed a poster of a mostly naked woman hugging herself. A sly smile spreading on her face, Sam pulled me into the store.

It was like a giant pink monster had barfed in the store and someone decided it was a good place to set up shop. I couldn't walk anywhere without bumping into a rack of bras that didn't require real boobs to go in them, or bins full of panties that were more like kite strings than things to call underwear.

Sam browsed slowly, gawking at the high price tags. When she came upon a silky sea green set, I knew I couldn't protest against the dollar amount.

Try it on, I wrote, blushing as I did. I wasn't quite sure we were in a place in our relationship that we could talk about this kind of thing. I had seen her in next to nothing, but it wasn't like we'd ever had sex.

That smile crossed her face again as she considered it. The sexy Sam smile. Grabbing the matching bra and panties, we made our way toward the back of the store to where the dressing rooms were.

I was about to wait outside when one of the workers spotted Sam about to walk in by herself.

"You're welcome to go in the changing rooms as well, if you want," she said, as innocently as if she was telling me it might rain that afternoon.

I kind of did this choking, silent laugh, covering my mouth and the awkward, cheesy smile that spread there. Sam stopped when the woman spoke, the sexy Sam smile spreading again. I could feel my face burning red when she took two steps back toward me. She grabbed the front of my shirt, bunching it in her hand, and pulled me into the dressing room.

"Guess if you're buying it's got to have your approval," she said as she raised one eyebrow and shut the door behind us.

It felt like my face was on fire as I sat down on the little bench. It was a huge dressing room. It must have accommodated two people often.

Turning her back to me, Sam slid her jacket off, followed by her long sleeved t-shirt. She half glanced back at me as she reached back and popped the snap on her faded pink bra.

One of my knees started bouncing up and down by itself. I couldn't keep my eyes off of Sam's curves, not that she had many left those days. I wanted to trace my fingers down her spine but kept them securely pinned between my knees.

After getting the new bra snapped, Sam looked over her shoulder. "You're going to have to close your eyes for this next part."

I thought I was going to die right then and there when I realized Sam was going to be about eighteen inches away from me with no pants and no panties on.

"So," she said a few moments later. "What do you think?"

Slowly, I let my eyes slide open, my heart seeming to skip a beat. Sam stood facing me, in all her barely clothed glory. The shade of green against her skin seemed to make her glow. I bit my lower lip to keep my tongue from falling out of my mouth.

"Guess that means you like it?" she said, that new smile spreading on her face.

I could only nod, reaching for her hips to guide her in my direction. She kneeled on the bench, a leg on either side of mine. My lips found their way to her throat, my entire body feeling alive and free.

Sam's fingers knotted in my hair as she tipped her head back, letting me continue to explore all that glorious skin of hers.

Somehow we made it out of that changing stall with our virginity intact, but with me walking pretty uncomfortably. I couldn't keep my mind from wandering back to that image of Sam, an image that would be gloriously engraved into my memory forever.

"I feel so spoiled," Sam said as we headed back out to the car just as the sky started to darken. "I don't think I've gotten new clothes since the beginning of last school year."

I pressed a kiss to her cheek, hoping the message of *you deserve it* got through.

My phone vibrated as we headed back to Anacortes to catch the six o'clock ferry back. Very illegally, I pulled it out and checked the text message. It was from Norah.

You hanging out with that girlfriend of yours tomorrow? Or would you like to come over and have some real fun at my party?

I just shook my head as I put the phone away.

Wow...

I'd never met someone who didn't get what *no* meant more than her. Norah didn't seem to care one bit that I had a girlfriend.

The water was pretty choppy as the ferry carried us back to Orcas Island. Sam and I just stayed in the car, the both of us lying on the backseat, enjoying the feel of the waves beneath a few hundred thousand tons of steel. Our notebook rested on the floor below us, another page mysteriously ripped out.

We seemed to have fallen into the habit of being quiet whenever we drove somewhere. It was easier. It was pretty impossible for me to write anything while I drove, and for some reason signing with Sam felt too… impersonal. So we drove silently back to the motorhome.

"Look at all this," Sam chuckled as I parked next to the motorhome and popped the back hatch to get her things.

You'll have to model a few things for me, I wrote on the back of my hand, our notebook still sitting in the back seat of the car.

She raised one eyebrow at me again, the sexy Sam smile spreading. "Well then, come on in."

My entire body jumped to life again as I followed her inside.

This was a dangerous road we were on tonight. I could feel things escalating and I wasn't sure where I wanted to or where I *should* draw the line.

"So what shall I try on first?" Sam asked as I closed the door behind us and set the bags on her cluttered tiny table.

Peeking into the bags we had just brought inside, I reached for three items.

"Interesting choice, Mr. Hayes," she said, taking them from me and walking back into her bedroom.

I pulled my coat off and threw it onto the back of the dining table chair. Checking my breath by breathing into my hand, I waited excited and nervous for Sam to make a reappearance.

Finally Sam opened the door again, standing with her arms braced in the doorway. She wore that sexy green number again, and a pair of dark wash jeans. And nothing else.

A growl almost… almost made its way out of my throat as I crossed the space between us. Hoisting her up, Sam wrapped her legs around my waist, my lips instantly meeting the skin at the base of her throat.

She gave a squealing giggle as we tumbled into her messy bed, her legs still wrapped around my waist. My lips moved to meet hers, our lips parting.

One of my hands slipped from the back of her neck, down her side, sliding down her hip all the way to her ankle. I was pretty sure I might die if something *else* didn't happen pretty fast.

"Jake," Sam said in a sigh that nearly sent me over the edge.

Sam, I internally moaned back.

Her lips moved with mine, an urgency behind them that had never been there before. It seemed there was no other possible way for the night to end other than the way I wanted it to.

"Jake," she sighed again. "I wish I could hear you say my name. Just once."

My entire body froze instantly.

It felt like my blood turned to ice.

I jerked away from her, propping myself up on my palms, looking down at her. I felt empty for a second as I processed her words again.

Something inside of me turned hard. Sam's face looked confused at my reaction at first, and then the realization of what she had just said filled her expression with horror.

"Jake," she said, her eyes wide. I pushed myself off of the bed and walked out of her room. "Jake, wait! I'm sorry!"

I grabbed my coat and furiously yanked it on.

"Jake! I'm sorry," she said as she followed me out, grabbing for my arm to pull me back. I yanked my hand away from her. "I wasn't thinking about what I was saying!"

I turned my eyes on her just once, everything inside of me feeling cold and hard. Her face looked horrified, her eyes wide and sad. I only shook my head once and stepped outside, slamming the door behind me.

Just before I peeled out of her driveway, Samantha stuck her head outside, screaming "I'm sorry!" again before she fell away behind me into the trees.

I heard a knock on my bedroom door late Sunday morning. I lay on my bed, staring blankly up at the ceiling. Everything in me felt hollow and sick. I didn't really want to talk to anyone, but I couldn't tell that to whoever was at the door.

"Jake?" Jordan said as she poked her head in. "Can I come in?"

I just shrugged as my eyes went back to the ceiling.

Jordan must have taken that as an invitation to come in. She closed the door quietly behind her and crossed the room. Stealing one of my pillows, she placed it at the foot of the bed and we lay head to toe, just like we always used to do when we were kids, protecting each other from the monsters in the dark.

"Rain asked me to prom," she said as she started picking at a hangnail absentmindedly. "Even through prom isn't until, what, like, May?"

I raised my eyebrows at her. *Oh yeah?*

Jordan nodded her head. "I'm pretty sure he likes me."

You like him? I pointed at her, my eyes questioning.

Jordan gave a little shrug. "I guess. He's definitely hot, and it's cool that a senior asked me out. I don't know. I guess I just always thought of him as your dorky jock friend."

By the uncomfortable look on Jordan's face I knew there was something she wasn't telling me. So I lay there patiently, my eyes on her face, waiting for her to spill.

"'K, it's kind of weird how clear your body language is these days," Jordan laughed, giving me this look like I had turned into a psychic goat or something. I couldn't help but smile, my chest doing one of those silent laughs.

"Fine," she said with a sigh. "I guess... I guess I kind of blame him for what happened to you. If he and Carter hadn't been with you, driving drunk, and probably high, you would still be able to talk."

My stomach churned as the whole crappy situation was brought up, and for the second time in the last twenty-four hours, someone was reminding me that I couldn't talk.

Looking over at the nightstand, I grabbed a notebook and a pen.

It was really stupid, and none of us should have been drinking. But it was mostly my fault. I was going to tell Samantha I loved her. Guess the booze made me grow a pair.

"Wow," Jordan said, her eyes surprised and sad. "Really?"

I just nodded.

I felt the back of my eyes sting. What was going to happen now? I wanted to believe I was big enough to forgive Sam for saying what she had. But that had hurt more than the actual accident had, because I could never do what she had wished for.

"Are you and Sam okay?" Jordan asked, her voice becoming small and quiet. "She's called the house a bunch of times. She seemed really worried. She said to tell you that she's sorry."

Feeling a little bit of moisture pool in my eyes, I turned them to the ceiling. I could only give a little shrug and a tiny shake of my head.

I heard Jordan shift on the bed and a second later she lifted my arm and snuggled up into my side. I felt a tear slip down my cheek.

What's wrong with me?

Jordan didn't try and say anything comforting, and I was grateful for that. I didn't want to cry any more than I already had and I didn't think I would be able to stop the tears if she had said anything. Instead she just laid there with me until we both fell asleep.

No matter what, Jordan always had my back.

2 days since the fight with Sam
7 weeks 'til her birthday

I didn't want to go to school on Monday, but Mom gave me no choice. She said she had too much to get done that morning and that I had to take Jordan, Jamie, James, and Joshua to school. So we all loaded into the Bronco and headed for school.

As soon as I dropped everyone off, I made a bee-line for Calculus, hoping and praying that I could avoid Samantha until I had to see her in second period.

Thankfully I was successful.

"Hi, Jake," Norah said as she sat down next to me first period. I hardly dared glance over at her for fear of what I'd see, but amazingly today she wore a pair of jeans and some kind of thick knitted sweater. The only flesh I could see was that of her hands and face.

I gave a little wave.

"Are you coming to my birthday party tomorrow? I think the whole school's coming," she said, giving me an almost bored looking smile. Wow. Strange behavior. Norah the Whora was finally calming down.

For some reason, I glanced toward the door. I caught a brief glance of Samantha, staring through the window of the door. As soon as our eyes met, I noticed hers were red. She held my eyes for just a second and then walked away.

Sure, I wrote, feeling my insides harden. *At your parents' house?*

Norah's face instantly brightened, her white teeth flashing in a brilliant smile. "Yeah? So glad you're coming! Here's the invitation," she reached into her backpack, then handed me a piece of paper that was shimmery purple and smelled like a girl. "That's good for one only, so don't forget it."

What I read between the lines was *Sam's not invited.*

I just gave a smile-less nod, and turned my attention to Ms. Sue as class started.

1 hour since pushing the self-destruct button
7 weeks 'til Sam's birthday

It was immature and stupid, I knew that, but I ended up skipping second, third, and forth period so I wouldn't have to deal with Sam. I didn't know what I was going to say and I wasn't ready to forgive her just yet. So I drove into town and waited for Carter and Rain to show up at Island Market for lunch.

"Okay, I heard you're going to Norah's eighteenth birthday party tomorrow," Carter said as we sat down to eat our lunch. "I'm confused."

I'm going, I scribbled, dripping ketchup on the page as I shoved Jojos into my mouth with my left hand.

"Have you forgotten that Norah hate's Samantha?" Rain asked, chowing down on a burrito. "This could turn into an all-out war."

Sam's not going.

Carter and Rain both suddenly stopped chewing. They shared a look with each other before looking back at me.

"Did you and Sam break up or something?" Carter asked.

I gave a shrug and shoved more food into my mouth.

"Dude, are you alright?" Carter asked. He actually set his food down. A true sign he was concerned.

I don't want to talk about it. I wrote, not meeting either of their eyes.

Neither of them said anything for a second and they shared another one of those looks.

"Well you know Norah's going to go all skank on you at her party, right?" Rain said, resuming the devouring of his burrito. "She's been eyeing you like you're a diet pill ever since she and Blake broke up."

I just shrugged, taking a long swig of my drink. I didn't want to talk about this anymore.

So you already asked my sister to prom? Change of subject.

"Yeah," Rain said with a chuckle. His face turned a little red. He had it bad for Jordan. "Guess you could say I jumped the gun a little. But she said yes!"

"Dude, it's only February," Carter laughed. "The *beginning* of February!"

"Shut up, man," Rain said as he glared at Carter and punched him in the shoulder. "At least I had the balls to ask her. You've been staring at Rivers butt for a whole year now and never said anything to her that didn't sound like caveman grunting."

Poor Carter. But I couldn't help but join Rain in laughing at him.

Apparently Samantha showed up at my house that night, asking to talk to me. I'd been up in the loft watching TV and Jordan had answered the door. She was all solemn faced when she came back up. Jordan said she told Sam I wasn't ready to talk.

I skipped school again the next day. My grades were starting to slip but I didn't care as much as I should have. All the hope and all the positivity I seemed to have found over the last few months was starting to dim. I was letting me feel sorry for myself again.

Once you start down the slippery slope of depression, it's hard to climb off of it.

And sometimes you don't want to climb off of it.

The crappy thing about living on such a small island, where everyone knows who you are and where you're supposed to be certain times of the day is there aren't many places to hide when you're skipping school. So I ended up out at West Beach, parked in a spot that looked out over the water. To the south side was a pottery shop, to the north was a resort. Both were tourist places, so I felt pretty safe hanging out there. No one would recognize me.

I pulled my journal out, running my fingers over its black cover. I hadn't written in it in a while. Really I hadn't felt a need to. But I felt like I was going to explode if I didn't get some words out of my head.

I hate Samantha for what she said. I didn't think that was possible.

How could she say something like that? She wishes she could hear me say her name? Why would she say that to someone like me? Could she have said anything worse?

First she tells me she doesn't believe in love. Seriously, what girl doesn't believe in love? Then she won't let me say it, and basically says she won't ever say it to me. And now this.

Part of me thinks I'm overreacting.

But sometimes I feel like all the crap in the world is building up inside of me, like all the bad is just filling me like a balloon. I push it all back, live my happy life.

But sometimes that balloon explodes and all the crap lands on everything around me.

I hate this.

I hate this.

I hate this.

I hate me.

1 hour 'til self-destruction
7 weeks 'til Sam's birthday

"You sure about this?" Rain asked, clapping a hand on my shoulder from the backseat. "You know how this is going down tonight, right?"

"Norah's got major plans for you," Carter said as he observed the long line of cars parked along Norah's driveway. "That's just the way Norah is."

My jaw clenched as I pulled into a parking spot, which was little more than a narrow shoulder before her driveway dropped down a steep ledge into thousands of trees. I pulled the keys out of the ignition and slid them into the pocket of my leather jacket. Slowly I nodded my head.

"Man, I have a bad feeling about this," Rain said as we got out of the car. "I know you're pissed at Samantha, but are you sure this is the way to handle it? I know Norah's going to do something crazy tonight."

I turned and glared at Rain and Carter. *Shut up.*

They must have gotten the message. They didn't say another word as we walked the rest of the way up Norah's driveway.

Norah's dad was older than dirt, her mom a good fifteen years younger than him, maybe more. Mr. Hamilton was some old time movie producer who made some major money back in like the seventies. He didn't get married until he was basically retired, and even though it was nasty, they had a kid.

A very spoiled, rich kid named Norah.

Norah the Whora, who drove her own BMW and lived like a princess in her castle by the sea.

I could hear the music blasting before we even got out of the car. Lights flashed and pulsed from the windows and I could hear people laughing and shouting.

Despite what Norah had said, I hadn't needed the invitation to get in. I'd half expected to find a bouncer waiting at the front door, that would have been Norah's style, but there wasn't. The air was thick and muggy as we walked through the massive front doors. The house was packed with about a hundred people. Everyone wore some kind of sparkly party hat, or a mask decorated in glitter and feathers. The entire place was black and purple, and everything was covered with glitter. There wasn't any sign of Norah's parents.

"Wow," Rain said loudly as we made our way through the crowd. "This is insane. How much do you think they spent on this party?"

I shook my head, looking around. There was a very sparkly and expensive looking disco ball hanging from the vaulted ceiling, black candelabras with matching black candles sat everywhere, some kind of large, glittery jewel things hanging from them. The party had been professionally decorated.

"The Shaw is in the house!" a loud boom suddenly rang out from the front door. The three of us turned to see Blake posing at the door, raising his hands above his head like some kind of professional wrestling hero. The crowd suddenly froze and then the whispers started breaking out.

Considering he and Norah had so recently broken up, there were sure to be an abundance of awkward moments before the night ended. Undeterred by that fact, Blake was swarmed with sophomore girls.

Carter, Rain, and I just shook our heads and kept walking toward the kitchen.

There were not one, but three cooks working in the kitchen, shuffling an endless supply of food onto the bar. Everything from shrimp to some kind of fancy cheeses, to food I didn't even recognize. Grabbing a clear glass plate from a stack, I filled it and turned to watch the crowd with Rain and Carter.

"No sign of Norah yet," Rain said as he scoured the crowd. I knew he was looking for Jordan, who had left with some friends about fifteen minutes before we did.

"Man, I got a bad feeling," Carter said. I saw his eyes locked on a few people with red plastic cups in their hands.

Something in me went cold when I saw those cups. I honestly hadn't expected everyone to stick to their pledges all year, but it still felt like a slap in the face to see them drinking.

"That's messed up," Rain said, shaking his head.

Tell me about it.

"Jacob Hayes," a silky voice said from behind me. "So glad you could make it."

I downed the rest of the food in my mouth in one painful swallow. I turned around slowly.

Norah stood there wearing this swooping dress made of purple silk, trimmed with black feathers in all the right

223

places. She also wore a black mask, her hair piled on the top of her head in a mess of curls and feathers.

She looked like a freaking Arabian Nights goddess. There was no other way to put it.

A wicked smile curled on Norah's face as she walked toward me, her black heals clicking on the marble floor.

I knew I was staring, and that was exactly the reaction Norah wanted.

I thought Rain whispered something like "don't give in to the Whora" but my brain was only processing legs and barely existent necklines.

"Are you enjoying the party?" Norah whispered as she leaned in right next to my ear.

I took a deep breath, my heart starting to beat in my throat. Norah's fingers curled around mine.

Everything about that moment, the whole night, felt wrong.

But everything about my life right then felt wrong too.

Norah took the plate I still held in my hand and shoved it in Rain's direction without even looking over at him.

"Come dance with me?" she said as she reached to a basket that sat on a shelf. I didn't even realize what she had reached for until she strapped a black Zorro type mask over my face.

She didn't give me a chance to answer, simply pulled me out into the mass of grinding bodies that moved to the pulsing music.

I tried not to think of Sam as Norah guided my hands to her hips. She wrapped her arms behind my neck. Norah knew all the right moves to excite any guy, the exact expressions to put on her face to make his body go crazy. Everything about the moment was intoxicating, the darkness of the room, the heady smell that reminded me of an Abercrombie and Fitch store, the masks and the sparkle.

Why is it so hard to stop doing something wrong, when you know that it is so wrong?

"Aren't you going to wish me a happy birthday?" Norah said with that wicked smile. She moved in closer to me. I wasn't sure how it was possible to move any closer.

How do you expect me to do that? I thought, giving her a look.

"Presents are always acceptable in exchange for words," she practically purred as she moved her lips in closer. It wasn't until then that I could smell the alcohol on her breath.

I realized that Norah was going kiss me at the same time I heard the voice from behind me.

"Jake?"

My head whipped around to see Samantha standing near the door. Horror and betrayal filled her face, her eyes reddening.

It felt like all my internal organs disappeared.

I took a step away from Norah, but not closer to Sam.

It was the wrong move.

She shook her head. I saw a single tear escape onto her cheek. She turned and ran from the house.

Everything in me knew I should go run after her. Now I was the one who had some major apologizing to do. I had just betrayed Samantha and she had found me with the person Sam hated most on all of Orcas.

But I just stood there.

"Forget about her," Norah said, placing a hand on my cheek, trying to pull my eyes away from the door and back to her. "Come on, it's a party. You're supposed to be having fun!"

I looked back at Norah and felt sick.

What was I doing?

Why had I even come?

Shaking my head, I turned to leave. Norah caught my arm in a vice grip that surprised me with its strength. Her face was livid, her eyes wide and wild behind the mask.

"Don't go after her, Jake," she said through clenched teeth. "You are at *my* party. This is *my* birthday."

"And *that* was his *girlfriend*," Carter's voice came from behind me. I turned to see him and Rain standing behind me, their arms folded across their chests.

Norah clenched her jaw again, her eyes shifting from me to Rain and Carter. "I think you all should leave now."

"Gladly," Rain said, already heading for the door.

My eyes were cold as I looked passed Norah and started for the door.

"Your *girlfriend* is going to regret showing up here uninvited," Norah said in a voice cold as ice. I just walked passed her.

Everything flared hot and red inside of me as I heard her words. I turned back once to look at her, my eyes spotting with dark patches. I curled my fingers into fists. Someone tugged on the back of my jacket and I was pulled through the crowd toward the door.

I felt like I could finally breathe again as soon as we got outside. And then I remembered how Sam had run out of there, looking crushed. But there was no sign of her.

"Seriously Jake," Rain fumed as he started shoving me toward the car. "You are such a freaking idiot! What were you thinking?!"

F off, I wanted to shout. I didn't need Rain telling me I was an idiot, I already knew that. I'd screwed up in a major way.

"Samantha is going to dump you, you know that right?" Carter said as he glanced over at me.

Shut up!!!

I grabbed one of the big rocks that lined the Hamilton's driveway and chucked it out into the middle of the lawn, letting out a silent scream into the black sky.

I hate this.

I hate this!

I hate me!

Digging the keys out of my pocket, I chucked them at Rain and climbed into the backseat.

Neither of them said a word to me as we drove back to my house.

I had thoroughly wrecked my whole world.

I really screwed up today.
I won't blame Sam if she breaks up with me.
What was I thinking?
I wasn't.
I just didn't want to feel.
But now everything's ruined.
And there's no one but me to blame.

6 days since everything fell apart
7 weeks 'til Sam's birthday

Samantha and I did a weird dance the next three days. I'd skip Physics and she'd find somewhere else to be during ASL. And then we'd sit as far apart as we could during AP English and Government. Awkward wasn't a big enough word for what those few days were.

Neither of us tried to say sorry, and neither of us had ever had so much pride.

I mostly felt like an idiot.

Sam and me fighting, or being broken up, I wasn't sure what it was, was hard on Jordan too. She and Sam had grown close, hanging out in the halls, and whatever the heck it was girls did.

But true to Jordan, she chose my side.

Even if she did yell at me for an hour straight when she found out about Norah's party.

But when you live on an island as small as Orcas, you really can't avoid anyone.

I had just walked into the lobby at the public library to drop off a book for Jamie when Sam walked out. We both froze there, staring at each other.

Sam looked terrible again. The bags under her eyes told me she'd been sleeping as little as I had since Saturday. She looked skinnier than ever, making me guess she'd had as good an appetite as me as well.

I love you, Sam, I thought. *I'm so sorry I'm such an idiot.*

"Hey," she said, shifting from one leg to the other like she was considering running.

Hi, I signed. I really hated sign language. It felt so cold and distant.

Sam's eyes kept dropping from mine to the floor.

She couldn't even look at me.

She must have totally hated me. And I couldn't blame her.

"I…" she trailed off. But she didn't say anything else. She just hurried past me and went out the door.

I wanted to scream.

6 weeks 'til Sam's birthday

The rest of the week continued like that. We'd dance around each other at school. Way beyond awkwardly say hi in the halls. And then we'd go home.

I thought what I hated the most was not knowing what we were anymore.

Was Sam still my girlfriend? The answer to that was probably not.

Did she totally hate me?

Would this ever get fixed?

Feeling too full of jumbled words, I pulled out my journal Friday night.

I just want to let out a string of cuss words, all the time, and never stop saying them these days. But Mom engrained the no-swearing-or-you-will-die thing into me too well.

Maybe this is what dying feels like. Slow. Painful. Uncertain.

That's kind of what I feel like inside. Dead. Maybe not though. Some say death is supposed to be peaceful. I don't think I could be more opposite of peaceful.

I miss Sam. I miss her so much my whole body hurts. I miss her hair in my face. I miss her million-flavored lips. I miss her constant seriousness and fanatic studying habits. I miss seeing her with my family.

How did I screw this up so bad?

How do I fix it?

A tiny knock on my window nearly scared the piss out of me. Snapping the journal closed, I shifted on my bed and silently slid the window open.

There, standing in the dark, was a terrified looking Sam.

What are you doing here? my eyes asked.

"Let me in," she whispered. Not waiting for me to respond, she reached for the ledge of the window. Giving her a hand, I helped her climb through. Then I realized there were tears streaking down her face.

What's wrong? I signed. I felt terror building up in myself, even though I didn't know what to be afraid of.

"Mike," Sam said as she paced my bedroom floor, ringing her hands. "Mike's here. My dad's on the island."

What?!

Grabbing a notebook from the dresser, I clicked a pen open. *What?!*

"Yeah," she said with a sniff. "I saw him talking to Officer Bennett in town earlier." By now her voice was sounding more desperate, on the verge of cracking. "Someone found out Jake! Someone ratted on me! And now my crap father's here and I'm going to have to leave and I'm going to lose everything." Her words were a jumbled mess, getting louder with each word.

I pulled her into my arms without even giving my body permission to do so. She instantly stopped moving, her arms gripping me so tightly it hurt.

"He's going to take me away Jake," she started sobbing. "I don't want to leave with him. I don't want to leave the school. I'm going to lose any hope of a scholarship. I'm going to lose my friends. I'm going to lose..."

Somehow I knew she was going to say *you.* But she stopped herself before she could admit anything.

"Have I already lost you, Jake?" she finally whispered into my chest. My shirt was soaked with her tears.

Never. I shook my head, squeezing her tighter. It felt like something in my chest released, finally letting me breathe. *I'm so sorry.*

"I freaked out when I saw you with Norah," Sam said, looking up into my eyes. Her cheeks were streaked with tears. "I knew you were mad about what I said, but... Norah?"

I'm so sorry. My brows drew together and I felt a sting behind my eyes as I released her.

Norah is nothing, I wrote. Nothing to me.

Sam bit her trembling lower lip. "I'm so sorry about what I said Jake. I really wasn't thinking. I was just... feeling." She suddenly blushed.

It's okay. I was just an idiot.

Taking my hand in hers, Sam led me back to the bed and she collapsed into it. I suddenly felt exhausted too. Lying back in the bed, Sam curled up into my side.

My phone suddenly vibrated, saying I had a text. Grabbing it, I opened it to find a message from Carter.

We're playing ball at the old gym tonight if you feel up to it, it read.

Something suddenly stirred in my brain then, something from the very beginning of the school year.

Scrolling up through my previous messages from Carter, I found what I was looking for. A video message Carter, sent from the night of the homecoming game.

"Oh Samantha!" my voice suddenly rang out. Sam's head whipped up, her eyes wide. Glancing from my face to the phone, she watched as my drunken self sang out my undying love.

I looked like a freaking idiot, but every word I said was true.

"Jake. You said my name," she said, her voice hazy sounding as she looked down into my eyes. Very gradually, as if in slow motion, she dipped her head until our lips touched.

It felt like finally breathing again after holding your breath for a full week.

"When was this?" she asked, her face still surprised and filled with awe.

Grabbing my notebook again I wrote, *The night of my accident.*

"What?" she said, her face filling with pain.

I nodded. *There's something I never told you before about that night.*

I looked up to see her reaction when she read my words. She looked at me, her face unsure. Something knotted in my chest. I'd tried telling her once before, but she hadn't let me.

I was drunk that night, I wrote. *But I meant what I said in that stupid song. Carter and Rain were taking me to your old house when we got into that accident. I was coming to tell you that I love you.*

I looked up into her face. Sam's lower lip was trembling, her eyes filling with tears. She clasped a hand over her mouth to hold in a sob, but it made its way out anyway.

Sam lay back on my chest and I just held her as she sobbed.

"I didn't know," she said, her voice shaking.

I know.

Slowly her cries quieted and we just lay there quiet and still. I traced my fingers up and down her boney back, feeling her slowly relax into me.

"Can I stay here tonight?"

Of course. I squeezed her tighter and pulled the blanket over the both of us.

I felt something tickle my cheek, my skin twitching. When something brushed it again, I slowly let my eyes slide open.

Sam was propped up on one elbow, looking down at me, our noses only about eight inches apart. It was her hair that had been brushing against my face.

Good morning.

"Hi," she breathed. The Jake smile spread on her lips. I hadn't felt as good as I did then in more than a week when I couldn't help but smile too.

"So," she said, her voice suddenly uncertain. "Are we... okay?"

To answer her, I placed my hand on the back of her neck and lifted my head from my pillow. Ever so gently, I let my lips meet hers, barely touching at first. I faintly detected coconut.

I love you. Always.

Sam backed away just a bit, her eyes meeting mine. They had their glow back. "I'd probably better get going before your parents wake up. Come over around lunch?"

My stomach instantly sank when she said she was leaving. But she was right. We couldn't get caught again.

What about your dad? I wrote in the notebook from the nightstand.

The glow in Sam's eyes instantly died. "It's pretty early. I doubt anyone will see me and I don't think he knows where I am yet. We'll talk about it later, 'k?"

Reluctantly, I nodded.

"Bye," she said, the Jake smile reappearing as she shifted forward for a lingering good-bye kiss. I waved to her as she crawled out my window.

My bedroom door opened the instant the window closed, and in walked Jordan. I hoped I didn't look as guilty as I felt.

Jordan gave me this look, like she knew something was up. "Why does it smell like Samantha in here?"

Busted.

Lying, I just gave a shrug. *What do you want?* I wrote.

"Mom's just about got breakfast done," she said, still eying me suspiciously.

Without waiting for her to figure things out, I hopped out of bed and walked past her to the kitchen.

I had a feeling things were about to get very complicated.

Sam decided there was no way that she could go to school until we figured out how to get rid of Mike. And we weren't sure how to do that yet. She also wasn't going to be able to go into town anymore without someone spotting her. It wasn't going to take long before everyone on the island knew Sam was living on her own.

They would all think they were being helpful, tracking Sam down so she could be reunited with her only living parent. But sometimes things aren't as story-book happy as they seem.

This also meant that Sam couldn't come over to my house anymore. It wouldn't be long before my parents found out about everything too.

I was going to become a lying fool.

One of the most frustrating things about it all was how close we were to Sam's birthday. There was less than six weeks left, only forty-one days.

Surprisingly, nothing happened until Monday, when school started back up from the weekend. I was dreading going to school without Sam, but I dreaded her being taken away even more.

"So," Carter said as us and Rain walked to our lockers that morning. "You and Samantha made up yet?"

Crap. I hadn't thought about that part yet. Everyone at school thought we were still broken up.

Which provided a perfect opportunity.

Nope, I wrote in a notebook. *Haven't talked to her since last week.*

Lie number one.

"Have I told you yet that you're an idiot," Rain said, shaking his head.

You have, I wrote impatiently.

"Just sayin'," he said as the bell rang and the three of us headed toward different classes.

I couldn't seem to keep my left leg from bouncing up and down like I'd had too much coffee as I went through my classes. Mr. Roy glanced in my direction when he called Sam's name for roll and she didn't answer. But it wasn't more than a glance. Thankfully we didn't get checked on too often for ASL, and Mrs. Morrison didn't make a big deal out of it that Sam wasn't there for our next class.

It was a little harder getting Sam's homework for her though without looking suspicious. Especially for those classes that I didn't have with her. It didn't help my story that we were broken up. I ended up having to con other students that were in Sam's classes into getting the work for me.

I was a freaking nervous wreck by the end of the day.

How were we going to keep this up until Sam's eighteenth birthday? Suddenly forty-one days felt like an eternity.

I knocked on the door to the motorhome five times to let Sam know it was me. She still looked edgy as she opened the door.

"So, how'd it go today?" she asked, her eyes scanning the trees behind me. She looked totally freaked out. "Any problems?"

None, I wrote in our notebook. *No one even seemed to notice you were gone. Got all your homework though.*

"Thank you!" she said gleefully, wrapping her arms around my neck and hugging me. "I've been so stressed out about all of this."

People still think we're broken up, I wrote when she released me. *Should make it easier to cover for you. I could just say that we had a fight last week and I don't know where you are.*

"Perfect," she said with a forced smile. She really was freaking out.

We sat and did homework for about an hour, ended up making out for about a half hour, and then I had to go home. Being there long was dangerous considering to everyone around us we were supposed to be broken up. Risking being gone after school would look suspicious.

Nothing seemed too different the next day at school either. Most of the teachers seemed surprised Sam wasn't in school, it was odd behavior for her, but it just seemed like normal concern, not suspicion. Again I got Sam's homework and took it to her.

But by Wednesday I heard whispers in the hall.

"They said her mom died over the summer."

"She's been living on her own all year."

"I heard she's homeless."

"No wonder she looks so shabby. Crap, I feel bad for saying anything about her."

"Why's she been hiding all this?"

240

Now the school was talking.

Stopping at my locker, I put some of my book in, taking other's out. I cringed when I saw Rain and Carter walking up to me.

Here come more lies.

"Dude," Rain said, his eyes wide. "Is Samantha really homeless? Her mom *died*?"

I didn't say anything, just pretended to be digging through my locker.

"You *knew*?" Carter said, his voice accusing sounding. "Why didn't you say anything?"

Don't go there, man.

"Everyone's looking for her, Jake," Rain said, his voice lowered. "Her dad's on the island. He needs to take her with him, they're saying. The cops have been at the school all morning questioning teachers. They're going to come looking for you."

Oh crap.

"Where is she?" Carter asked.

I felt like my heart was going to beat out of my chest and my palms started sweating.

We had another fight on Thursday, I wrote. Lies. *I haven't seen her since then. We're broken up, remember?*

"You think she took off after your fight?" Carter asked as we started walking down the hall.

I just shrugged. Hopefully my expression wasn't too freaked out.

I saw the way people stared at me as I made my way to Calculus. The whispers spread almost like a wave as I

241

walked by. Everyone would know about this before the tardy bell rang for first period.

Somehow I made it through my first class of the day. I had no idea what we were supposed to be learning, but somehow I survived the hour without having a total freak out. But as I walked to second period, everyone was staring at me as much as they did my first day back at school after the accident.

I should have known Principal Hill would send them after me during ASL, the class that was supposed to be just me and Sam. I slowed as I got to the end of the building and saw two police officers and Principal Hill standing just inside the room.

For a brief moment I considered just bolting. But how could that not look suspicious?

Hoping none of them would hear my heart freaking out in my chest, I put on a blank face and walked into the classroom.

"Jake," Principal Hill nodded to me, his face serious. I wondered if Sam's situation could get him into any kind of trouble. Teachers got a hard time for not noticing stuff like this. "Officers Blizen and Bennett need to ask you some questions about Samantha Shay."

Keeping my face as blank as I could, I nodded.

The two officers indicated for me to sit in one of the desks. Seeing they had no intention of sitting themselves, I chose to stand. I leaned against one of the desks, my backpack still on, and crossed my arms over my chest.

I saw them both eye my scars, unsure looks on their faces. Rolling my eyes, I swung my backpack to my front and pulled out a notebook and pen.

"We understand that you're... involved with Miss Shay?" Officer Bennett started. It was hard to take him seriously when most of the island saw him with the Oddfellows in the Solstice Day Parade costumed like a cross-dressing, thirteen-foot-tall clown.

Were, I wrote.

"I'm sorry?" he said, his face still so unsure looking, like I might melt if he spoke too harshly at me.

We were... involved. We broke up last week. Ask anyone in the school.

"Uh," he stuttered. He shuffled some papers, looking totally lost. He kept glancing at my throat. It was amazing how some people just didn't know how to handle communicating with people with disabilities.

Wow.

"May I ask what the reason was why you broke up?" Officer Blizen spoke up, saving Bennett. "It could be helpful in finding Samantha."

I hesitated, debating whether to lie. But it seemed simpler to tell the truth.

She said something about me not being able to talk, I confessed. *I freaked out and did something stupid with another girl.*

Let them think it was worse than it was. Should help my case.

"And I can imagine Miss Shay was very upset about this whole situation?" Something about Officer Blizen's questions seemed very routine. I had a feeling he wasn't from the island. A homeless girl going missing wasn't

243

something that exactly happened very often on the island. It seemed like he should be a little more concerned like Officer Bennett.

Yeah, I wrote. *She was upset. We had a big fight Thursday.*

"And have you seen her since Thursday?" he asked, scribbling something down on a notepad.

For a bit at school on Friday but that was the last time. Lie. How many more were to come?

"Jacob, were you aware that Samantha was living on her own, even though she is a minor?" He turned his green eyes on me, his expression almost daring me to come up with something that wasn't the truth.

I hesitated for a second. Honestly I wasn't quite sure what to say. Going either way could get me into a lot of trouble, more than I already was.

Should I be talking to either of you without my parents here? Now it was my turn to give them a "look."

"They've been called, Jake," Principal Hill said, his expression looking uncomfortable. I knew how my mom was going to react when she found out that Principal Hill had let the police question me before they got here. "Your parents should come any second."

Setting my notebook down flat on the desk, I crossed my arms over my chest, and stared Officer Blizen in the eye. I hoped he got the message that I was done talking for a while.

But while I was giving him the stare down, I was panicking on the inside. It was one thing to lie to these officers, which was pretty freaking bad; it was another lying to my parents about the girl who had spent hours, and many a night under their roof, as practically a part of our family.

244

It seemed like it took forever, but eventually my mom and dad walked through the doors of my classroom.

"They're already here?" Mom barely kept from yelling when she saw the officers in the room. "Tony, he's just a kid!"

"I am sorry, Jackie," he said, looking embarrassed. "They wanted to move quickly on this case. I'm just concerned for Samantha."

Yeah, his best student in five years...

"Is Samantha really missing?" Dad asked, folding his arms across his chest the exact same way I was.

"Are you all aware as to Miss Shay's living situation?" Officer Blizen asked them instead of answering Dad's question.

"What do you mean?" Mom asked, her brow furrowing.

Crap. Here it comes.

"She lives with her mom down Enchanted Forest Road," Dad answered, his expression not quite as sure as I would have liked it to be.

"Mr. and Mrs. Hayes," Officer Blizen said, trying to sound patient. "Miss Shay's mother passed away over the summer. Samantha has been living on her own somewhere on the island since about August."

The room got really quiet for a second. I refused to take my eyes from the police officer's face, not daring to look and see how my parents were reacting.

"I... I don't understand," Dad said, shifting his stance. "Samantha... Samantha's been on her own for the last seven months? How... how is that possible? Don't people like you step in when things like this happen?"

I finally glanced at Mom. She had her eyes locked on the floor, a million thoughts running through her head as her lips made tiny movements. She was trying to piece it all together.

The clues were all there if you knew to actually look.

Officer Blizen finally looked uncomfortable for the first time. "There was a miscommunication with social services as to who was to take custody of Samantha. Custody was granted to her grandparents, but almost the same day it was granted the grandfather had a heart attack and was soon moved to a long term care facility. Custody was then switched to Samantha's father but apparently he never got word it had been switched. Samantha... fell through the cracks. It wasn't until someone on the island told us they thought something was going on that we looked into it. No one on the island even knew that Samantha's mother had died."

I glanced at Mom again. She had her fist pressed against her lips, a few tears streaking down her face.

The back of my throat tightened in a way that had nothing to do with my muteness. My eyes dropped from Mom and glued themselves to the ground.

"Jake," Dad said, his voice firm. "Did you know about all of this?"

I debated with myself for a second. But there was no possible way he would believe me if I said I didn't. With as many hours as I supposedly spent at Sam's house...

I nodded my head.

"Jake," Mom said in a horrified gasp. "How could you not tell us about this? We could have helped her. That poor girl. She must have been terrified!"

"So, Samantha's missing?" Dad said. I was surprised to hear that he was holding back emotion in his voice.

"Oh gosh," Mom half moaned as she pressed her fist to her lips again and turned away from us all.

"Samantha's father has come back to the island to take her with him down to Auburn," Officer Bennett finally spoke up again. "He has not been able to locate her yet. It appears her old house was sold before the mother died, and no one seems to know her current residence."

Mom gave another choked off sob.

It felt like something in my chest cracked.

I knew Mom felt guilty for not knowing. But Sam and I had made sure to keep it that way. Anything Mom was feeling right now was all my fault.

"Everyone says Jacob and Samantha have been together for a few months now and that he'd be the one to know where she currently is." Officer Blizen turned those cold eyes on me again.

Both Mom and Dad's eyes turned on me at the same time. I felt everything in me go cold.

Trying to keep my hands from shaking, I grabbed my notebook and pen again.

Sam moved around a lot, I wrote. She'd work in trade for places to stay.

Lie. Lie. Lie.

As soon as I wrote the words I knew I'd made a mistake. It would be too easy for them to ask around and find out I'd

247

made it up. This was too small of an island for them not to figure that out.

"Do you know where she is now?" Officer Bennett asked, twirling his pen in his hand.

We've been broken up for a while now, like I said. Haven't seen her since Friday morning.

No one said anything for what felt like forever, as both the officers stared me down.

"Jacob," Officer Blizen finally spoke again. "I am curious as to why you seem so unconcerned that your... former... girlfriend has gone missing. While you may be broken up, I would think you would still be concerned about her."

Mom and Dad's eyes jumped to my face as if to say, *yeah, why aren't you more concerned?*

Just trying to put on a brave face, I wrote. *Trust me, I'm freaking out myself.*

Crap. Crap. Crap.

"Uh huh," he said, scribbling something down on another of those yellow notepads. "Samantha's father would like to speak to you sometime. Would you be willing to come down to the station this afternoon and meet with him?"

Did I have a choice?

But I looked over at Mom and Dad, knowing it was really up to them.

"We'll come down right after school's over," Mom said, trying to compose herself. "No reason for Jake to miss more school."

"Fine," the officer said. "Here's my card. We'll expect you at four."

248

Without another word, the both of them left.

"Seriously, Tony," Mom started in on Principal Hill. "How could you let them question him without us here?"

The two of them started wandering back toward his office, Mom chewing his ear off as they walked.

"Want to talk about this?" Dad asked, stuffing his hands into his pockets.

I just shook my head, my eyes glued to the ground.

"Okay," Dad said, giving a nod. "Have a good day at school then."

I just nodded again and Dad went to catch up with Mom, leaving me alone in the empty classroom.

Holy crap! Sam, I am totally freaking out here. The cops came to school to question me! They want me to come down to the police station to meet with your dad later today. I don't know what to do Sam. I don't know if I've ever been this scared. I don't want to blow this, but I'm afraid I'm going to say something wrong and they're going to figure out where you are.

I think I just might go crazy if they take you away. I think it's been you that's kept my head on straight through this crazy year. You didn't let me wallow in my self-pity. I needed you this year. There are a lot of dark places for someone like me, and I'm afraid I might slip into them if you're gone.

I can't let them take you away.

I sat there staring at the page I had just filled in our red notebook. The letters spilled out so fast I hadn't even thought about a single word I'd written.

I ripped the page out and stuffed it into my pocket.

Those were terrified words. Those were freaked-out words.

I had to hold it together right now. And I couldn't let Sam read how seriously scared I was about the very real possibility of her being taken away from me.

The entire school couldn't stop talking about Sam the rest of the day. And they couldn't seem to leave me alone. Except for Norah strangely. I kept finding her eyes on me the whole day, watching me, like she was waiting for me to lose it.

I worked out by myself during weight-training. All the guys were watching me, just as the whole island would be by the end of the day. I just bench pressed, and stared blankly up at the ceiling.

With a dead knot in my stomach, I knew how this was all going to end. And I didn't think I could stop it.

I had never actually been to the police station before. It was hard to even call it that. From the outside it looked like nothing more than a small house. There wasn't much more than a waiting area, a few small rooms, and a kitchen area in the whole building.

Officer Blizen ushered my parents and me into one of the rooms. It had a large table in it with half a dozen chairs surrounding it. We sat down at one end, Officer Blizen sat down at the other end. I wondered where Bennett was.

None of us said much of anything as we stared at one another. Our eyes kept flickering to the clock on the wall, watching the second hands work their way past the four. We watched the door, waiting for someone to come through it.

"You said four o'clock, right?" Mom asked. I could tell she was trying to keep her voice patient.

"Yes, Mrs. Hayes," Blizen said, lazy and annoyed. "I am sure Mr. Garren will be here soon."

And the clock continued to tick away.

Samantha's dad wasn't going to show. I could feel it.

He really was as unreliable as Sam had said.

"Okay," Dad said, resting his elbows on the table, leaning forward. "We've been very patient. We've just been sitting here for over a half hour. We've got four other kids at home waiting for us, I've taken an hour off of work, and now had my time wasted. Can we go?"

Blizen turned cold, narrow eyes on Dad.

Where did this guy come from? He couldn't be less of an islander.

Blizen's eyes suddenly flicked to my face, almost making me jump. "Of course you're free to go. But you need to understand, Jacob, that this is a desperate, bad situation. There is a girl out there, underage, who isn't old enough to take care of herself. And her family is here to take care of her. If you know where she is, you need to tell us."

Feeling everything in me harden against this man, I just sat there with my lips pressed together.

No one could keep a secret quite like me now.

"We're going to go now," Mom said, grabbing my upper arm and pulling me to my feet. She was a lot stronger than she looked.

"That guy's got a lot of nerve, to just not show up like this," Mom fumed as we walked out toward our cars. "Do you know anything about the man, Jake? I've got a bad feeling about all of this."

I just shook my head. I really didn't know much about him, just that he wasn't a great guy and there was no way Sam wanted to leave the island with him.

Pulling her cell phone out of her purse, Mom checked a text message.

"Great," she said with a sigh, texting back. "Joshua just puked all over the bathroom. He said he wasn't feeling good this morning but seemed fine after school."

Just one more reason I was glad I wasn't Mom.

"Jake, honey, could you run and get a few things for me at The Market for dinner tonight?" she asked. She was already digging an old receipt and a pen out of her bag. I just nodded. It was the least I could do after everything I was putting my parents through.

"See you in an hour," Dad said, pressing a kiss to the side of Mom's head. "I've got to go back to work for a bit."

"'K," she said, kissing him back. "Dinner should be done around seven."

Dad left and Mom gave me her list and hurried off for barf duty.

I debated going over to Sam's then, to drop off her homework and tell her about the events of the day, but ended up chickening out. Blizen was watching me now. I couldn't risk leading him right to Sam's motorhome.

I saw the look in people's eyes as I gathered things for Mom at the Market. They wanted to come up and question me about the Sam situation, but they also saw those scars on my throat and wondered how I was going to answer. I made sure I held my head high so everyone could see them. I didn't want to have to lie any more than I already had.

I was just taking the two bags of groceries out to my car when I spotted someone stumbling through the parking lot to go into The Market. I set the bags down on the passenger seat, and took a closer look.

The guy looked like he was in his mid-forties. He had thick brown hair, looks that would probably be considered attractive if he'd taken care of himself.

Even from where I stood, I could tell he was drunk.

The Lower Tavern backed up to the parking lot of The Market, and that was the general direction the man had stumbled from.

As he came closer to me, headed for the doors of the store, he tripped and landed flat on his face just a few feet from me. Reacting on instinct, I lurched for him, but was nowhere near fast enough to stop his fall.

The man groaned as he started picking himself up, my hands under his arms to help him. He let out a string of cuss words and I could already smell the alcohol on his breath.

Suddenly, he looked up at me. His eyes seemed unfocused at first, but they slowly narrowed on my face.

"You're that kid from the accident," he said, his words slightly slurred. "The one who can't talk that everyone's been chattering about these last few days. You're my daughter's boyfriend."

My insides went cold as familiar facial features suddenly stood out. He had the same exact jawline as Sam, had the same brow and cheekbones. It seemed obvious now.

"Everyone's been sayin' you're hiding her from me," he said, his eyes growing hard. "But she needs to come home with me. You're a bad boy for keeping her from her family."

Mr. Garren finally pulled himself to his feet, swaying where he stood. He had this mean look on his face that I had seen people get when they'd had too much to drink.

There were a lot of things I wanted to say to that man right then.

"Don't know what she'd want to hang out on this island for," he said, looking around like he could see and judge our whole island right there from the parking lot. "Couldn't possibly be for a scrawny, broken kid like you."

My jaw tightened and my fingers curled into fists.

"Never should have knocked that girl up all those years ago," he murmured to himself. "Now look what it's gotten me. Stuck with a sad little rat."

My fist exploded in pain as it connected with Mr. Garren's jaw. I knocked him clean off his feet, flat on his back.

Don't you ever talk about Sam like that again!

Spitting on the ground right next to me, I held his cold eyes while he rubbed his jaw.

"I will find her," Mr. Garren said, his voice just daring me to take another swing. "And I will take her with me."

Instead of doing something stupid like kicking the man while he was down, I turned to climb into my car. I froze solid when I saw Norah by the front doors, paper bag in hand, watching our confrontation. Everything in me hardening all the more, I looked away from her and slid into the driver's seat. Not even caring to check and make sure Mr. Garren was out of the way, I pulled out of the parking lot.

I rapped on Sam's door five times, letting her know it was me. I stormed passed her as soon as she opened it, pacing the tiny space, and cradling my throbbing hand.

"Jake," Sam said, her voice alarmed. "What happened?"

Meeting her eyes, I made the sign for dad. When she didn't seem to understand, I pointed at her once and again made the sign for dad.

"You punched Mike?!" she half yelled, finally understanding why I was cradling my hand. "Are you okay?" She opened her tiny freezer and pulled out an ice cube tray and wrapped a handful of them in a towel.

I nodded, letting her doctor my hand.

"He doesn't know where I am?" she asked. "Right?"

I shook my head, reaching for the notebook. *Don't think so. Cops showed up at school today and questioned me. Was supposed to meet your dad down at the station at 4, but apparently he was too busy at The Lower to show up.*

Sam swore under her breath as she continued to hold the ice to my hand.

I think maybe we should move you tomorrow, just to be safe. I can come over after school.

"'K," Sam said in a small voice with a nod.

There were unspoken words between us. We both knew what was going to happen and it was going to happen soon. Sam couldn't hide for forever.

6 weeks 'til Sam's birthday...

There was a sick feeling in the pit of my stomach the next day. The kind that causes your hands shake and makes you feel like you're going to hurl. Something felt wrong.

I went to school as I normally would have. Eyes still followed me like I was some kind of criminal, whispers slipped out as I walked by. Despite their best efforts, my teachers looked at me differently.

But what scared me most, was the smug look that Norah gave me at lunch.

After school, I headed for the motorhome. That sick feeling bubbled up in my stomach and I nearly had a panic attack when I saw two cars parked next to the small cabin. One of them was a police car.

I parked and ran toward the motorhome.

Sam!

The door to the motorhome was wide open and I could see two men moving around inside. I burst in to see Mr. Garren gathering Sam's things, the policeman filling out some kind of form.

As soon as Sam saw me, she leapt at me from the dining seat, throwing her arms around my neck.

"They say I have to go Jake," she immediately started sobbing. "I don't know how they found me but they showed up an hour ago and he's taking me on the next ferry. I don't want to go, Jake, I don't want to go."

I ran a hand down Sam's hair, my eyes meeting Mr. Garren's as he stopped and looked at me. He had a smug smile on his face, one that practically screamed *I told you so.*

Turning to the officer, I searched his face for any sympathy.

"Sorry, Jake," he said. I was thankful it wasn't Blizen. Unfortunately it wasn't Bennett though, who would have been a little more understanding. "She's still a minor, she has to go."

Sam kept muttering "I don't want to go, I don't want to go," over and over into my neck.

I wanted to rage. I wanted to punch the lights out of Mr. Garren. I wanted to stuff Sam in my car and just drive away from all of this. I wanted to turn back time twelve hours so I could hide Sam better. If only we'd moved the motorhome yesterday.

But all I could do was hold Sam and watch as her father gathered her things up and took them out to his car.

Had I still been able to talk, this entire scene would go down a lot different. I would have been yelling, screaming, fighting against Mr. Garren and the officer with everything I had in me.

I felt weak for not being able to fight for Sam.

It felt like she was already becoming less and less solid in my arms.

"It's time to go," Mr. Garren finally said, backed up by the police officer.

Sam placed her hands on either side of my face, her eyes locking with mine. "I will be back," she said, her voice shaking. "As soon as I'm eighteen. I'm moving back the second I turn eighteen. It's just a few weeks away."

And a few weeks away felt like eternity.

I love you, I thought for the millionth time.

Sam pressed her lips to mine, tears rolling down her face. I kissed her with urgency. Would I ever taste her mango flavored lips again?

"Take care of this while I'm gone, okay?" Sam said as she pressed a set of keys into my hand. She wiped her tears on the back of her hand. "Help me find a new place to put it when I get back?"

I could only nod. A single tear leaked out onto my cheek.

"Come on," Mr. Garren said, his voice impatient.

Not so gently, he directed Sam out of the motorhome, and toward his rust bucket of a car. Without even giving us the chance to say good-bye, he sat Sam in the passenger seat and closed the door. She pressed a palm against the window, her eyes locking on mine. And just a few seconds later they rolled down the driveway.

The police officer started typing something into the laptop in his car. I ducked back into the motorhome and grabbed a notebook and a pen.

Who told you? I wrote. Walking back out to the police car, I pressed it against his window. The officer looked startled at first, and then he rolled the window down.

"We got a tip from someone at your high school who said she had seen where Miss Shay was staying."

Norah.

She'd seen the fight yesterday and followed me right to Sam's.

And then she'd told the cops.

Did you guys ever stop to wonder why she went missing as soon as her father showed up on the island? I wrote and flashed to him again.

"Sorry, kid," he said, which only pissed me off more. "I know this can't be easy."

Without another word, I turned and got in my car and drove off.

I didn't even remember the drive back to my house. Suddenly I was just at home, slamming the front door behind me, my hands pulling at my hair.

"Hey!" Mom shouted at me from the kitchen. "You trying to break our house?"

Mom then walked out of the kitchen and saw my break down.

"Jake?" she said, her voice filling with panic. "What's wrong?"

A few more tears leaked out onto my cheek. I signed Sam's name.

"Oh no," she breathed, her expression hardening. She steered me into a seat. "What happened?"

Grabbing a notebook, I explained.

By the time I had finished my long, detailed description of what had happened, including where Sam had actually been living, half the family had come into the living room. And then Dad walked in just as everyone else finished reading my explanation.

"I can't believe she's gone," Jordan said, her voice breathy. "How can they just make her leave like that?"

"She doesn't have a choice," Mom said, her hands shaking. "The system is set up so it's either him or a foster home. I'm not sure which would be worse."

"Come on, Jake," Dad said, grabbing the keys to his truck. "Let's go get her motorhome."

I looked up at Dad with surprise in my eyes, my entire body feeling like it was in shock.

"We'll go get it and store it here until she gets back," he said. "Maybe... maybe she can just stay here after her birthday. In the backyard of course."

I rose to my feet and wrapped my arms around him, something I hadn't done in a very long time.

We rode in silence to Sam's place. Dad wasn't one for a lot of talk, especially about these kinds of things. But I appreciated his understanding and support, even if it was silent.

We pulled the truck up to the motorhome and I watched Dad's reaction as we walked up to it. He kept his face pretty blank, but I could see a sadness in his face that he'd never vocalize.

"So you want to drive the truck home or this thing?" Dad asked as he stepped inside after me.

I patted the driver seat.

I didn't want to be in there. Everything reminded me of Sam and the fact that she was gone. It was still way too fresh. But having my dad drive it felt like an invasion of Sam's privacy.

"Okay," Dad simply nodded. He glanced around for a moment longer, his eyes lingering on Sam's tiny kitchen, on the space heater I knew he would recognize. But without saying anything, he just turned and walked back outside.

Together we unhooked everything, making sure to leave no evidence to the owner of the house that Sam had been there.

I slid into the driver's seat and put the key Sam had given me in the ignition. The thing whined for a minute, but finally turned over. It groaned and creaked the entire drive back. With Dad holding the gate open, I pulled it into the backyard and parked it in the corner.

I tried not to look back at it as we walked into the house. I suddenly didn't want it there. It was a huge hulking reminder that Sam was gone.

5 weeks 'til Sam's birthday

I talked to Sam's teachers the following Monday when we went back to school. And I finally told them the horrifying truth. They agreed to work with Sam so that she could continue doing all her schoolwork with them, just long distance.

As best I could, I ignored Norah. Everything in me wanted to get revenge. She'd ruined my life so it was human nature that I wanted to ruin hers. But revenge wouldn't bring Sam back. And Norah was finally cold to me. She wouldn't even look at me.

"How you holding up?" Rain asked me as we sat down at The Market to eat our lunch.

I just shrugged as I bit into my burrito.

"I can't believe he just took her like that," Carter said as he squirted ketchup all over his Jojos. "She doesn't even really know the guy, does she?"

I shook my head and clicked a pen open. She hadn't seen him since she was six.

"Dang," Rain said, shaking his head. "At least she turns eighteen soon."

I nodded.

"A bunch of the guys are going backpacking up Constitution and camping out Thursday since Friday's off for school," Carter said, tactfully changing the subject. "You want to come?"

I thought about it for a second. Really all I wanted to do was curl up in a little ball and lie comatose for a few weeks. But I couldn't just stop living for the next thirty-three days.

Sure, I wrote.

5 weeks 'til Sam's birthday

That night, I sat on the computer in the loft, and mindlessly scrolled through the internet. I was reading something on Facebook when a box in the right corner suddenly popped up.

Message from Samantha Shay: *Hey! You there?*

My heart jumped into my throat. I'd had no way of contacting Sam as she didn't have a cell phone and I hadn't gotten the chance to get Mr. Garren's number.

Jake: *Hey! You're like, never on Facebook! You're dad let you on the computer?*

Sam: *Ugh, no. I'm at the library. Some creepy dude keeps staring at me from the computer across from this one.*

Jake: *Want me to kick his butt for you?*

Sam: *LOL! If only you could.*

Jake: *I miss you like crazy.*

Sam: *It's only been two days.*

Jake: *Still miss you.*

Sam: *Miss you too. This sucks.*

Jake: *I got all your homework. Teachers are going to let you keep going through you're classes while you're away.*

Sam: *What would I do without you?*

Jake: *I do what I can.*

Sam: *Dad's been gone almost the whole time I've been here. Comes home at like three in the morning, totally wasted.*

Jake: *Maybe I'll have to come kidnap you.*

Sam: *Don't think that would be a good idea. He's super* paranoid. *Won't hardly let me leave the house.*

Jake: *I'm worried about you.*

Sam: *I'll be fine. I don't think he'd do anything.*

Jake: *Wish I KNEW he wouldn't do anything.*

Sam: *I've got to go. I'm only supposed to be on here for* fifteen minutes and I used most of that time for homework.

Jake: *Can you talk again tomorrow? Same time?*

Sam: *I'll try.*

Jake: *Counting the hours already.*

Sam: *Sleep good.*

I love you, I typed out, but only in my head.

And then it showed that Sam was offline.

"Jake?" Mom called from downstairs. "Dinner's ready."

4 weeks 'til Sam's birthday

"Like this?" Jordan asked, trying to manipulate her fingers into the sign for sister.

I shook my head, moving her fingers to the right position and showing her the movement again.

"I probably look like such a dork," she laughed, finally doing the sign right.

No more than usual, I wrote.

She responded to that by punching me in the arm.

"Show me, show me!" Jamie said excitedly as she walked passed Jordan and me in the living room. She hurtled herself across the room and landed on the couch next to me with a big bounce.

Silently laughing, I showed her the sign.

"Someday I'm going to be really good at sign language," she said as she did the sign flawlessly the first time. Jordan just glared at her. "And me and you can talk like we're just talking normal."

I smiled at her, everything inside of me warming.

"Hey," James said as he wandered out of the kitchen, a box of crackers tucked under his arm and a knife and a block of cheese in the opposite hand. "What are you guys doing?"

"Jake's teaching us some sign language," Jamie said gleefully.

Glancing upstairs where his Xbox awaited him, James changed direction and joined us in the living room.

"James!" Joshua yelled from upstairs. "Hurry up! I'm totally killing you!"

"Hang on!" James yelled, stuffing a piece of cheese sandwiched between two crackers in his mouth. "Be up in a minute!"

"What are you doing?" Joshua yelled. I heard an explosion from the TV.

"Bonding!"

Everyone burst out laughing at that.

Suddenly we heard Joshua tromping across the floor and a second later his feet pounded down the stairs.

"What's the sign for dork?" James asked, making up his own sign.

Jordan punched him in the arm too. "Be nice," she said, half scowling at him, half trying not to smile.

It had been a week since I first talked to Sam online. I'd gone on the overnight hike with the guys. We built a fire and one of the crazy guys I didn't know well from school actually cooked a rabbit he'd captured over it. I tried not to hurl when the guy started eating it.

Sam and I talked briefly online whenever she could manage to get to the library. She didn't do much. Her dad was gone all day long but she just stayed at his house, doing homework and trying to keep sane. I mailed her homework to her every other day.

I had been struggling to concentrate at school and not let my grades slip any further than they had. All I could think about all day long was Sam and how much I missed her.

"Show me the sign for chocolate," Jamie said as she bit into the chocolate chip cookie she'd been holding.

"What's this?" someone said as the front door suddenly opened. In walked John and Jenny. "Sibling council meeting?"

Joshua practically launched himself across the room at the two of them. I couldn't help but smile as my two older siblings dropped their bags by the door and came and sat down next to the rest of us. The room had gotten really crowded, really fast.

"I heard about Samantha," Jenny said as she pulled her boots off. "That's so crazy. And you knew about it the whole time?"

Letting my eyes drop, I nodded.

"I'm not judging you," she said as she ruffled my hair. "I think it's cool you helped her out all this time."

"Yeah, we can't blame you for keeping your little love shack a secret," John teased. "I would have kept it a secret too."

Grabbing a pillow, I chucked it at him, hitting him square in the face.

"What's the sign for making out?" he teased, launching the pillow back at me.

"Ooo," Joshua said, puckering his lips. "Sam and Jake in the love shack."

"Shut up you little dork," Jordan said with a laugh as she grabbed Joshua around the waist and tucked his skinny body into hers. "You don't even know what you're talking about."

"Yes I do!" he protested, trying to worm his way out of her grasp. "It's just like I saw you and Rain holding hands at Teazer's yesterday!"

"What?!" half the siblings cried, including me, just soundlessly.

"Seriously?" Jamie said, glancing back and forth between Jordan and me.

Is there something I missed?! I quickly scrawled.

Jordan blushed so hard her entire body looked red. "It's nothing guys! We just went for some coffee and a scone and he… just… held my hand as we were leaving."

"Jordan and Rain, sittin' in a tree," Joshua chanted. "K-I-S-S-I-N-G!"

"Okay, that's enough!" Jordan said, tackling Joshua to the ground and tickling him until there were tears running down his cheeks he was laughing so hard.

I laughed silently as I observed my siblings, teasing each other and wrestling and talking over one another. I may have been missing Sam, but I was certainly never alone. My family would always be there for me, no matter what.

3 weeks 'til Sam's birthday

The keys to my car stared back at me, daring me to pick them up, to put them in the ignition, and let the road fall behind me. It wouldn't be hard. I'd gotten the address. All I had to do was pack a few things, get in the car and go get her.

Because not knowing what was happening was killing me.

Nine days. That was how long it had been since I'd heard a word from Sam.

Anything could happen in nine days. I tried not to let my imagination get away with me. Not to let things like thoughts of Mr. Garren driving them somewhere, drunk, getting in car crashes, dying, thoughts like him doing things to Sam that he shouldn't, go through my head. Thoughts like him accidently lighting the curtains on fire and burning the house down with Sam in it. Things like him turning into a vampire and draining Sam dry.

My imagination was getting away with me.

I stood and grabbed my keys off of the dresser. I opened the door to my bedroom and walked into the kitchen.

"Jake?" Jordan said from the bar where she worked on her homework. "You look... green. Are you okay?"

I shook my head, my teeth clenching together.

I was so far from okay.

"You haven't heard from her today either, have you?" Jordan put the pieces together. I shook my head again. "How many days has it been?"

I held up nine fingers.

"Crap," she breathed. She slid off the bar and crossed the space between us. She wrapped her arms around me, squeezing me tight.

I held up the keys in my hand, staring at them. Jordan released me and looked at the keys too.

"I know how bad you want her back," Jordan said, a trace of fear in her eyes when she looked back at me. "I want her back too. I want her to come home. But you know what will happen if you go and get her. You've already had one fight with her dad. You got lucky that time. You go at it with him again and you could get thrown in jail or something. And then think of what he might do to Sam?"

I just stood there frozen for a second. I hadn't thought about that part. I hadn't thought about what it could mean for Sam if I showed up when I wasn't supposed to. I hadn't thought about what might happen when I actually got there.

This was nothing short of torture.

I wrapped my arms around Jordan, hugging her so hard I knew it had to hurt just a bit. One tear slipped down my face, followed by two more, followed by a whole flood.

I didn't care that I was crying like a baby. And Jordan didn't seem to either, she just hugged me back and didn't let go until I was finished.

"I've got something to show you," Mom said one day after school. Only seven days until Sam's birthday. "Come outside with me."

Setting my backpack down on the dining table, I followed Mom out the back door. I nearly tripped over one of the chickens who sat at the bottom of the steps. She hustled away with a loud squawk and a flurry of feathers.

Mom crossed the lawn to Sam's motorhome and opened the door. I followed her in and she flipped the lights on. Dad must have hooked up the power.

I had never seen the motorhome so clean. Sam wasn't a total slob, but she wasn't exactly a neat freak. Mom had scrubbed everything, from the cabinets to the floor to the ceiling. She'd also painted the dingy, dated cabinets a fresh, bright white and it looked like she had taken the paint to the entire trailer. Everything looked fresh and bright.

She'd put in new soft yellow curtains in the main area of the motorhome. As I wandered back toward Sam's bedroom, I saw that Mom had also gotten a new sea green bedspread and decorated the bedroom to match.

It was like stepping into a completely different motorhome.

"What do you think?" Mom asked, her face beaming with pride.

It's amazing, I wrote.

"You think Samantha will like it?" she asked as she straightened one of the curtains.

She'll love it. I couldn't help but smile.

"I've been spending most of the day out here this last week while everyone's been in school," she explained as she sank into the seat at the dining table. "Dad went and got all the paint, as well as some other things that needed to be repaired. It's actually been really fun fixing this thing up."

I nodded as I looked around, amazed at how much better it felt with just a simple coat of paint. I suddenly wished I'd thought of doing this. But it really did mean a lot that my parents had gone to all this trouble. It meant they cared about Sam too.

"How's she doing?" Mom asked, her eyes locking on me.

I slid into the seat opposite her, placing the notebook in front of me.

I really have no idea. I haven't heard from her in forever, I wrote. *Her dad doesn't let her leave the house much. She just stays home all day and is basically doing homeschool.*

"I hope she's alright," Mom said, her eyes sad. "I've been worried sick about her. It doesn't sound like her dad's a real great guy. Not that I should judge."

He's not, I simply wrote.

"It will be nice to have her back," she said, a small smile forming on her face. "I've missed her."

Me too. My chest ached from how much I missed her.

"Have you told her yet?"

Told her what? I wrote and looked up at Mom with confused eyes.

"That you love her." Mom's eyes were serious, but she was smiling.

274

I felt my face instantly blush, my heart doing a weird little skip. For a second I thought about denying it, but there was no use doing that with Mom. Of course she knew.

I've tried, I explained. Sam... doesn't believe in love, she says. I don't know, I think she's just scared of it considering what her parents went through. Her dad leaving her and her mom really screwed up her idea of relationships.

"The L word is a scary one for some people," she said, reaching across the table and placing a hand over mine. "She loves you, Jake. She just can't say it quite yet."

I gave Mom a small smile, silently hoping and praying that it was true.

Jake: *You're killing me! It's been sixteen days!!! I thought you must have been dead!*

Sam: *Sorry. Dad's been super sick the last week and he's treating me like I'm some kind of slave. I haven't been out of the house in two weeks, except to go pick up food.*

Jake: *He hasn't been around enough to deserve you helping him out.*

Sam: *No argument there.*

Jake: *I miss you.*

Sam: *I miss you too. I thought I was going to throw up today I miss you so bad.*

That brought a smile to my face.

Jake: *I've got a question for you. It's quite a serious one and you might break my heart if you say no.*

It was a full fifteen seconds before Sam responded.

Sam: *Yes?*

Jake: *Will you go to prom with me?*

Sam: *LOL! K, you scared the crap out of me for a second there!*

Jake: *HAHA*

Sam: *I don't know, maybe not after that!*

Jake: *Come on, you know you want to see me in a tux.*

Sam: *Well, when you put it like that...*

Jake: *So is that a yes?*

Sam: *YES!*

Jake: *Touch down, number nine, Jake Hayes!*

Sam: *HAHA. I can't wait!*

Jake: *Me either.*

Sam: *Dang it. I'm getting waved off this computer.* Guess I got to go.

Jake: *Alright. I'll talk to you soon.*

My fingers hesitated, wanting to type out *I love you.*

Sam: *Talk to you later.*

Every day until Sam's birthday felt like three. I couldn't help but watch the clock every period, counting them down until Sunday when Sam would turn eighteen. My leg would bounce up and down as I counted in my head how many hours were left. Rain and Carter made fun of me, making whipping sounds and jerking their hands as they'd walk by me in the halls.

I didn't even defend myself. I *was* whipped.

And I didn't mind in the least.

Saturday was the worst day of all. Dad must have anticipated this, as he put me to work in the yard all day. First we cleaned out the chicken coop. Next we started prepping our half-acre garden to be planted in a few weeks. After that he had me help him build a nice and sturdy staircase for Sam to get up to the motorhome. Lastly he had me mow the lawn, even though it was barely starting to grow with it only being the end of March.

I was grateful for all the work Dad made me do. I collapsed into bed that night and didn't wake up until Mom pounded on my door at eight the next morning, yelling at me to get dressed so we could make the 8:50 ferry.

Mom and Dad put Jordan in charge of the other kids for the day. Normally Jordan would have complained, but she was nearly as excited as I was about Sam coming home.

Home.

The drive to the ferry felt like it took forever. I cursed the forty mile-per-hour roads as we wove between the towering evergreens. Not that it would have mattered if we could have driven faster. The ferry would still leave at 8:50 either way.

We finally loaded on the boat and headed up to the passenger deck. It was pretty quiet, though picking up a bit from the dead of winter. I spotted a few tourists, taking pictures out the windows at the shoreline of Orcas and the marina just off from the ferry dock.

Leaving Mom and Dad to sit and talk at a table, I wandered out onto the deck that wrapped around the boat. Resting my elbows on the painted green railing, I took in my surroundings.

Living in a place like Orcas for so long, you eventually stopped seeing the beauty that was always around you. There weren't many places like this in the world that had as many miles of shoreline and ocean view. You couldn't drive long anywhere on the island and not see ocean. Ancient trees hung out over the water, some threatening to cave into the ocean, others blown that way by the wind into permanent position. There had to be at least five hundred trees to every person on the island.

Hearing the engines kick up, the boat pulled away from the dock and started out across the water toward Shaw Island. Dozens of small islands fell behind us as the ferry moved slowly through the water. Blakely, Lopez, Decatur. It suddenly seemed a shame I had never been to more of the small islands. There were only four islands in the San Juan Islands that had ferry service, but you could always take a small boat or kayak to the smaller ones, and there were hundreds of them.

I decided that summer that I'd take Sam camping on one of them. We'd load up two of Carter's kayaks and just take off.

There was a reason people paid crazy amounts for property, groceries, and ferry rides to be out on the islands. There were few places on the Earth that were more beautiful.

The ferry ride to Anacortes went surprisingly fast. I actually had to run down to the van since I wasn't paying attention and hadn't realized we were suddenly docked.

And then my parents and I were headed to Auburn and toward Sam.

Was I supposed to have some sort of romantic reunion planned? Suddenly I wondered if I was supposed to have thought of all kinds of cheesy things to say, or rather write. But I hadn't thought of anything. All I had gotten her for her birthday was a framed picture of the two of us, the one I had snapped on my birthday. It didn't seem like near enough. But I'd had too many bigger things on my mind to come up with anything better.

There were three words I wanted to say to her as a present, three words I'd wanted to say to her for forever.

Would she ever let me say them?

After two hours of driving, the GPS on Mom's phone said we were only half a mile away. I started getting a little worried as we pulled into the neighborhood. It was mostly trailer homes, lawns filled with broken down cars, broken outdoor furniture, and mangy looking dogs lying on porches. *This* was where Sam had been living the last six weeks?

"Oh my," Mom breathed as she took it all in.

Crap.

And then we pulled in front of the address Sam had given me. It was one of the smaller trailers, looking dirty and half broken down. The porch sagged and looked ready to cave in. The lawn was filled with winter-dead weeds, a dozen or so empty cans and beer bottles lying in front of it.

Crap.

Dad put the van in park and I hopped out as soon as it stopped moving. My heart was hammering as I walked up to the front door. Just as I was about to knock, the door swung open and there was Sam.

Her eyes locked with mine and the both of us froze, just standing there looking at each other.

I'd hoped that Sam might gain some weight, living with an adult who should be putting food on the table every day, but Sam looked skinner than ever. Her eyes looked sunken, like she hadn't slept since she left the island.

A single tear slipped down her face before she rushed forward and wrapped her arms around my neck. Her entire frame trembled. I wrapped my arms around her and never wanted to have to let go.

"I want to go home," she said, her voice cracking. I felt her tears slip down her face onto my chest.

I backed away just a bit, pressing my lips to hers, everything inside of me hurting.

The whole situation just felt ten times worse when her lips didn't taste like anything.

Where is your dad? I signed as she took half a step away, wiping her tears from her cheeks.

Her face went hard and angry as she stepped to the side, letting me see into the trailer. And I saw him there, lying on a couch, totally passed out, three beer bottles resting on the floor.

"He's been wasted since yesterday," she said, her voice hard. "He probably won't even remember that I was ever here when he comes to. *If* he wakes up."

"Come on, Samantha," Mom said as she and Dad walked up to the porch. "Jake and Johnson will get your things."

Sam just nodded, pointing to a small pile of things by the front door. She walked back to the van, Mom's arm wrapped around her shoulders. Sam wrapped her arms around Mom's waist, leaning her head on Mom's shoulder.

"Crap," Dad said in a low voice as we stepped inside and started picking up Sam's things. "What a dump."

A dump was right. There was garbage everywhere, stains on the carpet, on the walls, on the ceiling. The place just needed to be burned to the ground. It had to be a health hazard.

"Think we should wake him and let him know we're taking Sam home?" Dad asked, hesitating before leaving.

I glanced at Mr. Garren. There was a line of drool coming out of the left side of his mouth onto the couch. He snored softly.

I shook my head and walked back out to the van.

Dad and I put Sam's three small bags in the back of the van. I climbed in the first row of passenger seats next to Sam and slid the door closed behind me. None of us said anything as we pulled away from the curb and made our way back to the freeway. After a few minutes, Sam laid her head in my lap and closed her eyes like she was trying to hold something bad and breakable in.

I didn't know what to say and it didn't feel right to say anything in front of my parents. So I just ran one of my hands over her hair, and held one of her hands securely in my other.

As my dad pulled the van into Costco in Burlington, I signed to Sam, *You okay?*

She just stared vacantly out the window as we parked.

We all piled out of the van and grabbed two shopping carts on our way inside. Sam held my hand as we followed my parents through the aisles. If Sam wasn't acting so out of it, she might have seen my parents whispering to each other, grabbing a few articles of clothes for her, and grabbing other things like shampoo, girl things, and a whole extra stock pile of food just for her.

Sam may not have had parents to take care of her for the last eight months, but she had them now.

By the time we all got to the ferry at six that night, Sam seemed to be feeling better. She had livened up a bit and talked to Mom the whole ferry ride home about prom dresses, hair and make-up. They made plans to go off-island again with Jordan in two weeks to go shopping.

I couldn't help but smile as I watched the two of them together. Sam really was family.

We backed the van into the driveway and Dad honked the horn for everyone to get outside and help haul things in. Sam nearly got mauled to death by everyone when they saw her. I saw how tears pooled in her eyes as she hugged them all back.

And when we walked into the house, we found the entire place decorated with pink, orange, and white balloons and streamers. All the younger siblings had spent most of the day getting ready for Sam. Jordan and Jamie had baked a cake and Joshua had organized a bunch of birthday games. Tears really did stream down Sam's cheeks when she saw it all.

But around nine, Mom gave the knowing smile, and gave me the "go ahead" nod to take Sam out to see her big surprise.

I shouldered two of Sam's bags, and we crossed the yard hand in hand.

"You have no idea how good it feels to be back on the island," she said as we slowly crossed the damp grass. She let her eyes slide closed, her face upturned slightly. "I never would have guessed I'd miss it so much."

I pressed a kiss to her temple as we hesitated outside the door to the motorhome.

I never would have guessed how much I could miss you.

"Home sweet home," she chuckled as she opened her eyes. She got a huge smile when she saw the stairs Dad and I had built. "Such handy boys," she teased. I just shrugged and gave a smile.

It seemed like it took her forever, but she finally opened the door to the motorhome and stepped inside.

"Oh my..." she trailed off when she flipped the light on and took everything in. Her face was filled with pure wonder, her eyes wide and her mouth hanging open just slightly. "What...?"

Mom, I signed.

"This..." she struggled to put how she was feeling into words. "This is amazing. It looks totally different. Everything feels so... clean!"

I gave a silent laugh, feeling like I might burst from how happy I felt for her. I knew it wasn't enough to erase all the bad she'd experienced over the last six weeks. Heck, over the last year, but I hoped it was enough to give her something to look forward to in the weeks and months to come.

Mom worked her butt off fixing it up, I wrote on our notebook. It felt so good to have it out again. *Dad too. It should be tight as a tin can by now.*

"This is so amazing," she said again, wandering back toward her room. "This looks like an actual bedroom now, not just a frumpy closet."

I followed her back, wrapping my arms around her from behind as she took it in. Resting my chin on her shoulder, she placed her palm against my cheek.

"Jake," she said, her voice filling with emotion. "You and your family have been amazing to me. You're the best thing that's ever happened to me."

She turned in my arms then, her chocolate eyes meeting mine. There were a million emotions behind her eyes, but none of them were the sadness or anger that had been there earlier that day.

There was just hope, joy, appreciation, and I hoped... love.

She pressed her lips to mine, slowly melting into me, and me into her.

It was perfect moments like that that made all the bad ones worth living through.

And you're the best thing that has ever or ever will happen to me.

Sam threw a rock out into the water, her hair blowing all around her face. Since we'd gotten home I hadn't pressured her into talking about what had happened while she was with Mike, but I sensed that Sam had something to get off of her chest.

She threw one more rock out into the ocean and turned and walked back to where I sat on the rocky beach. She sank next to me, resting her forearms on her knees.

Without any prompting from me, she answered the question I was silently asking.

"It was pretty bad," she said, her eyes staying glued in the direction of the water, though they looked glazed over, like she was seeing the past six weeks again. "That trailer was disgusting. Everything was filthy, not much of anything worked. I didn't think it could get much worse after living in the motorhome for so long, but this was so bad. You got nothing more than a drizzle out of the kitchen sink. The toilet plugged every time you tried to flush it. You could get hot water for maybe three minutes. And there was mold everywhere."

She took a big sigh, shaking her head as her jaw clenched. "I slept on this sleeping bag in the tiny dining area, I was too afraid of that disgusting couch. There wasn't anywhere else for me. It was dirty and smelly. But it would have been bearable if it hadn't have been for Mike."

I didn't want to hear the rest, to have all those blanks filled in. I'd wondered every second Sam was gone what was happening to her, but suddenly I didn't want to know.

"I don't think he was sober more than twenty-four hours while I was there." Her eyes fell to the rocks beneath us. She picked up a handful of small stones and threw them out into the water. They fell with a soft *plink*, sending endless ripples out to mix with the waves. "We had no food in the house, but there were always more than enough six packs around.

"He'd come back to the trailer from the bar with a different girl almost every night. His bedroom was only across the eight foot living room from where I slept." Sam gave an obvious shutter. "It was..." she trailed off, her eyes sliding closed. I wrapped an arm around her shoulders as she shook her head. "Sickening. And it was every night."

My fingers balled into fists.

"And he wanted me to be his little slave. He yelled at me all hours of the day to clean this, cook that up. I could only get homework done after he'd pass out or when he was at the bar. One time I tried telling him that I had an essay to finish and he slapped me and told me not to talk back to him. Flat out slapped me."

Call the police! I signed, rage and revenge filling me.

"No, Jake," she said with a sign, shaking her head. "I don't want to have to deal with him anymore. I just want to be done with him. And it was only the once, about four days before you came to get me. I thought it would be easier to wait the last few days out than to stir up an investigation. I just wanted to come home."

I looked at Sam, she finally meeting my eyes with her last few words. I brought my fingers up, tracing the very last shadows of a bruise on her cheek. I leaned forward, pressing my lips to hers.

I didn't ever want to have to let her go again. I never wanted to not be there to fight guys like Mike off.

"I just had to keep reminding myself that six weeks wasn't forever," she said quietly. "And I just kept telling myself that you were going to be there when that six weeks was over. You kept me sane."

This time it was Sam who leaned in and pressed her lips to mine.

"I dropped my History textbook on his nuts the night after he hit me," Sam said with a chuckle as she backed away. "While he was passed out. He couldn't walk straight for a day and a half later and had no idea what had happened."

A silent laugh rumbled around my chest. Soon I was laughing so hard I was on my back, hugging Sam into my side.

2 days since everything fell into place

Sam might not have been the most popular girl in school but neither of us could have guessed how much she was missed while she was gone. She was mauled when we got back to school. I thought almost everyone in the school came up to her, hugged her and said welcome back. Well, everyone except Norah. Sam was practically glowing as she walked down the halls at school.

We easily fell back into our routine over the next three weeks. Classes went about as usual. Sam worked harder than ever to keep her grades perfect. She was still on track to be Valedictorian. We continued to work at sign language. I was actually getting better at it than Sam was. Guess all my hours with Kali were finally paying off. Kali had moved back out just two weeks after Sam's return.

And Sam was just like another one of the family, just one that lived outside and I made out with. She ate every meal with us, spent her evenings studying with the rest of the kids at the dining table or lounged out on the living room floor.

One day we both got a big envelope from the University of Washington, both saying we had been accepted. Sam got her full ride scholarship. We'd spent hours online looking at student housing. That picture I'd had of the two of us down the road in college was looking a little more solid.

The day came at the end of May that I was instructed not to go upstairs as Sam and Jordan got ready for prom with Mom's help. I hung out on the couch downstairs, prepping myself for at least an hour of hanging out in my tux while the girls got ready.

A knock on the door a half hour later brought me to my feet and I opened it to find Rain.

"Hey man!" he said, clasping my one hand and pounding me on the back with the other. "You look sharp Hayes!"

I lifted my chin at him as I stepped away. *You too.*

"Thanks! So I'm assuming the ladies are upstairs prepping for the night?" he said as he closed the door behind him and flopped down on a couch.

I nodded and grabbed a notebook from the coffee table. *I've been exiled from setting foot on those stairs.*

"Best to heed their warning," Rain said, his face suddenly serious. "River just about clawed my eyes out for trying to use the bathroom while she was doing her hair just before I left the house."

Who's she going with?

"Just a group of girls boycotting having to go with a date," he said, rolling his eyes. I wondered if he knew River's secret yet. He had to have his suspicions.

Carter finally gave up then?

Rain chuckled. "Yeah, he's taking some sophomore named Daisy, or Rose, or some flower name like that."

I suddenly remembered. It was Lilly. Lilly Ridd.

"How long you think they're going to be?" Rain asked, his eyes floating in the direction of the stairs.

I shrugged my shoulders.

Half a second later I heard Mom yell from upstairs. "Is that you Rain?"

"Yes ma'am," he replied, a smile crossing his face.

"Alright," she yelled again. "You boys be prepared to have your breath taken away."

Feeling silly and formal, but dumb for not, Rain and I both rose to our feet. We checked each other to straighten ties and jackets then turned toward the staircase.

Jordan came down first. I had to admit, she looked good in her rosewood dress that hugged her in all the right ways. Her hair was piled on her head in an intricate mess of curls and braids.

I thought Rain was going to piss himself when he saw her. Rain took Jordan's hand in his when she got down the stairs, pressing a very formal kiss to her knuckles.

I just rolled my eyes and turned back to the stairs.

And then there was Sam. A smile crossed her face as our eyes met and she started down the stairs.

It sounded cliché to say she looked like an angel, but there was no other way to describe her. Her knee length dress was silver with frills and gathers that made her look even more perfect than she already was. She finally put on some weight over the last month and a half, giving her some curves back. She wore matching silver stiletto's that made her legs look nothing short of amazing. Her hair fell down her back in a cascade of perfect curls.

Even if I wasn't mute, I doubted I would have been able to say a thing as she stopped in front of me.

"What do you think?" she said, biting her lip-glossed lower lip, her eyes shining.

I didn't answer her. I simply kissed her to the point I knew most of my face was going to be covered in lip gloss too.

"Ooo…we!" Mom said as she walked down the stairs, camera in hand, flashing away at our public display. "Now that's a kiss!" She was all smiles.

Everyone just laughed.

"Alright," Mom said. "Now I want a picture of the four of you together. It's too bad Carter isn't here too. Then it'd be just perfect."

We all squished up together, wrapping our arms around each other. Mom snapped one picture, then gave me one of those looks.

"Jacob Hayes," she said in a Mom voice as she grabbed a tissue from the box on the coffee table. "Have a little decency." She then set to wiping Sam's lip gloss from my face.

Grapefruit.

After snapping about fifty pictures, Mom finally sent us on our way.

Prom was one night most of the restaurants on the island were actually busy in the spring. Rain and I had chosen to take the girls to a little Italian restaurant.

"Welcome you guys!" the hostess greeted us warmly. She had only graduated one year ahead of us. Some people never could escape the island. Leading us to a seat right in the window, she left us with menus.

"I can't believe the school year is almost over," Jordan said as she opened her menu and started looking it over. "You guys are going to be graduating in only three weeks."

"Three weeks could not be soon enough," Rain said as he shook his head. I just barely caught the slightly saddened look on Jordan's face. I would be surprised if the two of them made it to the end of the night without having their first kiss.

"Have you written your speech yet, Samantha?" Rain asked as he bit into a piece of bread the waitress set on the table.

Sam gave a crooked smile, her face blushing. "It's not a guaranteed thing yet," she tried to defend.

"Yes it is," Rain and Jordan said at the same time. Everyone laughed.

"Okay, fine," Sam said, shaking her head and grinning. "I've worked on it a bit. I'm really nervous to give it. I've had more than a little too much attention this year."

"Yeah, between everyone finding out about you being homeless and hooking up with the town pity boy, I don't think you could have possibly drawn much more attention to yourself this year."

I took a swing at Rain but he just ducked out of the way, laughing as he did.

"It's been a memorable year," Sam said. She placed her hand on my knee under the table. "That's for sure."

I met her eyes, a thousand thoughts running behind her own.

After we finished eating dinner we finally headed out to Rosario Resort where prom was being held that year. The decorating committee, which mostly consisted of parents, had gone all out. The entire mansion was lit up with a thousand Christmas lights, the walk up to the doors illuminated and glowing. Music softly poured out the open doors.

You ready for this? I signed to Sam as I parked the car.

"This is going to be the best night of this whole year," she said, a smile creeping onto her face. She leaned forward and pressed a kiss to my lips briefly.

"Party's waiting!" Rain said, clapping a hand on my shoulder, ending the moment. I was starting to question doubling with Rain. It certainly wasn't giving Sam and I any privacy. Not that I had any secret plans for the night.

Arm in arm, Sam and I followed Rain and Jordan up the steps and into the ballroom that overlooked the water. Most of the high school had already arrived it seemed, the room packed and hot.

Jordan immediately took Rain's hand and led him to where others were dancing, pulling his arms around her waist. Yeah, there was definitely something going on there.

"Let's go look at the water," Sam said, taking my hand in hers and leading me to the opposite side of the room.

There was a door that let out onto a narrow deck that hung above the still, calm ocean. Seeing we were alone out there, I wrapped my arms around Sam's waist, leaning against the railing toward the ocean.

"It's so peaceful out here tonight," she said, her voice thoughtful. I pressed my lips to her cheek, just letting them linger there. Everything in me felt relaxed, like this was exactly where I was supposed to be.

We stood out there for a few minutes longer, just enjoying the cool night air and the calm, before we went back inside and joined the others. We found Carter and Lily, the both of them looking awkward together, like things weren't quite clicking. He seemed relieved when we joined them and danced and talked for a good fifteen minutes.

The DJ the school hired wasn't the best and there was often long pauses between songs while he tried his best to figure out how to work the equipment in front of him. But no one seemed to mind. Everyone was having a good time.

A slow song came on and I pulled Sam into my arms. She rested her head on my chest, taking in a deep, relaxed breath. I rested my chin on top of her head, feeling her heart beat against my chest.

It could have been only the two of us as we slowly moved in a small circle, the music swaying us in the dark. We didn't need to talk. At this point in our weird, challenged relationship it didn't even feel like we needed words. I could feel Sam's contentment just by the way she held her body, by the way her head rested on my chest, by the way her hand laid in mine. And I knew she could feel all those words she wouldn't let me say, just by the way I held her.

Towards the end of the song, Sam lifted her head to look at me. I could tell there was something on her mind, could see it in her eyes. She looked full of emotion and thought. Very slowly, she leaned forward until her lips met mine. She let them linger there for a moment, just holding them still, almost as if in anticipation of what was to come.

But then she pressed them to mine a bit more forcefully, her lips parting just slightly, her tongue tracing my lower lip. One of her hands came to the back of my neck, pulling me closer to her, if it was possible. My hands circled her waist, my entire body humming with life.

This was one of those perfect moments they made cheesy movies about.

"Either get a room or come play!" Rain suddenly shouted next to us. As my eyes slid open, he grabbed my arm and was suddenly dragging me to one corner of the room. Barely managing to keep hold of Sam's hand, we were dragged over to a gathering crowd.

One of the science teachers stood before everyone with a microphone.

"Make sure you write your name on the back of one of these tickets and get it put in this bowl here," he said. He held what looked like a round fish bowl under one of his arms. "Don't miss out on the chance to win the thousand dollar raffle prize!"

Pens and tickets made their way through the crowd. As Sam wrote our names on two of the tickets, I peeled my tux jacket off, tossing it on the back of a chair and rolling my sleeves up. When I walked back to the crowd, I found Sam sitting up on a table, her shoes discarded underneath her.

Smiling at seeing her so relaxed, I sat next to her, taking one of her feet in my hand and rubbing it. She smiled at me as she twirled one of the black permanent markers between her fingers absentmindedly.

Out of the corner of my eye, I noticed Norah staring at me with a mix of distain and jealousy on her face. I almost felt sorry for her that she hadn't come to the dance with anyone she actually cared about. She certainly didn't care about junior Anthony LeFray who stood at her side.

"Okay," the teacher said. "Everyone got their tickets deposited in the bowl? Yes? Okay. The first drawing is for a twenty dollar gift certificate to Teazer's."

He reached his hand into the bowl, mixing the tickets.

"So did you have a good school year?" Sam whispered into my ear as she watched a freshman girl get her name drawn.

Realizing I didn't have anything to write on to respond, Sam held out her arm and extended the permanent marker to me. *Are you sure?* I raised my eyebrows at her. She smiled and nodded her head.

Don't think it could have been better, I wrote in small letters on the inside of her arm. For some reason it made me smile, to see my handwriting on her skin.

Another guy cheered as he won the next prize.

Taking the pen from me, she put it to the skin on the inside of my arm.

No regrets? She wrote in her neat handwriting.

Looking up at her and catching her eyes, I thought about it for a long moment. There had been a lot that had gone wrong that year. There was the obvious. There'd been fights and hardships between us. There'd been a million unsure looks from most of the island and an evil, spoiled princess that had tried to rip us apart.

But I had become a different person. One who looked at things in a new way. I appreciated life a whole lot more than I had last year.

And best of all, Sam was there by my side.

Not a one, I wrote on her arm.

Me either, she inked my skin.

"And the winner of the $1,000 raffle prize is..." the teacher drew out dramatically. Everyone got real quiet as they waited to find out if they won. "Jordan Hayes!"

The room broke out in cheers and a few boo's. Jordan jumped up and down, higher than I thought it was possible for her, clapping her hands. And sure enough, she turned and planted one on Rain's lips, right then and there.

I felt Sam writing something else on my arm, but didn't bother looking yet. I just smiled and pumped my fist in the air, cheering for my sister. She bounded toward the front of the room, laughing and it looked like tears were pooling in her eyes. I thought the smile was going to break her face as she accepted the rolled up wad of green bills the teacher handed to her.

I was happy for Jordan for winning. She'd had a lot of weight on her this year, and I knew helping out with me and always having to worry about me had worn on her. I couldn't help but feel a little bit like I had somewhat ruined her junior year. It was nice she could have something cool like this happen at the end of the year. She'd have an awesome summer with it.

"Alright everyone," the teacher said, picking up the microphone again. "That's all we've got for tonight. Have fun dancing, and be safe out there tonight."

The crowd quickly disbursed back onto the dance floor as the music picked back up. I jumped up to my feet and started rolling my sleeves down, about to take Sam back out onto the floor with me, when my eyes fell to my arm and what Sam had written.

I'm kind of tired, she'd written. Is it okay if we go home?

I looked up at Sam's face, disappointment sinking in my stomach. She looked uncertain, something else hiding behind her eyes, I just couldn't pinpoint what it was.

My mood falling slightly, I gave a small nod.

After retrieving my jacket, we found Rain and let him know we were leaving. He said he and Jordan would get a ride home with Carter.

I wasn't sure what to think about Sam wanting to leave the dance early. She didn't really seem tired and she had seemed like she was having a good time. I wondered if there was something else going on and tried not to let the uncertainty make me sick. Sam didn't seem upset or anything. She held my hand tightly in hers as we drove home, tracing small circles into the back of mine with the fingers of her other hand.

The house was dark when we got home, which seemed weird. I wondered where Mom and Dad had taken all the younger kids.

Still hand in hand, Sam and I walked slowly walked to the front door. Just as I had guessed, the house was completely silent when we walked inside. I flipped the lights on, shrugging out of my jacket and draping it over a chair.

I glanced once at Sam, my eyes questioning. She was being oddly quiet.

Very slowly, almost so slowly I didn't notice it happening at first, the Jake smile crept onto her face. Running her fingers over her lips like she was zipping them closed, she crooked her finger at me, telling me to follow her. She took one of my hands in hers again, and led us back toward my bedroom.

For half a second I got nervous and excited. Sam had wanted to leave the dance early, none of my family was here.

The house was dark and we were alone... Could Sam be planning...?

But the thought left as soon as it came. This was Sam, she didn't make those kind of plans. That was Norah's style, not hers.

Sam glanced back at me once, her eyes excited and nervous at the same time. My eyes questioning her again, she placed her hand on the knob, and pushed the door to my bedroom open. She flipped the light on and we stepped inside.

I didn't understand what I was supposed to be seeing at first. Sam looked at me, as if waiting to see what my reaction was going to be to whatever there was supposed to be inside.

And then I saw it. The entire wall above my bed had been covered with pages. Pages with rough edges and little tags of paper that looked like they'd been ripped from a spiral notebook. But there had to be more than fifty pages. There hadn't been that many pages ripped from our notebook.

I glanced at Sam once before I walked closer to the wall. She gave a nervous smile before nodding me to get closer.

It all just looked like a jumble of words at first, some pages completely full, some pages with only a few words on them.

And then my eyes picked out four words that kept repeating throughout all the pages.

I love you, Jake.

It was there, written in the middle of pages, surrounded by words like "scared to say it," "not sure how to say it," and "maybe I'll tell you tomorrow." And there were dozens of pages with only those four words written on them.

I knew a lot of those pages were the missing sheets from our notebook. And some of those pages had been missing for weeks and weeks.

I felt Sam come to my side and she slowly started rolling my right sleeve up. Not really believing what I was seeing on my wall, I looked down at her and watched as she rolled it up to my elbow.

And there those three words were, inked on the inside of my arm, in the black permanent marker she'd stained my skin with earlier that night. I'd never even realized she'd written them at the dance.

I love you.

My eyes jumped up to Sam's. She looked so uncertain, like she didn't know what my reaction might be. But I saw in them that she meant what she had written. It was there all over her face.

Stepping closer to her, so that there was only a half inch between us, I placed a hand on either side of her face. My eyes studied hers, wishing with everything I had in me that I could vocalize those words I'd never gotten to say.

I love you, my lips formed. I may have only been able to mouth it, but it didn't make the words any less true.

"I've wanted to say it for a long time now," Sam said, her words coming out in a rush. "I've just been… afraid. I didn't want to say them and get taken away, or have something terrible happen. I know I haven't been fair about letting you say it, but I didn't want you to say it and me not be ready to say it back. But I do, Jake. I love you. More than I thought it was possible. And I thought it was totally impossible."

She brought her hands to the back of my neck, resting her forehead against mine. "I had this notebook with me while I was at Mike's and I tried to find a good way to write it down every day. I wanted to tell you so bad it made it hard to breathe, as ridiculous as that sounds. I nearly filled the entire notebook but I couldn't just send it to you and not be there to really tell you myself. I love you and I've loved you this whole year, even if I couldn't tell you."

I chuckled at hearing Sam stumble over herself like this. But it didn't matter. She was saying those words. The ones I feared she never would.

Taking one of her arms in my hand, and grabbing the permanent marker I'd slid into my pocket before we left the dance, I pulled the lid off.

I love you, forever, I wrote.

The Jake smile spread once again on Sam's face as she wrapped her arms behind my neck and pressed her lips to mine.

I hoped our words would never wash off.

1 day 'til the rest of forever

I tugged at my cap, feeling like it wouldn't sit on my head quite right. I fiddled with the blue gown I wore, cursing under my breath. Who came up with this get up for graduation? Were we not in the twenty-first century?

I turned in my seat, catching the eye of all six of my siblings, both my parents, and my Hayes grandparents. My family filled half the stands in that tiny gym of ours. Mom and Jenny waved at me, flashing bright and proud smiles. I waved back and turned back to the front of the gym.

"And now I'd like to present to you our senior class Valedictorian, Samantha Shay," Principal Hill said, clapping his hands as he stepped away from the podium. The entire gym erupted in cheers and clapping, its volume deafening.

Sam rose from her seat in the front row of students. She was already blushing but she was beaming.

The cap and gown may have looked stupid on me, but Sam looked perfect in anything.

"Thank you," she said, a small laugh bubbling up from her throat. Her face flushed even more red when the cheers only got louder. I clapped so hard my hands hurt. Catching my eyes, Sam laughed again, covering her face with her hands. Finally, almost a full minute later, the crowd started calming down.

"Wow," Sam said, her voice breathy. Her eyes looked like there might be tears pooling in them. "Thank you, so much. You're support means everything to me, especially after the year we have all had."

Sam shifted from one foot to the other, pushing her hair over her shoulder. She was uncomfortable and nervous, but she looked adorable. I had never been so proud of her.

"This year has been one of change, for all of us," she started. "We started it out, feeling like normal teenagers, doing things normal teenagers do, screwing things up and making poor choices. No one blamed us. It was expected if nothing else.

"But sometimes hard lessons have to be learned. Sometimes we need a loud wake up call for us to make changes for the better. I don't even have to state what that wakeup call was, we all know. While this year could have turned to one of tragedy and sorrow, a year of regrets for our actions, we all decided to make a change. We made a commitment to do better, to be better.

"We learned we didn't have to have alcohol or drugs to have a good time. We learned that our families extended beyond blood. We learned to let others help and uplift us."

Sam lifted her eyes from her speech, and suddenly met mine. "We learned to love this year, in ways we never knew we could." Her voice cracked just the tiniest bit on love. I gave her a smile, feeling a sting behind my own eyes.

"So we fell this year, we rose, and now here we are, triumphant and ready to take on the rest of our lives. Let us never forget the lessons we learned this year. Let us never forget how to grow, how to live, how to love. Let us never forget each other."

Sam gave a little bow of her head, letting everyone know she was done. The gym erupted into cheers again. As I looked around to the thirty-six other students who were graduating with me, I wasn't surprised to see tears in many eyes. Rain clapped his hand on my shoulder from behind, giving it a hard squeeze. I patted his hand, and smiled. Carter, who stood right next to me, wrapped an arm around my shoulders.

"Congratulations, Orcas High School senior class," Principal Hill said as he stood next to Sam, wrapping an arm around her shoulders. "Welcome to your future."

As the chaos started, all the families mixing with the newly freed students, Sam worked her way toward me in the crowd. She was glowing, a brilliant smile on her face. I thought I was going to pop from all the pride and joy I felt then.

"How'd I do?" she asked as she stepped into me, our arms wrapping around each other.

Perfect, I signed, pressing my lips to her cheek.

"We wouldn't have had the year we did without you," she said. "Things would have been a lot different."

I just smiled and pressed my lips to hers once more.

"Congratulations you two," Mom's voice said from behind. Suddenly Sam and I were wrapped in a giant

Mom hug. She pressed kisses to both me and Sam's foreheads. "I'm so proud of you two. Neither of you had an easy year, but you both came out on top."

And it was true. It would have been really easy to spiral down into drugs or alcohol that year, for both of us. But instead we were there, together. We'd taken all the bad things that had happened to us and turned them around into something good and bigger than the two of us.

I smiled as I looked back at Sam.

What I didn't say before no longer mattered.

We had the entire future before us to say everything else.

Author's Note

I've debated with myself (a lot) about putting this note in here. In a way I almost feel like I have to have a reason why I'm allowed to write this type of story. It's one that has to be handled very carefully, and it's touchy, and was quite a scary one for me to write.

But this story is very personal to me.

When I was fifteen, a sophomore in high school, I suddenly got very sick. I'd been dizzy for a few days, feeling nauseous all the time. Within a day or two, I couldn't even get out of bed, the world was spinning so bad. I couldn't keep anything down and it felt like my right ear would never pop.

And eventually I couldn't hear anything in that ear.

Those seven days or so were a blur. To be honest I don't remember a lot of details, I just remembering thinking something really, really bad was happening to me.

I fought my parents for a few days about going to the doctor. But eventually I caved and they took me in. The doctor I saw said I had seasonal allergies, and that was why my ear was so "stopped up." He gave me some pills and said it would clear up in a week or two.

Except it never did. My hearing never came back in that ear and when I went back to the doctors, they couldn't figure out why. The closest they could figure was that I had gotten some kind of virus. But they knew one thing: my hearing wasn't going to come back.

So I was fifteen and already half deaf.

It felt like the end of the world.

It was humiliating and terrifying.

I couldn't have someone sit on my right side and have a conversation with them because I couldn't hear the majority of what they said. Someone would call out behind me in the halls and I wouldn't hear them. I had to constantly ask people "what?" or ask them to repeat what they had said. Being in a loud, crowded room made it impossible to follow a conversation.

And I was embarrassed to let people know. Telling a new boyfriend this was nerve-wracking, always wondering if he was going to think differently of me when he found out. Telling anyone was awkward and uncomfortable.

The world kind of sucked for a while.

Like Jake, I had a choice to make in my life. I could let this drown me, I could get mad at the world, and I could let this define me.

Or I could learn something from it.

It didn't happen quickly, but loosing half my hearing taught me to appreciate a lot of things. I really, *really* appreciated the fact that I could still hear out of my left ear. I appreciated that I could still see, that I could still talk. You don't think about those kind of things until something is taken away.

I learned to see that things could be so much worse.

I still struggle with being half deaf every day. I don't like telling people about it, thus I wasn't sure I'd be able to write this note. I frequently have a hard time following what people are saying. When I have to sit in a room with other people I plot out where I'm going to sit so that the majority of people are on my left side.

But I know that there are so many people out there who have things so much worse than me. I still have the things I need. I have a house, I have food, I have an amazing family. I may not be able to hear very well, but I have everything else.

So when life seems impossible, when it seems so bad that you can't go on, just stop for a second to take a look at all of the things that you do have. I bet the list will grow pretty fast. And even if it doesn't you have to power to decide if you're going to let the bad or the good take control of your life.

If you've never heard it before, I encourage you to look up the song "Somebody wishes they were you" by *Adelita's Way*. I consider it to be the theme song to *What I Didn't Say* and I think it is something we should all think about.

"Nobody is trial-free, but we have a choice. We can choose to allow our experiences to hold us back, and to not allow us to become great or achieve greatness in this life.

Or we can allow our experiences to push us forward, to make us grateful for every day we have and to be all the more thankful for those who are around us."

- Elizabeth Smart

Acknowledgments

This book was an absolute work of love and it would have been almost impossible to write without a lot of help from a lot of people.

First I have to say thank you to the team at home. Thank you to Justin, as always, for his support and love, for putting up with me and all of my craziness. Thank you to my kids who inspire me every day. Thank you to my family, both immediate and extended.

Thank you to my real deal Orcas teens, who answered my questions and made sure I didn't sound like a total idiot: Jessica, Courtney, and Taylor. And a huge thank you to Rachel. Your answers to my questions were vital and you and your family are inspiring.

Thank you to Britney and Jenni for beta reading. Huge thank you to my editor Steven.

Thank you to the blogging community. I never expected to find such amazing friends through this world. I wouldn't be where I am today without all of you.

And most importantly, thank you to my Heavenly Father, for this precious gift.

Keary Taylor grew up in the foothills of the Rocky Mountains where she started creating imaginary worlds and daring characters who always fell in love. She now resides on a tiny island in the Pacific Northwest with her husband and their two young children. She continues to have an overactive imagination that frequently keeps her up at night.

<u>Also by Keary Taylor</u>
FALL OF ANGELS
Branded
Forsaken
Vindicated
Afterlife: a Fall of Angels novelette

EDEN

To learn more about Keary and her writing process, please visit www.KearyTaylor.com

CPSIA information can be obtained at www.ICGtesting.com
Printed in the USA
LVOW061627121112

306980LV00004B/47/P